"Not happening." Even through her chattering teeth, the tone of her statement was sharper than she'd meant. "I mean, something between us. After the kiss. The kisses. I don't want to lead you on."

"Trust me, that's the last thing I'd ever expect from you. The leading me on part. As for kissing you, hell, Trina, it's been five years. We had amazing chemistry when we were together, and that's not gone away."

"We had more than chemistry." She wasn't letting him off so easily. "If it was only a physical attraction, you going off the radar by allowing Justin to officially die wouldn't be such a big deal."

"I thought you were married, Trina." His quiet words weighed heavy with what sounded an awful lot like pain. Regret.

"Not good enough, Rob. Even if I'd remarried, was still married, whatever. What we shared deserved more than you walking away when you saw me again." She fought to keep her words aboveboard, fair. Her heart screamed at her conscience, telling her that if she were really fair she'd tell him about their son, how she'd really felt about Rob.

* * *

We hope you enjoy the Silver Valley P.D. miniseries.

* * *

**If you're on Twitter, tell us what you think of Harlequin Romantic Suspense!
#harlequinromsuspense**

Dear Reader,

Welcome back to Silver Valley! *The Fugitive's Secret Child* was a natural fit for the SVPD series as we're beginning a miniseries within the series. This time, instead of a crazy, lethal cult that plagued the town and our heroes and heroines in books one to four, the Silver Valley police are facing the effects of Russian organized crime as it stretches its tentacles into the otherwise picturesque, serene town.

Trina is happy as a US marshal and the mother of five-year-old Justin, but her heart has never healed from losing the love of her life during wartime. She'd been a navy pilot and he was the navy SEAL she'd fallen in love with while supporting his missions into enemy territory. The darkest day of her life was when she was told that her future husband was KIA. But he left her with one gift—their son.

Rob was in fact not killed but taken into enemy captivity, which he survived, and then went on to fight as an undercover operative. This lends well to his current job as a Trail Hiker agent. When he and Trina meet again, it's surreal and yet the most right thing that's happened to either of them since they were torn apart.

There is so much happening in Silver Valley and it's covered in detail on my website. Please visit gerikrotow.com/contact to sign up for my newsletter so that you don't miss any exciting news. Also connect with me on Facebook—I'd love to see you there: Facebook.com/gerikrotow.

Peace,

Geri

THE FUGITIVE'S
SECRET CHILD

———

Geri Krotow

HARLEQUIN®ROMANTIC SUSPENSE

Recycling programs
for this product may
not exist in your area.

ISBN-13: 978-1-335-45640-3

The Fugitive's Secret Child

Copyright © 2018 by Geri Krotow

Printed in U.S.A.

Former naval intelligence officer and US Naval Academy graduate **Geri Krotow** draws inspiration from the global situations she's experienced. Geri loves to hear from her readers. You can email her via her website and blog, gerikrotow.com.

Books by Geri Krotow

Harlequin Romantic Suspense

Silver Valley P.D.

Her Christmas Protector
Wedding Takedown
Her Secret Christmas Agent
Secret Agent Under Fire
The Fugitive's Secret Child

Harlequin Superromance

What Family Means
Sasha's Dad

Whidbey Island

Navy Rules
Navy Orders
Navy Rescue
Navy Christmas
Navy Justice

Harlequin Anthology

Coming Home for Christmas
"Navy Joy"

Harlequin Everlasting Love

A Rendezvous to Remember

Visit the Author Profile page
at Harlequin.com for more titles.

To Alex—you inspire me every day.

Prologue

Winter wind blew off the Atlantic as he got out of his car across from the Norfolk, Virginia, address with the speed and agility of an eighty-year-old. At twenty-five, it sucked to be so fragile. He leaned against a wide oak tree and checked out the town house she'd purchased last year—he'd found that out on the internet.

Two years was a long time to wait. Justin Berger wouldn't blame her if she hadn't. A five-month affair in the desert during wartime didn't qualify as lifetime vows. Even if memories of their time together had gotten him through a year as a POW, several near-death experiences and torture by the enemy, and led to his eventual escape and rescue. It'd be different for her; she thought he was dead.

He'd spent the last five months recovering in the best rehabilitation center on the planet, Walter Reed

National Military Medical Center in the greater Washington, DC, area. Before that he'd been in Landstuhl, Germany, where they'd saved his life. The pain had been worth it. Torture with a purpose.

He still needed the cane, and the doctors were certain his femurs and pelvis would never be completely pain-free when he walked. But he was young enough to bounce back and he had the ability to return to his life. A lot of his SEAL teammates didn't. There was no person on earth he wanted to celebrate his survival with other than her.

Finding her had been easy. He'd asked his higher-ups where she was stationed. Because of the top secret mission, an operation that had officially never existed, his assumed death and actual time as a POW were classified, too. He could have told his parents if he'd had any. A product of the foster system, he didn't. He only had his brother, who he'd gained permission to inform he was still alive. He could tell her, too, and start life over as a civilian. If she still wanted him. His other option was to work for the CIA under a new name. It would make it nearly impossible for any future targets to research him and find out his full capabilities.

Before he walked across the street, an SUV pulled into her driveway. His gut tightened; his throat closed against the immediate lump at the sight of Trina getting out of her car, her hair pinned up as part of her Navy uniform. Her face, the long, lean lines of her feminine body, was more beautiful than he remembered. If he thought his voice could reach her, he'd call to her, give a slight wave. Anything to connect.

She opened the rear driver's-side door and leaned in, probably for her laptop or groceries. Another car eased next to hers in the two-car driveway. A man emerged from behind the wheel. Tall, broad-shouldered, in a business suit and topcoat. Dread combined with months of fearing this exact scenario. It poured through his veins, temporarily paralyzing him on the spot. They wouldn't notice him as the street was wide, with several cars parked along both curbs. The tree provided him excellent cover. Protection he hadn't expected to need.

He watched as the man walked over to Trina, who waited for him with a large bundle in her arms. A child, a toddler, dressed as a boy. In a bright green parka, with a cartoon hero ski cap, the little tyke clutched a construction truck in his mittened hand. The man took the boy into his arms and laughed, holding him overhead for a quick moment before hugging him to his massive chest and leaning down to kiss Trina on the cheek.

She hadn't waited. She'd found another and had a child. Trina had her own family now. He'd known it was possible, probable, but still, he'd have bet against it. Hoped she'd mourned for him, needed him. He was caught between the tragedy of his own sorrow and disappointment, and the darkly sick humor of having to struggle to stand upright, quietly, under the large oak tree. If she looked over she wouldn't recognize his shattered silhouette; she'd only see what looked like an older man with a cane. But he didn't want to take any chances that she'd see him. If she got the quickest glance at his eyes, she'd see without a shred of doubt that he was a man with an irreparably broken heart.

As soon as they disappeared into the townhome, he arthritically folded himself back into his vehicle and drove away, refusing to look back.

So it was to be the CIA job. Justin Berger had been dead to her, to the world, for two and a half years. Now it'd be forever.

Chapter 1

Three and a half years later

Rob Bristol was pissed off, tired, hot and horny. Not all in that order, but close enough for government work. He shot back the rest of his electrolyte-enhanced water, keeping his gulps silent. As he stretched his neck with a couple of creaky turns of his head he remained vigilant, doing a 360-degree scan of his perimeter. Once settled back on his stomach, he wrapped his arms around his precision sniper rifle and adjusted the sight. His shoulders ached, as did much of his skeleton. Another reminder that his days as a top-secret operative were nearing their end, twenty years earlier than for most.

"Gosh-damned boonies." The Trail Hikers had once again sent him out to the most dangerous, remote operation the government shadow agency was involved with.

In the continental US, anyhow. He couldn't complain about his employer, though. Rural northern Pennsylvania was still better than Kandahar or the depths of a jungle on the worst day. It was his home country and he had quick access to anything he needed, from weaponry to foodstuffs. He enjoyed life as a civilian secret agent almost as much as he'd loved being a Navy SEAL or CIA agent. He dug the added benefit of being able to choose his missions these days. For the most part. He'd wanted to participate in another especially tricky op that involved travel to Ukraine and Russia. Claudia Michele, his boss and Trail Hikers director, had nixed it. She didn't care that he'd already completed several successful missions against Russian organized crime in Eastern Europe and New York City. Said his talents were better spent in the former honeymoon capital of Pennsylvania, where a ROC crime boss was reportedly holed up. A mobster who'd eluded the FBI and all other law enforcement agencies.

The irony of this mission, so very unromantic in what was considered a romantic area, wasn't lost on him. Anger fueled his motivation to take down his target, the man who'd helped ROC bring the ugliness of high-stakes crime to this beautiful area. Rob's weapon's sight was trained on the one building on the planet that the world's most sought-after crime bosses were operating from. He'd followed the dirtbag for the last six weeks. Dima Ivanov was the head of a major Russian organized crime group on the East Coast. Yuri Vasin was number two, Ivanov's right hand. Ivanov led up to two thousand criminals and a plethora of illegal enterprises. The most recent was human trafficking, and that's what had pushed the FBI to ask for Trail Hikers' help. Several dozen underage girls had been smuggled into the US via the Canadian border in Maine and trucked down to the Poconos. From here they were about to be dispersed to the winds of the ROC sex trade.

Time was of the essence.

Ivanov was an old badger, but he wasn't stupid. In his most recent photos he'd looked older, less energetic than the younger ROC member he'd been. Back when Rob had been with the CIA he'd trailed Ivanov to Russia, Ukraine and back without ever being detected by one single ROC member or any government officials. Rob had helped bring down an entire branch of the East Coast crime ring over a three-day period in the hot hell of New York City and Trenton, New Jersey, last year. It was during a summer heat wave that included power outages and heat-induced rage. He'd come face-to-face with Ivanov. Close enough that the criminal spat in his face as the FBI cuffed him and carted him off. Ivanov had gotten off on a technicality, thanks to the best attorneys money could buy. That was a year and multiple lifetimes ago, as far as Rob was concerned. He'd participated in countless missions since then.

But this was his favorite. He'd majored in Russian in college and knew Russian history inside and out.

Come on out, Ivanov. Rob forced his muscles to relax and drew upon years of experience as he waited for his prey. If he could disable the son of a bitch and his guards, allowing for law enforcement to come in and apprehend the criminals, he would. If not, he'd at least take out Yuri Vasin, who was responsible for ordering hits; nearly two thousand deaths were known. Countless victims' bodies would never be found. One of Vasin's main trademarks was leaving no trail of human remains. Vasin didn't care about getting credit for a hit.

Hot summer sun beat on the back of Rob's neck and through his drab olive T-shirt and cargo pants. The Poconos were beautiful when snow covered, or drenched in green as they were now. But the July humidity was oppressive, soaking his clothes after only an hour on target.

He'd thought Ivanov would have shown his face by now. There'd been no sign of him since last night, when Rob spotted him taking his last smoke break before bed, around nine o'clock. He knew Ivanov chain-smoked and had come out for fresh air, a risk when he had to know he was a wanted man. Ivanov and Vasin had been surrounded by guards. If Rob wasn't on such strict orders from Trail Hikers headquarters in Silver Valley to keep collateral damage to a minimum, he'd have taken out both monsters and their thugs in that moment. His mission was to disable Ivanov and Vasin, call in other law enforcement agencies, or LEAs, and then get the hell out of Dodge. Typical of a Trail Hikers op, there were to be no fingerprints of his government shadow agency's involvement.

Rob liked to think of Trail Hikers as the helping hand for all other LEAs, national and local. A Trail Hikers agent enabled an FBI agent, state trooper, sheriff or local cop to come in and finish the job. And take credit for it.

The real reason he'd gone with Trail Hikers instead of another shadow agency was for his mental health. After three years of ignoring the regret of not crossing the street to let Trina Lopez know he'd lived, he'd sought counseling six months ago. And discovered he still needed to finish what he'd tried to do in Norfolk. Trina was with the US Marshals in Harrisburg, and Silver Valley was only twenty minutes away across the Susquehanna River. He'd made the move to Silver Valley a month later, so that he could face her again, put to right the lack of initiative on his part three years ago. As far as he knew she was still with someone else, had her own family, but he still needed some kind of closure, if only to wish her well. It was for his own sanity.

The beauty of Trail Hikers was that he could live anywhere in the country and work for them. He'd grown to like Silver Valley over the past several months, and it would be nice to stay, but he didn't think permanently living that close to Trina would be healthy, even with closure.

A gnat flew into his eye, and he swatted it away.

He wondered why Ivanov was staying inside so much today. Usually he liked to go for a walk, at least twice a day if not more often. That sense of dread Rob identified as his instinct waved a warning flag. Did Ivanov and Vasin know Rob was out here?

Ivanov had puffed on his cigarette with Vasin and four other men around him, as if he knew he was hunted, that his enemy was close. Of course by now the criminal had to be downright paranoid, considering his constant need to be on the run. Add in his love of women, vodka and tobacco and he probably had at least the beginnings of cirrhosis and lung cancer. Ivanov's mind and sense of trust in humanity were pretty much shot, Rob figured.

That Rob understood.

A glint of metal in the sun was his only warning

before the building's door opened. He took the safety off, positioned his fingers to shoot without hesitation.

He waited. And waited.

Nothing. The door was open, but nobody came out. With experience wrought only from years of tortuous situations, Robert ignored his annoyance, his impatience. He could outwait the best of them. As he watched, a tiny figure appeared at the edge of the doorway. An animal? Peering through the scope he discovered he was looking at a puppy.

A *dog*? He'd seen a lot of strange things in his years as a SEAL, CIA operative and now Trail Hikers secret agent, but he'd never seen a dog, much less a puppy, around Vasin. Unless it was a guard dog with killer instincts. He hadn't seen any sign of guard dogs or any strays around this compound of sorts. He swiped at the sweat on his nape, the bandanna around his head unable to keep it as dry as his temples as sweat streamed off him, making rivulets through his sunscreen. He sensed a slight breeze around his neck and shoulders and went still.

"We meet again, Robert Bristol." Hearing his name spoken by the all-too-familiar bass voice chilled him to the bone and made him grateful he'd heeded the CIA's suggestion and changed his name after he'd been presumed dead as a Navy SEAL. The cold metal of a gun barrel pressed painfully into his temple. "Get up slowly, and leave your rifle. You won't be needing it."

Rob did as instructed. He knew the voice, the heavy accent. His captor was no one to brook argument.

Once Rob was standing, his nemesis shoved the gun more deeply into the side of his head, the pressure making white floaters appear in Rob's vision.

"You try my patience, Bristol. Put your hands up and turn around."

Robert turned, his arms at shoulder level, dreading whom he'd see.

"Vasin. Fancy seeing you in the Poconos, of all places. I thought Jersey City was your jurisdiction."

"Go to hell, Bristol. Your time is over." Vasin's voice pulsated with acrimony as he stared at Rob, surrounded by four henchmen who also carried the best handguns money could buy. Vasin had stayed as lean and lethal as when Rob had tracked him in a CIA operation three years ago, and ended up in actual hand-to-hand with him. It had been a fight that started with knives and ended with several broken bones, on Vasin's part. Rob had suffered three butterfly stitches over his left eye that one of his fellow agents had tended to on their helo ride out of New Jersey.

"How're your ribs, Vasin? I see you can at least breathe again."

Rob saw the polished tip of Vasin's Italian loafer close in a nanosecond before an explosion of pain shattered his vision. His body collapsed with zero fight. A kick to the balls did that to a guy.

Dirt. The ground is hard. The grass is like straw.

Thoughts to take his mind off the pain, keep him detached from the anguish to come. Vasin knew a sadist's way around the human body—what hurt the most, what would elicit a confession the quickest. Rob and cruelty were on a first-name basis. He knew every torture method intimately. So did his bones.

"Drag him by his feet to the ATVs." Vasin's thugs grabbed his legs and started the laborious trek over hardened field grass and mud. Rob sucked in his gut as hard as he could despite the quaking tremors from his groin. It was enough to hold his neck up, away from the ground. Enough to protect it from the excruciating jolts, enough to be able to observe that Vasin and his dirtbags were facing front, not looking at him as they trudged to the waiting off-road vehicles. In an instant he grabbed the knife he'd tucked in his front pocket and threw it with little preparation. His target arched his back and dropped. The man let out a loud *whoosh* as he hit the ground. Satisfaction cleared some of Rob's pain-addled vision.

One punctured lung.

The second knife was in his left hand, raised to throw it, when one of the remaining men turned and crushed Rob's arm with one fierce stomp of his foot. Rob saw Vasin's shoe again through a shroud of unbearable pain before his throat was pressed closed and darkness prevailed.

US Marshal Trina Lopez looked at the map, her phone GPS and the email from her boss. She was four hours into what was supposed to be a two-and-a-half-hour drive, and all of her coordinates indicated she was in the right spot. But instead of a resort complex as described in her target's case file, she was looking at a warehouse of sorts. A single, nondescript warehouse that in any other part of the country, on the outskirts of a city, would look normal. If it were lined up with other warehouses. If it had trucks coming and going. If it had access to an interstate highway.

Instead, this building had none of the above. It was in a place she'd expect to see a log cabin, maybe, or some kind of ski lodge. At the base of the mountains in a beautiful, scenic Pennsylvania valley, the desolate building was incongruous with its surroundings. Under the cover of the thick summer foliage, it was no wonder it had looked like just another camping gear storage building. An afterthought of sorts.

She'd had to maneuver along a narrow dirt road in her company car to get here. The Ford Fiesta wasn't made for the sudden dips and dried-out potholes from last winter. Why had she chosen today to take the agency's small car and not the company SUV?

Because another mission had priority. It wasn't her job to question her superiors. Yuri Vasin was wanted for a number of crimes, with drug and human trafficking at the top of the long list. Drug runners abounded, and with the current opioid epidemic the US Marshals had a lot of pressure to bring in any drug-related fugitives. Still, the right equipment for the job helped, and someone hadn't done their homework right. This site was far more rural than the case file had described. She was supposed to be taking him in from a resort hotel room, not from a camping site. Her partner was coming in from the other side of the mountain and waiting to hear from her to bring in backup.

Rechecking her GPS, she confirmed she was in the right spot before she turned her car back around and drove out a mile to hide her vehicle under a pile of woodland debris.

Car in place, walking to building, she texted her partner. His reply was immediate, and predictable.

If it's ugly, don't go.

Mike always played the big brother. Or maybe wannabe lover, she wasn't sure. And didn't care. She had no interest, no attraction to him.

Roger.

Her military reply indicated she'd received his text. Mike Seabring was a great partner, and she enjoyed working with him. But his protectiveness could annoy her.

It'll never be like working in the Navy.

More like it'd never be as natural a fit as working with fellow Navy pilots and one special Navy SEAL— had been.

She steered her thoughts quickly away from that emotional quicksand and kept walking. The hike back through the woods would have normally refreshed her. She breathed in the pine scent, hoping to feel revived. But it was too hot and her day was growing too long to feel anything but tired, sweaty and cranky. By the time she reached the clearing again she was ready to get the show on the road. Or more accurately, get her fugitive and take him back to Harrisburg or have Mike do it. She wasn't in it for the credit—she wanted this bad guy caught and put away, no matter how they had to do it.

Trina adjusted her holster, as it was digging into her waist. She thought about shedding the leather jacket she wore over her body armor and thin white T-shirt. It was too warm for the jacket, but she wasn't going into a strange building without her weapon, and didn't want to open-carry her Glock .45, either. She rustled her thick, unruly hair into a ponytail holder she found in the front jacket pocket, needing to feel prepared and without any possible distractions. Vasin's case file said he'd always gone easily into custody when caught alone, or she wouldn't have been sent in solo to apprehend him. Mike would be next to her instead of a mile or so out, checking for signs of a perimeter patrol. Still, she never knew what was behind a closed door.

Her practical, steel-toe combat-style boots stirred up the dirt that surrounded the aluminum building, and thin billows of dust rose to her hips. It was the middle of a long, hot summer, and the record-breaking heat had taken its toll on the grass undergrowth. One short spark and this place would become a forest furnace.

She was confident that Yuri Vasin's arrest would go smoothly, but her instincts were warning her to be on high alert. Whether it was the drive she'd had up here from Silver Valley, the isolated look of the building she approached or just nerves, she didn't know. Nerves were part of her job—they let her know she was paying attention, aware of her risks. Her stomach started to flip, and she reminded herself that this was supposed to be one of the more routine apprehensions—not that she ever considered catching a fugitive "routine." But her work had been pretty stable for the past several years, allowing her to be home for dinner most nights. A plus for her and her five-year-old son, Justin, but she'd called him Jake because she couldn't bear to hear his father's name on a regular basis.

Justin Berger. It didn't hurt anymore, most days, when she thought of her little boy's namesake. Because she *did* think about Justin every day, the man who'd fathered her son and given the ultimate sacrifice serving as a SEAL in the Mideast. Back in another life, when she'd been a Navy P-8 pilot and had worked with the special ops teams to help root out the bad guys.

Trina physically shook her head as if it'd rid her mind of the errant memories. It was approaching the anniversary of Justin's death; it was only natural she'd think of him now.

She turned her thoughts back to the present, back to the work in front of her. Arrest Vasin. Call in Mike to take him or get the jerk into the back of her tiny vehicle. She'd place a call to her team manager as soon as either of them had Vasin in cuffs. Take him to the nearest federal facility for processing, which in this case was Harrisburg.

Movement in her peripheral vision made her stop and reassess. A tiny furry creature crawled out from the other side of the building. Phew. A rabbit. She continued forward. But then the creature whimpered.

A puppy. Jake would be elated if she came home with a puppy to add to their growing menagerie at the farmette she'd recently purchased for them in Silver Valley, Pennsylvania.

No way.

Crap. This was not a canine rescue mission. Yuri Vasin was her man, the fugitive wanted for money laundering in New York, Connecticut, Pennsylvania and New Jersey. With new charges of human trafficking coming out of Wilmington, Delaware, this morning.

Vasin was Russian, five feet eleven inches, one hundred and eighty-five pounds. He definitely was not an approximately ten-pound caramel-latte-colored fuzz ball with big brown eyes and large paws on a too-skinny body. As the puppy stumbled along toward her, tail wagging tentatively, its whines turned to yips.

"Shhh!" She had to stop its noise. Bending down, she hoisted the little guy up and went to gently muzzle his puppy snout with her hand. He wriggled his face out of her grasp and licked her chin, his tiny body quivering with excitement. Or maybe relief?

Vasin couldn't be that bad, not if he had a new puppy. Although he needed to feed the pup more—this little guy was skinny. She looked around, making sure she was still alone. There weren't any visible cameras on the outside of the building. It looked abandoned, in fact.

Except for fresh tire tracks that ran from where the front door was to the surrounding grasslands. She saw the tracks emerge from the fields, and as she turned the corner with the puppy in her arms, she found the three ATVs that had made the tracks parked alongside the corrugated metal building.

The flips in her stomach turned to alarm bells.

Vasin wasn't alone.

Rob lay on the concrete floor of the warehouse and willed his aching limbs to stay still as he listened to Vasin and his men. His labored breathing made it difficult to ascertain the colloquial Russian, but he understood enough of their conversation to know two things.

First, they said they were hiding out in the Poconos to protect Dima Ivanov who was in his "bunker." That meant that Ivanov was nearby. This was new intelligence that the Trail Hikers didn't have—they knew he was close but didn't realize he had a full-on shelter. No one had suspected Ivanov would risk remaining so close to New York City and his usual operation area, not while the heat on him from all federal agencies was so heavy. But most importantly, Rob hadn't heard the all-too-familiar sneer of Dima Ivanov's voice, however. Which meant Vasin was running this current op, whatever it entailed. Rob could handle Vasin. Ivanov's voice was one he dreaded, because he knew if he heard the heavy, smoke-addled voice, Rob would be dead.

The last time he'd come face-to-face with Vasin and his immediate circle, Rob had had the upper hand. He'd been deep undercover and had helped blow the headquarters of a drug and money-laundering operation out of the water, literally. Ivanov had been operating his command center from a yacht in the Atlantic, just off the Jersey shore. Vasin ran the op on land, and Rob's CIA team took it all down, working hand in hand with FBI, ATF, DHS and local LEAs. Rob had escaped with his life and that of his team's—except for Jazz.

Goddamn it, he still saw her eyes right before the bullet blew her apart. The shock of losing a teammate never left him. Their memory never faded. But Jazz's loss had been the impetus for him to try to find closure for the other part of his life, a relationship he could have put to rest three years ago if he'd only had the courage to cross the damned street. To face for the last time the woman he'd loved when he'd still been named Justin.

A shuffle of chairs and rapid-fire Russian conversation filled his ears. No more thoughts of the woman he'd lost to distract him from the pain. He had to interpret their dialogue. His language skills weren't what they used to be, but they were good enough.

Hell and damnation. They were going to kill him sometime before tomorrow morning. Something about him being in the way of their "most important mission."

Robert opened his left eye a slit, since their voices came from his right side. He took in racks of weapons, ammo, explosives. Dang, they were loaded for bear. Just who were they expecting, the national guard? He wouldn't mind a unit to show up and rescue him right about now.

He knew no one was scheduled to come in here until after he'd secured Vasin—the risks were too great. Vasin and his boss Ivanov were known for retribution; last month six ATF agents had been slaughtered in an ambush in Newark, New Jersey. ROC didn't get its hands dirty, of course, but intelligence had proven it was clearly done on Ivanov's orders.

The powers that be had decided that taking out Ivanov alone was best to allow them to begin to dismantle the entire North American ROC from the inside out. It was going to take months, even years. Rob couldn't worry about that—he still had to complete his mission to neutralize Vasin. Somehow, someway, despite all these men around him.

He tested his binds. They'd used plastic zip ties on his wrists, which remained painfully strapped behind him and forced his back into an excruciating arch. His ankles were shackled, probably by chains, judging from the weight holding him down. The victims he'd witnessed captured by the ROC in New Jersey had been similarly restrained. It was signature Vasin. The man was a sadistic sociopath.

Vasin asked for something, then the sound of pounding on a table—a bottle, maybe?

Liquid pouring, a toast. Then another. Then a third. *Keep drinking, you son of a bitch.*

Fortunately for Rob, Vasin liked his vodka. Judging from the larger size of Vasin's nose, the obvious veins mapped over it, Vasin's alcoholism had progressed over the last two years even as his physicality didn't appear weaker. And it sounded like he wanted to celebrate tonight, before the big party tomorrow—Rob's murder party.

Steps shuffled on the floor, toward Rob. A solid hit to his chest forced his eyes to fly open.

Vasin laughed and spoke in a flurry of Russian. His spit hit his face with obvious satisfaction. Rob considered it a win that he felt it on his swollen skin. No extensive nerve damage. Yet.

"I didn't come here for you." It hurt so much to speak, damn it. Flashes of a previous time at the mercy of captors. He ignored them, fought off thinking about the one sure thing that got him through that torture.

"No, of course you didn't. You want my boss, no? But you'll never get him. No one touches Dima Ivanov."

"Maybe not, but I know who's coming to get him and all of you, and when." Another sign Vasin was losing it; he'd said his boss's name, blatantly unafraid of Rob. Yeah, Rob was a goner—they were going to kill him. Maybe sooner than tomorrow.

Vasin's eyes narrowed at Rob's dig, his breathing hitched. *Bait.* He'd believed the overblown statement.

"Everything you say is a lie. Who do you work for—the same people?"

"Yes." Let Vasin think he was still CIA or FBI. Vasin had accused Robert of being CIA when they'd blown apart the New Jersey op. There was no reason to correct him. The Trail Hikers were far more clandestine than the CIA, and Rob was certain Vasin and in fact the ROC had no idea who the Trail Hikers were.

"And who are they, your employers?"

Robert stayed silent. He'd never tell Vasin whom he really worked for. Or that he'd been a SEAL. Vasin was smart enough to know that no agent worth his or her training would ever give up their employer.

"Tell me." Vasin's meaty fist hit his temple, and an explosion of lights floated over his vision. The blackness threatened, but he hung on.

"Never."

"Of course you won't. So tell me, who's on their way to get us? The bogeyman?"

Hook.

"Two thousand agents. National Guard, DEA, local teams." The lie came easily even through his aching jaw. Vasin's breathing increased.

"When?"

"Tomorrow. Before sunup."

Vasin straightened and turned toward his men, but not before Rob saw the frown drawn on his face. He watched them squirm in their seats as Vasin asked his team if anyone knew about the LEAs. Then he asked how many of the ROC men were expected to arrive over the next day. Rob let go a small, painful sigh when the men stated they only expected a dozen or so.

Vasin lowered his head, and Robert saw the flicker of worry cross the bastard's face. After what felt like hours, Vasin motioned with his head toward Rob, shouting orders to his goons. "Get him up and let him take a piss. Then put him in the chair at the table."

He faced Rob again and leaned in, his breath heavy with vodka and bile. "I'm going to let you tell me everything you know. If you're lucky, I'll leave you for dead here, before my boss shows up."

Rob didn't have to ask what would happen if he wasn't lucky. Vasin would torture him until he begged to die.

Time to reel the monster in.

* * *

Trina peered around the corner of the building, her weapon drawn. The puppy had given her enough time to see the ATVs before she'd done something stupid and unforgivable for a US marshal: walk into a danger zone uninformed. Someone hadn't done their job, because clearly Vasin was not alone and all of her reports indicated otherwise. She'd worry about the lack of communication later. Right now she wanted Yuri Vasin in cuffs.

Security cameras were mounted under the roof's overhang on the four corners of the building; she'd only discovered them once she was up under the eaves herself.

She flattened herself to the side of the wall and started to inch her way back toward the opposite side of the building where she'd noticed the other, probably faux, doors. But she had to determine if she could see inside the structure and make out what the hell was going on. Trina sent a quick text to Mike, telling him to head in. She'd wait for him to apprehend.

As she crept along the twenty yards of solid steel building, she was conscious of the puppy shadowing her, quiet and stealthy. She couldn't risk the noise of shooing the dog away, and was annoyed that he distracted her at all. Her fingers hit the corner of the building and she made sure the area was clear before she turned the corner and made straight for the doors. The security cameras had to not be working, or she'd have been stopped by someone by now.

When she lined up with the "doors," her fingertips felt the smoothness of the corrugated steel—and the paint that had been used to create the illusion of entrances.

Except in the middle of the one large garage-style door, where she immediately felt the cut of steel-on-steel. An opening. Maybe not one that was used much, but an entrance or exit of some sort. Further inspection revealed a painted-over window. She slipped a razor out of her front pocket. Slowly and carefully scraped away the black pigment. She kept her free hand over the working one—she didn't want to alert anyone inside with a flash of light. The paint was thick and chipped off in the tiniest of pieces. That was fine. All she needed was a pupil's worth.

As soon as she had enough of an opening, she stood on tiptoe and looked inside. Shelves, all stocked with what appeared to be cans of paint—no shocker there— and ammo, the boxes emblazoned with US ARMY. It was hard to see much farther than five or six rows of shelving.

Ammo. *Crap.* She couldn't see past the stacked army boxes. *Double crap.* Either this was some kind of clandestine military ammunitions depot she didn't know about, or she'd been mistakenly sent to get this Vasin dude at his place of business. He was supposed to be alone, separated from the ROC and far from its head honcho, Dima Ivanov. Intelligence reports revealed that Vasin might have had a falling-out with Dima and that's why he was working alone. That was another factor that supposedly made him an easy suspect to bring in. But it looked like Vasin had decided to protect himself in the process. And whoever was with him in the building.

Trina sank down onto her haunches, lifting her cowboy hat enough to wipe the sweat off her brow and out of her eyes. She had two choices: go in with Mike, or call for backup and wait to go in with Mike.

She sent a quick text to both Mike and their team leader, Corey. They had to understand that Vasin was not alone, and she told them that she needed direction on whether to abort the apprehension or not. While she waited for the return texts, she headed back to the front of the building. Her boss would need exact details for whatever additional law enforcement they sent in, and she wanted to tell him the license plate numbers on the ATVs.

A sharp rustle behind her startled her and she whipped around and trained her weapon on the source. She let out a sigh of relief as it was only the puppy, making funny growling noises as he ran in a circle in front of her. Her relief turned to trepidation as she realized he was trying to tell her something.

"What, boy?" She mouthed the words as the back of her neck prickled. The tiny animal didn't want her to go any further and was trying to keep her from moving forward. Intuition tightened her gut and her hold on her weapon but as an explosion sounded in the building she realized she might be too late.

Chapter 2

Rob had done it. He'd convinced Vasin that he was worth keeping alive. For a bit longer, anyhow.

It was enough time to get hold of the tear gas that was on the shelf. If that was what was in the box marked US ARMY TEAR GAS, that is. He'd also spotted several box cutters scattered around the shelves.

"I have to piss." He spoke to the ROC member through swollen lips, dried blood tasting foul from where his teeth had cut through his cheeks with each blow from Vasin earlier. He played along with Vasin's order to let him use the bathroom.

"No funny business, or *phwwwt*." One of Vasin's men swiped his finger across his neck while his smug smirk dared Rob to challenge him. Rob had no doubt that the finger would become a switchblade with little provocation. He also knew he'd take this little jerk down.

"I can't go without my hands, man."

"Let him go, Aleksey." Vasin's voice slurred from the vodka, but the thug listened to him nonetheless. Vasin's word was law, drunk or sober, superseded only by Ivanov's.

Two clicks of the very knife Rob feared freed his wrists. Painful jolts of pins and needles hit his arms, hands, as his blood flow returned full force. He fought to flex his fingers and roll his shoulders.

"I give you both but you only need one for your small dick." The man with the smirk laughed at his poor humor. Rob remained silent and waited for the feeling to return to his hands and fingers.

"The bathroom?" He spoke through clenched teeth.

"The bathroom for *you* is over there." Aleksey took him past the ammo and to a small latrine, which was little more than a hole in the ground. Nothing Rob hadn't experienced before.

Aleksey left him alone so that he could walk over to the table where Vasin sat. He shot down a glass of vodka that Vasin had poured for him, his *ura* an underscore to the laughter and leers at Rob from the other men. That was the Russian military response to a toast, or more historically, a battle cry similar to the U.S. Marine Corps' *oorah*. Aleskey, and the others, were trying to intimidate him.

Have your fun now, suckers.

As they mocked him, he mapped out his route and plan of attack. It might be his last. But he'd have accomplished his mission—take out Vasin and in the process, Ivanov. Rob wouldn't be the one to actually kill Ivanov, but he'd make damned sure the other LEAs knew where to find him with little effort.

Trina.

He couldn't risk not surviving this mission, after all.

Because Rob knew Ivanov was in this building, or somewhere very nearby. Most likely in a basement. The type of underground, clandestine, over-the-top living structure that ROC was famous for. Ingenious locations with even more clever hideaways.

Rob forced himself to urinate, finding that indeed, he'd had to go. Funny how pain distracted one from basic needs.

"Can't find it, you capitalist pig?" Vasin laughed and slammed down another empty shot glass. Rob bided his time, acting as if he were fumbling with his zipper.

Truth was, he'd be hard-pressed to re-zip his pants right now with his fingers still so stiff and swollen. But he had enough range of motion to open a box with a box cutter, grab a tear gas canister and launch it. He'd use his teeth to get to it if he had to.

Another boisterous toast. The men clinked glasses and Robert ran.

"The agent!" Slurred words from one of them.

"Don't shoot him! We need his information!" Vasin unwittingly gave Rob the precious seconds he needed by making the men halt in their tracks.

He grabbed the box off the shelf and heard the yells, the sounds of vodka-hindered feet. The carton opened with little effort, spilling dozens of canisters at his feet. He kicked them toward his attackers as he clutched one, armed it and threw. It landed in the center of the group of four men. Then he shoved against the shelf in front of them as hard as his battered body allowed him to. A loud squeaking rent the air as the metal contraption yielded. He looked at his captors as the canister fell toward them. The men wore various expressions of shock, fear and dread. They reflexively reached for their weapons, despite their boss's order, as if bullets would stop hundreds of pounds of metal and ammunition aimed at them. It was too late. The shelves came down, and he didn't stick around to see how many were trapped. The loud *crack* of the detonator was immediately followed by the appearance of a misty cloud of tear gas. Rob held his breath and ran for the exit.

Trina texted her boss again with the minimal vital details of her plan and what she expected but still hoped she wouldn't find in the warehouse. Before she added a third text, he called her.

"Get out, Trina. Don't go in there alone. One explosion leads to more. Mike is on the east side of the clearing if you need him, but I want you both out of there *now*."

She heard her boss's voice over the Bluetooth connection in her earbuds and let out a sigh of relief. "I was thinking the same thing," she whispered as she looked at the puppy and decided not to tell Corey that she was taking one thing from this mission—a new family member. She and Jake had the space now, so why not?

"Stop! Where are you now exactly, Trina?" Corey's sharp query startled her.

"Next to the building. Heading out." She read off the GPS coordinates, in case Corey had lost her signal. Keeping her voice in a whisper, she crouched down to grab the puppy.

Corey swore over the connection. "Damn it, change of plans. Trina, you're closest. I need you to get someone who's in there, from another op. Damn these mixed comms!" Corey was obviously taking a call from another LEA.

"Who, Corey?"

"Hang on." She heard another loud bang inside the building and the puppy jumped, moving away from her. Damn it! "Robert Bristol. Don't come back without him."

"Got it." And she'd get the man. There wasn't time to ask Corey specifically who the man was, if he was wanted by the agents from another op, or was LEA himself. It'd all come out soon enough.

She shot one last look at the door she'd surveyed. Was she going to have to go in there, after all? This Robert Bristol dude had better know she was going to get him. Looking around the building and the surrounding forest, she saw no one. Disappointment weighed on her. As she turned back toward the building, the door burst open and a hunched over yet ambulatory man barreled out amid a cloud of white smoke. Coughing as if he had TB, he appeared a little dazed. Tear gas. *Crap.*

Trina drew her weapon and pointed it him. "Stop. Hands above your head."

The man complied, albeit stiffly. She watched his arms rise and noted his hands. Why were her eyes drawn to his hands? They were so familiar. As if she'd seen them, seen *him* before. She stared at his face. Her insides froze. Was this how it felt to lose your mind? How crazy felt? Because she felt like she was looking at a ghost.

"Gotta go, boss." She spoke into her mic, never taking her eyes off the man. The man who looked exactly like the man she'd given her heart to years ago. Justin Berger.

"Trina, wait—" She yanked her earbuds and Corey's voice out. She left her phone on, though. Headquarters would at least have a recording of whatever was about to go down. Hopefully it wasn't her sanity.

"Stay still. Identify yourself."

The man looked stunned as he turned toward her voice, arms raised. Tears streamed down his cheeks thanks to tear gas. They fell from dark eyes. That is, one of them was a dark brown, the other swollen to a narrow slit. His body, at least the parts visible to her, was unbelievably bruised. He wore only a T-shirt that had once been greenish but was filthy and torn, and his cargo pants were unzipped, and God, she could see his briefs and what should be tucked away *inside* his briefs.

Acting on pure instinct born of years of training, she visually inspected him from head to toe, looking for weapons. Even if he had a weapon he appeared too battered to use it, but Trina knew no matter how much pain either a criminal trying to escape, or a trained agent was in, they'd figure out a way. She still wasn't sure who this man was—friend or foe. Her orders were to get him but she'd rescued agents from tight spots before, under the guise of taking them into custody. She had to treat him as suspicious until either he proved he wasn't, or Corey told her to trust him.

"Keep your hands up and turn around."

He complied, and she swiftly approached him and patted him down. No weapons, but the way his pants fit him, the way his form was achingly familiar, had her wondering again if she was having some sort of psychotic break.

He had an air about him that distracted her, made her

think she knew him. She shook her head, her weapon still on him. Focus. She needed focus.

"Turn around. Who the hell are you?" Her voice usually commanded response, but this man only stared after he turned around to face her. He lowered his arms.

"Keep them up."

"You know I'm not armed. Look, our time is short—"

"Who are you?"

"Rob Bristol. Who the hell are you?" He was her last-minute target, after all. She forced out a breath.

"US Marshal Lopez. You're coming with me."

Gunfire erupted before he could reply, and "Rob" looked at her. Because she was beginning to feel that she wasn't crazy. That this was Justin.

"Who were you here for, Marshal? Originally?"

She stared him down, refusing to answer. Was it hotter than she thought? Was she dehydrated? Because this man, this apparition in front of her, looked and sounded exactly like Justin.

The ghost spoke. "I'm with the government, too. There are too many of them for us to handle."

Trina remained silent.

"Let's go before they kill us both." His voice was taut and he'd obviously had the crap knocked out of him, but the tone, the way he measured each word even under pressure, it was unique. She'd only ever known one other man to act like this in the midst of a firefight.

"I don't suppose you have ID?" She'd never had to guess at whether she was taking in a good guy or not. They'd always been bad guys.

"You're kidding me, right? Look at me. I've had the crap knocked out of me." The harsh words softened with a tone she'd thought was only for her. It was the same method Justin had used to convince her his tactic was best.

She was going to put in for two weeks' leave the minute she was back at headquarters. Mental health preventive. Because she had to be losing it. Right here, in the middle of what was supposed to be a routine apprehension.

More gunfire and a cloud of what she assumed was tear gas poured from the crack under the door. Once again she tried to stare him down, make him flinch. "Can you run?"

Rob nodded once, his hands still high.

"Follow me."

She ran not away from the building, but toward it, and she sensed his hesitation, his desire to run in the opposite direction. When she held up the key she'd hid in her pocket and pointed at the ATV she was headed for, he followed.

As they ran, the puppy loped alongside her. "Buddy, there's no room at the inn. Go home!" She spoke under her breath as she ran, shooing away the too-cute creature. Robert Bristol needed a quick ride out of here, and she intended to keep them both alive while doing it.

This was the craziest apprehension she'd ever had, especially since she wasn't leaving with her target but a stranger her mind thought was Justin. And now a puppy was trying to join them. As if it were all some kind of fun escapade and not life-and-death circumstances. They came up to the first ATV and she faced the gaunt man, her Justin-come-to-life, ready to put her weapon on him again if she had to.

"Raise your hands again." She looked him in the eyes and faltered. Blinked. What the hell was wrong with her? Justin was dead. This man who looked like the one man she would have ever been willing to sacrifice everything for had to be a genetic anomaly. He couldn't be Justin. Justin was dead. Killed—in action in a war-torn Middle Eastern country during a civil war— five years ago tomorrow. A date etched in her mind but seared on her heart. The part that had never healed.

The eye that wasn't swollen widened, and she ignored the screaming of her subconscious. So the doppelgänger had the same eye color.

"Who are you?"

He didn't say anything. With no fanfare she patted him down more intensely this time, noting again that he was clean of any weapons. He'd sustained several bruises and a possible fracture on his ulna. Yet he still held his arm up. His muscles were tight under his dirty olive T-shirt and cargo pants, but that wasn't her problem. Or advantage. His ass, at once familiar and strange, could solve her obvious mental stress. Justin had had a tattoo on his butt. Certainly this man did not.

She forced herself to not try to find said tattoo and straightened. She looked him in his good eye. "Mess with me and I'll kill you. Got it?"

"Roger."

Gunshots erupted again, and this time they were followed by the sounds of footsteps outside the building. Three men had emerged from the structure, but Trina didn't wait to ID them. She had her man and she had wheels. Time to make their escape.

The puppy's whimper tugged at the part of her that had nothing to do with being a hardened US marshal. Huge, liquid-chocolate-brown eyes pleaded for her mercy as he sat at her feet.

"Damn it." Trina reached down and grabbed the pup and handed him to the man named Rob. "Here. Keep him between us. Use your good arm to hang on to me. Get on."

The puppy seemed to sense this was for the best as he settled without fanfare between Trina and her captive. Rob Bristol reached his good arm loosely around her middle, keeping the puppy safe on the seat. The tiny sparks she imagined dancing on her skin weren't any kind of awareness; she simply noticed that his fingers brushed her waist. *He's probably a criminal anyway, not a government agent or LEA.*

And he wasn't, couldn't possibly be, Justin, no matter how many times she'd fantasized that Justin had somehow survived that secret mission all those years ago. They'd never recovered his body, though. That had always haunted her.

"Hang on." It was her only warning before she gunned the engine, zigzagging over the road she'd memorized, and aimed for the main highway. One thing she knew about bad guys, they usually didn't like to travel during the day on a major thoroughfare. Too risky. If she could get herself and this unknown-government-agency-dude there, they'd be in the clear.

He kept his arm around her waist, holding more tightly on the bumpy patches, remaining silent save for an occasional unintelligible murmur. Groans of pain, she guessed.

All she had to do was get them to the car, move the branches out of the way, and drive out of here. If she was taking him to Harrisburg, she'd make the most of the few hours' drive. Trina had a lot of questions for this man once they were free of their pursuers.

* * *

"Ma'am, the US marshal from the Harrisburg office is on line one." The Trail Hikers receptionist's voice came over Claudia's computer speaker.

"Thanks, Jessica." Trail Hikers agency Director Claudia Michele pressed the key that put the secure, encrypted call through. A retired US Marine Corps two-star general, Claudia thrived on live ops and knew her agents were the best in the world. She trusted that Corey from the US Marshals had followed through and one of his team had managed to get Rob out of the ROC op gone wrong.

"Hi, Corey. I hope you have good news."

"Absolutely. My marshal reports that she's got a man who says his name is Rob Bristol, but won't say who he works for. That sound about right, General?" Corey and the US Marshals as a whole weren't privy to what Trail Hikers was all about, but like other LEAs in the area he had been told enough to be able to help out Claudia when one of her agents was at risk. She'd gone straight to Corey when she'd found out he had two marshals already in the area.

Claudia sat up straight. "Yes, that's him. Where did she run into him?"

She listened as Corey related the details of his marshal's situation, and as he spoke she worked on her computer, finding the affirmation she needed. There'd been no word from Rob since earlier today, and it wasn't because he'd lost comms due to weather or gear failure. He'd been taken by the notorious ROC member Yuri Vasin, if what Corey relayed was correct.

Claudia started to tell Corey to have his marshal go to a location where another TH agent would get Rob.

Then she stopped, remembering the reason Rob had moved to Silver Valley, temporarily.

"Corey, do you mind telling me the name of your marshal?"

"Lopez. Trina Lopez."

Claudia had to stifle a long whistle, an old Marine Corps habit. She knew all there was to know about her agents—it was part and parcel of hiring someone to be a Trail Hiker. As much as she wanted to see Rob put his old demons to rest, she would have never picked a live firefight as the time to do so.

"Tell you what, Corey. As long as Rob is good to go for now, without medical attention, have her bring him back to Harrisburg. We'll arrange for a pickup from your office. If he needs medical assistance, have them either call in or go to the Lehigh Valley medical center in Allentown. We have a special team there for this type of circumstance."

"Will do. I have another marshal in the area but I've called him off. In light of your man's appearance, the fewer eyes on him the better, I figure."

"You're absolutely right." Claudia finished working out details with Corey and then disconnected the call. Rob wasn't going to be happy he'd run into Trina in this manner, but sometimes fate nudged things along. She knew that firsthand from her working relationship with Silver Valley PD's chief, Colt Todd. What had started as a business connection turned into much more as they spent time together. She fingered her wedding band, which Colt had slid on not too long ago. Claudia wasn't one to stick her nose in her agents' personal lives, but if she helped any of them come to resolution over a private matter, it was better for their entire Trail Hikers team.

TH work was fast-paced, intense and often deadly. The more emotionally stable her agents were, the better.

Of course, the US marshal Rob was interested in was married, at least she had been three years ago, from what he'd said. It pained her whenever one of her agents was hurting, physically or otherwise. But if this was the "ripping off the bandage" work that Rob needed to do to move on with his life, she was all for it.

She shifted in her executive chair and moved her mouse over the satellite image of where Rob and Trina had reunited. Reports were coming in that Vasin had been taken into custody, but there was no sign of the big ROC boss, Ivanov. Vasin had better talk, because Ivanov was still at large.

Rob couldn't believe it. He'd taken the temporary Trail Hikers position to be closer to where he knew Trina had settled down. She'd returned to her family's native city of Harrisburg, Pennsylvania. Since he'd finally realized he needed to see her again, gain closure from the intense affair they'd had, and admit to her that she'd been the one thought that got him through it, that is. His counselor as well as his boss at Trail Hikers both confirmed what he knew but hadn't wanted to follow through on. He had to face Trina one last time, no matter if she was happily married and settled down with another. It was crucial to keep the PTSD from flaring up again and messing up a mission. Not that it ever had, but he didn't want it hanging over his head forever.

When he'd first met the counselor and decided to gain closure with Trina, he thought he'd drive up to Silver Valley for a day, face her, then drive back to the

condo he owned in Arlington, Virginia. Then the Trail
Hikers opportunity had opened up six months ago when
he'd turned in his CIA resignation. He was done with
the hard stuff. But his CIA handler knew that a man
like Rob never retired from clandestine ops. He'd connected Rob with Trail Hikers and the rest was history.

At least, the last six months of his life's history. He'd
told himself he'd approach Trina soon. He knew she
was a US marshal; Claudia said she could help him
make contact.

But it was supposed to be on *his* time schedule, when
he was ready. Not in the middle of an op gone wrong.

He'd thrown himself out of the building, not sure he'd
survive. He was too hurt to outrun the ROC on his own.
Trina had appeared: a savior with the face of an angel
and a killer body. He'd tried to figure out how quickly
he could disappear into the fields and forest surrounding Vasin's hideout even as Trina patted him down.
He'd entertained hot-wiring one of the ATVs, whether
or not she came with him. Fifteen seconds was his record. But with swollen hands and fingers, he didn't
stand a chance.

Then Trina had shown up as if his mind had willed
her to.

When she'd jangled that key in midair he'd wanted
to whoop. Until he caught the glimmer of her eyes, the
slant of her cheekbones. Until he'd looked, really *seen*
her body. Same curves but fuller. Somehow stronger
than before, which was incredible since she'd always
been able to keep up with him on training runs around
the airfield. And then she'd spoken. Her voice was unforgettable. Tragedy and fate might have put several

lifetimes between them, but he'd recognize her voice anywhere.

Trina was a US marshal. And just as memories of her and what they'd shared in the godforsaken desert saved him in the depths of POW torture, she'd plucked him from certain death today.

Bullets strafed the dirt on either side of the ATV as they sped away. He had to fight from telling her what to do. If she was a US marshal, she knew what she was doing. Judging from how quickly they put Vasin's men behind them, she was for real. Did she even have a clue who he was? Had he imagined the flicker of recognition that crossed her face, the initial look of shock?

She buried you a long time ago.

"You okay back there?"

"Fine." He leaned his torso against her back. The hell with it. Aches and repeat injuries to his rib cage and jaw weren't as easy to ignore as they'd been five years ago. His thirty-year-old body had the aches of a seventy-year-old at the moment, thanks to Vasin's attention to detail. Rob realized he'd been lucky to transition to the CIA after his SEAL time, and then into Trail Hikers. However, maybe he'd bitten off more than he could chew by signing up for this particular Trail Hikers op. There were other, less lethal ops to take on.

No. Not a thought he'd entertain while escaping certain death, while Ivanov remained out there. Trina took the ATV through a rough field, and the jostling made stars stab at his closed lids. Oh yeah. He'd taken a decent beating this time.

"Hang tight. It's going to get a little rough, but we'll be in a regular car soon." The commanding tone reflected her years of training. First as a Navy combat pilot and now as a marshal. He'd have pegged her as a shoo-in for the commercial airlines, but her will of steel no doubt made her an excellent marshal. The best.

He leaned against a woman who'd changed as much as he had in five years. Yet her body felt as if it still belonged to him. He cursed himself for paying attention to anything but their getting out of range of the ROC's bullets. She was married, most likely to the man he'd seen her with. And she had a kid. There was no future with Trina, only this present space as he leaned against her. But no matter what he tried to think of to keep his heart from pounding with exultation that he'd found her again, it was pointless.

It was as if no time had passed.

Wrong, buddy. Five years have passed. Five years in which she never tried to find him. Assumed he'd died. Would he have believed she'd died if presented with the same circumstances?

Anger washed over him. She had no idea that her threat to kill him if he tried to escape meant nothing, no clue that he could kill her with his bare hands. Speeding ATV and multiple injuries be damned.

Sure you're not overestimating your capabilities?

More like underestimating his injuries. Rob groaned, and for the umpteenth time refused to acknowledge his mortality. At least the pain kept him grounded, which he needed. Trina wasn't his angel or savior. She wasn't *his* anything. The ATV hit a large bump, throwing them airborne for a solid second. He held on to the woman and let himself enjoy the physical contact with her, no matter how brief. Even though he'd crushed her chances of happily ever after with him. Or rather, the war and extenuating circumstances had. He would sure as rain jump off this vehicle if he had to. No matter if it killed him. At least it would be on his terms and not Vasin's. And Trina need never know it was him.

You'd never leave her to face them alone.

No amount of bouncing on an ATV with his most certainly bruised if not broken ribs could cause enough pain to keep him from facing the cold truth. It mocked him with each jarring movement.

He'd never stopped loving Trina.

Trina changed her focus, from the trail as she swerved off it onto avoiding tree trunks in the dense forest. It was the perfect spot to keep them out of sight and more importantly, out of bullet range of Vasin's men. The intensity of the wooded route allowed her to hang on to what felt like the last remnants of her sanity.

It was as if her fantasies had materialized in the form of a man who said he worked for the same team she did, and who looked, sounded and walked exactly as Justin had.

His breathing was shallow as he kept his arms around her waist, and she winced with him at each outcropping, each shale rock that the wheels hit. As if it really were Justin. As if maybe, somehow, he'd survived that explosion, crawled out of the detonation crater and lived.

His loud groan of pain tensed her muscles. Now she was feeling his pain. This wasn't how to work an apprehension.

"Hang on and I'll get us off this as soon as I can. It sounds like we may have lost them." Not that the loud roar of the ATV was any way to elude detection. She only had to get them near her vehicle and they'd have the upper hand.

If her mind would stop playing tricks on her.

Chapter 3

"You're awfully quiet. Hang on, we're almost there. Don't even think about jumping—it'll make it hurt more." The vibration of her voice felt comforting under Rob's uninjured arm as he continued to hang on to her.

It was as if Trina had read his mind. That gave him pause, made his heart lurch at the possibility they still shared their unforgettable connection. As steely and official as her tone was, she couldn't shake the seductive edge of it. When she'd been a pilot helping him in support of SEAL missions he'd heard it, looked up from his tablet to pinpoint who was speaking in such rich notes. Her voice had been what initially drew him to her, how he'd learned there was so much more to the accomplished Navy pilot than met the eye.

"I'm not going anywhere." Not this time. Not until he leveled with her, told her he'd survived. And wished her well to her face. She had to know, or suspect strongly, that it was him. Trina was too smart not to see the similarities. She had to be at least comparing him to the man he'd once been. A man she'd thought dead for the past five years.

"Damn right you're not going anywhere." Her words weren't directed at him as she didn't shout over the engine or wind, but he felt her breath, heard her words as his ear rested on her back. He wondered if she could feel how well they still fit together.

"Ugh." His grunt came out louder than he'd planned, but the ATV rode like a truck without the shock absorbers. Holy hell but Trina knew how to maneuver it, as well as she'd flown the P-8 they'd met in. More importantly, how to evade a pursuer. Within minutes they passed through a copse of birch, pine and fir trees and drove up onto a paved road. A real highway.

It was pure bliss to his bruised ass and kidneys, as well as his sore crotch.

With no fanfare, she stopped the ATV and dismounted, indicating he do the same. She took the puppy from him as he stiffly executed a controlled fall off his seat. At least he was on two feet.

Trina's gaze assessed him, but if she thought it was the man she'd once loved, her expression revealed nothing. She'd had the time she needed to regain her composure.

"We have to move quickly. Can you still run?"

"I'll do my best."

Her cool gray eyes met his. Awareness, tight and immediate, thrummed between them. He held his breath, waiting for her to acknowledge she recognized him.

"Damn right. Let's go." She tucked the damned dog

under one arm and grabbed his upper arm with the other. She propelled him forward, leading them back into the deeper part of the woods, away from the highway. For someone with such a lean body she was remarkably strong. And fast. Just as he remembered.

His breath hitched, and the air felt like fire as it entered and exited his lungs, scraping as it went. The raspy sound would have alarmed him if he weren't afraid they were both about to get shot to pieces by one of Vasin's men. He was pretty sure Vasin was down for the count, with a shelving unit and tear gas to fight through. He'd caught the other thugs unawares, too, but at least one if not two of them had escaped and shot at them. He had no doubt they were close behind on the remaining ATVs. His ears strained to hear their roar. He was afraid that they'd alerted Ivanov to the breach of their inner sanctum. The ROC would unleash hell on earth to stop Rob and anyone who threatened their dominion.

"Come on! Don't slow down now." No compassion laced Trina's urgent order.

"Going. Fast. As. I. Can." He gritted his teeth, but his swollen cheeks didn't make it the pain-relieving experience it should have been as his jaw screamed in protest.

The roar of an ATV reached his ears just fine, however. Cold sweat would have broken out on his neck if he weren't already overheated from the physical demands of the run and his pain non-management.

Trina heard the engine as well. She kept moving, kept up their forward momentum as she half pushed, half dragged him by his good arm. "Come on, buddy. Pretend you're in shape and have to score the winning touchdown in the Super Bowl. You're a wide receiver, running with the ball toward the goalpost."

In shape? Couldn't she see he was freaking injured, not out of shape?

"We're headed to that spot over there, by the way." He looked at her out of his good eye, which made him turn his head, and he tripped. Sharp rocks and hard dirt raced up toward him, filling his limited vision, before a hard yank on his shirt collar had him upright. His neck howled in pain.

"Aggggh." He stifled the scream, and it sounded like a damned frog. This was definitely an example of how not to run into a former lover.

"Stay with me." Trina's voice strained as she dug in with the heels of her work boots and kept him from falling face-first onto the forest floor for a second time. She held on to his collar as she pulled him up next to her, her silver eyes steady on him again. "You okay?"

He grunted.

"Then get in this car, back seat, now." She'd led them to what he'd thought was a huge shrub but she pulled the branches off to reveal a small hatchback—a Ford Fiesta. If he had the breath he'd whoop and hug the tight-assed marshal. She was his ticket out of hell. Until he told her he was, had been, Justin. That he was still alive. Would she even care?

"Okay, get in." He bit his lip as he held on to the small car's roof with his arm, holding his injured arm against his middle. After he got into the seat, Trina put his seat belt around him, and he caught a whiff of her scent. When he breathed in sharply she stilled and stared at him, her expression wary. Frightened.

Yeah, she'd noticed the resemblance.

The buckle clicked into place and Trina straightened outside the car. "Keep an eye on the dog." The mangy pup was placed on the seat next to him, where it immediately curled up and went to sleep. Rob envied the dog's ability to give in to basic instinct.

He'd be fighting his the entire time he was with Trina.

The shooters had come so close to them but never noticed the car under the branches, between two full bushes.

Only minutes earlier, getting killed by fugitives had been her biggest worry. Not whether or not she was sane, thinking the man behind her was Justin. Justin was dead. But if he'd lived, if this was him, she'd have to tell him about *her* Justin Berger, his son, Jake.

No, you don't.

Yes, she did. Protecting Jake from strangers was one thing, but from his father another. Although the man in the back seat was virtually a stranger. He couldn't be Justin.

It's improbable but still possible.

As she cleared the remaining branches off the car, she used the small space from Rob Bristol to get it together. She refused to look back as she took off her cowboy hat, threw it across to the passenger seat, and slid into the driver's seat. Trina waited as the sound of the Russians' ATV engines faded, making certain they were gone before she started the car.

The man remained silent as she drove up onto the highway. After a few miles on flat pavement, she checked him out in the rearview mirror. His head was tilted back as if he'd fallen asleep. Or unconscious. Panic gripped her chest.

"Hey! You still with me?"

Nothing.

He could be messing with her. But then he lifted his head, and she saw the tortured expression on his face. Compassion pierced her defenses.

"Are you all right? I've got pain meds in the first aid kit."

"A-okay, baby cakes."

Realization slammed through her, blowing away her cobwebs of disbelief and denial. Unless this was a ghost, and she'd imagined the entire time between seeing him stumble out of the building that was housing Vasin and now, this had to be Justin. He was the only one who'd ever called her "baby cakes."

Justin was still alive.

She headed east, called her boss and refused to look her passenger in the eye. She gripped the wheel, waiting for Corey to pick up.

"Trina, why the freak haven't you checked in?" Corey Blumenthal's voice rumbled in her earpiece. She couldn't use the speakerphone, not with an unknown in the back seat, no matter that he was probably a fellow LEA agent or officer.

And he wasn't unknown, but a freaking practical ghost.

"Handling things. I'm safe. I should be in Harrisburg in about two hours or so. I've got Rob Bristol with me."

"Thank God! We've got reports that the warehouse you went to had an event. Where are you?" Her boss's voice remained professional, but she heard the concern in it.

She gave him her coordinates so that he could confirm her GPS unit was working. "I'm within two and a

half hours of base. Unless you tell me to go elsewhere."
The puppy chose that time to bark. Of course.

"What the hell is that?"

"A dog. He wouldn't stop following me."

"You're a US marshal, Lopez, not a dogcatcher."

"Yes, sir." She and Corey were on first-name basis,
but she liked to rankle him by reminding him he was
two decades older.

"So, you have Bristol. Well done. Just to be safe, describe him to me."

What the hell? He never questioned her like this.

She looked in the rearview mirror as she drove,
catching quick looks at Justin—God, it *was* Justin—
but not enough to get them in an accident.

"Shaved crew cut, blondish, graying scruff on his
chin, dark eyes, well, eye—one of them is swollen
shut—about six feet, maybe two hundred, two-twenty."
And all of it hard muscle, if he was anything like he'd
been when they'd made love under the desert stars,
making the baby she'd raised on her own.

"Lopez. What about ID?" Corey's impatience bris-
tled more than usual because she got it—she was annoyed, too.

"Not possible. I asked. No ID, no papers on him.
Not saying who he's with." Her fingers betrayed her
as she spoke, burning with the memory of patting him
down—there'd been nothing under his clothing except
hard, sinewy male body. Justin's body.

"Ask him." Her boss's voice shook her from her lust.

"He claims he's an agent of some type. I trusted my
gut. He's been beat to hell by the ROC members."

"Robert Bristol. TH." Her fugitive croaked out his
name again but this time added the "TH." Trina locked

gazes with him in the rearview mirror, fighting the urge to slam the car to a stop, get out and pull him out to get to the bottom of his identity.

"He says his name is Robert Bristol, TH, whatever the hell that means."

Was that a sparkle of glee, amusement or demonic intention in his good eye?

"That's all the identification we need. You've got the right man, Trina. Bring him in." Corey paused, the line crackling in her earbud. "Well done, Trina."

"Yes, sir." She finished her conversation with Corey and turned her attention to her passenger.

"That's not your name and we both know it. Where the hell have you been?" Trina wasn't playing his game any longer. The initial shock was wearing thin and she had to know whom she was transporting back to head-quarters, at least, whoever he used to be. Before he called himself Robert Bristol.

"Please keep your eyes on the road, Marshal Lopez."

"Shut the hell up." Backed into an emotional corner, she relied on good old sailor-speak.

"Trina, what the hell is going on out there? Are you okay?" Corey's concerned voice filled her ear. She'd neglected to disconnect. Just great.

"I'm okay, boss. We're having a little 'whose LEA is bigger' contest, that's all."

This time she made sure to disconnect.

"Damn it!" Trina slammed her palms on the steering wheel of the small economy car. A cheap rental, judging from the clean smell of the upholstery and lack of air-conditioning. At least she'd opened the windows and let the clean air stream in. "Want to explain why your name is Rob Bristol these days?"

"Self-preservation."

He liked the way her gray eyes looked almost black each time she glanced at him in the rearview mirror. Her hair was escaping the ponytail holder, and long, wavy wisps floated around her as the air blew in through the front two windows she'd lowered halfway.

He couldn't help it; he laughed. And then groaned.

"Are you in pain?" Her tough countenance fled. Did she care if he suffered? It could be a good sign if she did.

He shook his head. Nope, couldn't go there. Trina was married, and he had to gain closure with her for their time in the desert. Nothing more. Achieve point A, move to B.

"Stop." He choked out the word.

"I can't stop—we have to make it to Harrisburg." Same tiny lines between her brows when she frowned, if a bit deeper and definite. The years had been tough on each of them, it appeared.

"No, I mean, stop making me laugh. It hurts my ribs."

"It's going to hurt a lot more if you don't start talking. What were you doing in that warehouse? Did you lie to me about working for the government? Do you work for ROC?"

"Hell no. I was trying to take Vasin out." The words escaped and he realized he had to reel them back in, but couldn't. He'd never let classified information spill before, no matter how much pain he was in.

"Take Yuri Vasin, second to only Dima Ivanov, out? What's your definition of 'out,' by the way?"

"Actually, it turns out I had to take out Vasin first.

And before you get upset, know that he's under a huge metal shelf sucking in tear gas. He's as good as caught. The local authorities will have no problem apprehending him. Ivanov remains unseen and at large, but I'd bet my life he's near the warehouse, if not in it." She had to know about the basements and concealed structures-within-structures that ROC was famous for. Nothing about that was classified.

"Well, that's reassuring." Her sarcasm tore at him, and he reassessed his initial appraisal of US Marshal Trina Lopez. Or rather, added to it. She'd come a long way from the serious but always chipper Navy pilot he'd known. She was still spot-on with her job, but her demeanor was more sober. Wiser. She hadn't made a misstep when she'd taken him into pseudo custody—she'd hedged her bets, in fact. As a well-trained, intelligent US marshal would do. The few he'd worked with over the years had been all business, the epitome of professional. Trina proved no exception.

No other US marshal had been the love of his life, however. And not one of them had thought he was dead for the past five years, come back to life as if in a dream.

More like a nightmare. Yeah, he supposed he was Trina's worst nightmare, in many ways.

That made him laugh again. Ouch.

Freakin' ribs.

Trina's deep shock at seeing Justin alive wasn't going to dissipate anytime soon, but she had to take care of what was in front of her nose. She was concerned about his injuries, wondering if he was internally bleeding as they sped across the state.

She sighed and focused on a few deep, calming

breaths as she drove, certain they'd left the criminals behind them. She didn't want to see anyone in pain, and especially not a man who wasn't a bad guy. Was in fact, the guy she'd fallen for and gotten pregnant by. He was a *different* kind of guy now, though. He'd been in the vicinity of very, very bad men. And he knew who Vasin and Ivanov were. Not usual LEA targets. More like FBI, even CIA. The Marshals had been called in to nab Vasin only because they hadn't received the intelligence that he was with other men and protected. Trina wasn't fazed by running across an agent from another LEA—it happened all the time. But in this instance, and with "Rob" not revealing which agency he worked for, her hackles were at attention. It had nothing to do with the sexual attraction she was imagining between them. *Seriously, in the middle of an op?*

A quick look at her rearview mirror revealed Rob with his head laid back again, maybe trying to escape the incredible discomfort he was in. She'd call in for a doctor as soon as they were an hour out from the Harrisburg station. Giving him first aid unless he was facing imminent death wasn't an option, as they had to make time and put road between them and ROC. Rob had said he was fine, that he didn't need to stop at Lehigh Valley medical center. She chose to believe him. Stopping to clean wounds and place bandages was a luxury when being chased by bad guys.

She should have checked him over for any bleeding wounds. And internal bleeding—it was pretty clear he'd probably snapped a rib or two, either from his escape out of the warehouse or from Vasin and his posse whaling on him. But her mind, her heart, had been vibrating from the effort to assimilate what she witnessed.

The resurrection of her son's father. A man come back to life.

Her phone buzzed and the ID indicated it was Corey on a secure line.

"Hey, boss."

"Any more information from Rob Bristol, Trina?"

"Nothing more than what I told you. He says he's Robert Bristol, that he was working to find Ivanov and Vasin. He's got a lot of bruises, maybe a cracked rib. But nothing serious, hopefully."

"He's telling you the truth, Trina." Corey never spoke with such a dramatic tone of conciliation unless he thought she was about to lose it from a particularly rough operation, or when he was insistent she take time off.

"Okay, fine, so who does he work for?"

"I'll fill you in when this is over. All of it's above my pay grade. Bottom line is that he's not a suspect or fugitive. He's one of us, but with a different group. You can trust him. And if you need to, follow his orders."

Trust the man who let her believe he'd died during a failed raid in the Mideast? Who'd obviously lived but never came to find her afterward? Who didn't know their passion, their uncontrollable lust for each other, had made a baby who was her precious Jake?

"Okaaaaay." She couldn't help drawing out her response. Just a little.

"I've called because you've got new orders, Lopez."

"Can't they wait until we're in? We're only sixty miles out." She wanted to be home with her son, in her house. The sooner the better.

"Nope. You're not stopping in Harrisburg. As a matter of fact, you're going to pull off in three miles and get a new rental, then head south on I-81. Use your company card and find a hotel when you need to, and hole up. You need to take three days to get back here. You need to practice maximum evasion—not just for his sake but for yours and Justin's. These are the worst of the worst, Trina. ROC don't leave anyone alive who's pegged them."

"We have to do this all weekend?"

"Yes."

"Where do we end up, then?" She tried to sound calm, professional.

"Ultimately, you'll bring Rob Bristol back to his home base."

The hair on her nape prickled, and she massaged her neck with one hand on the wheel.

"And where is that?"

"Silver Valley."

"As in where I just bought my new house?" What the hell was Rob Bristol of "TH" doing in Silver Valley?

Corey was quiet for a moment. "Yes. I can't say anymore on this line. Stop along the way. Stay in more populated areas, at regular hotels. Nothing fancy. You're just another couple playing tourist. Charge everything to the company."

Trina groaned. The "company" was of course the US Marshals. This was official business. She blew out a deliberate, angry puff of air. This was *not* happening to her. Yet inexplicably, it was.

"Roger, boss. Got it."

"Check in as usual."

"Will do."

"And Lopez?"

"Yes, sir?"

"The dog food is on your tab."

Corey disconnected the call, and Trina would have screamed at the top of her lungs if she were alone.

Alone. Her gaze flew to the mirror and collided with the blue laser that was Rob Bristol's stare. *Justin's.* The glance that had set her on fire at one time, made her wet before he'd stroked between her legs with his fingers. Made her entire body quiver in anticipation.

She gulped. "Your left eye appears to be getting better—the swelling is going down."

"What did you have on your schedule this weekend?"

Dang it. He'd heard the call. Or her side of it, at least.

"Nothing that can't be rearranged." She wished her heart, her soul, felt as calm and easygoing as her reply. Trina had her family and Jake's friends' families to rely on. Since they'd moved, though, his friends were forty-five minutes away, north of her office in Harrisburg. They hadn't set down roots in Silver Valley yet. But he'd be able to stay with her parents, or her brother would stay over at her place with him. She need only make the call.

"There was a time when you would have done anything to spend an overnight with me, Trina."

Chapter 4

Right now she needed to pee, gas up and find a hotel as Corey had told her. A place to hole up. She pulled into a familiar convenience store, her favorite pit stop, and up to a fuel pump. "Do you want something to drink or eat? Can you get out and use the bathroom?"

"I'd rather wait until we hunker down at the hotel. I know a couple of places that no one would think to search for us around here."

She looked over her sunglasses at him. Emotion sideswiped her, knocking her confidence over as easily as a gull's feather in the wind. "What's going on here? You're not really Rob Bristol."

His mouth was a grim line, albeit with a swollen lip. It barely moved as he opened it to speak. "Justin died out in the field, Trina. All that's left is Rob. It's been my name since I escaped, practically."

"Escaped?" It felt like it was her ribs that had taken the beating. Her heart had nowhere to escape to, and there wasn't enough room to fill her lungs. Hell, there wasn't enough air on earth to keep her blood oxygenated right now.

"Didn't it ever occur to you I'd been captured by the enemy?" Bitterness laced his tone.

"Every conceivable outcome occurred to me, Justin."

"Rob. I told you, Justin's dead."

"Fine. *Rob.*" She barely kept herself from shouting at him. "We'll talk about our history later. I'm going to fill up the tank before we exchange this car for another, use the facilities, and pick up some snacks. Last chance to ask for anything or you're stuck with what I get you."

His stare was unholy. As if she were the one who'd done something wrong.

"Water would be nice."

She slammed her door shut because she could and hooked up the nozzle to the gas tank. As soon as the gas was running she went into the store. Rob was still in the car. He was capable of watching to make sure it all went safely.

With dogged determination to keep her wits about her, she ordered them each two sandwiches and iced lattes from the touch-screen menus. As she walked back to the refrigerator section for water, she called her brother.

"Hey, Nolan, it's me. I'm involved in something I hadn't expected. Can you watch Jake this weekend?"

"Of course I can. I saw Mom and Dad at the diner this morning and they were saying how they'd like to take him to the water park at Hershey."

"Sure they were. That's way too hot for them."

Nolan laughed. "Relax. I'll take him. He and I will have fun. Have you told him yet, that you'll be away?"

"No. Can you get him from day camp in an hour? I'll talk to him once he's at your place. Or you can stay at our place. I have plenty of boxes to still unpack if you're bored."

"Sure thing. You be safe out there, Trina."

"Will do. Thanks." Her arms full of blissfully cold bottled water, she went to the register and paid her bill. She picked up the bagged food as soon as the server called her number and went outside. As she looked across the lot to the car's back seat, her strength left her.

It was empty. He was gone. Again.

A cramp the size and pain of ten charley horses stabbed through her middle and she doubled over, dry heaving on the pavement in front of the convenience store. She'd indeed lost her freaking mind.

Rob made his way out of the men's room toward where he'd spied Trina ordering food on the fancy terminal. She was gone, and he looked out the store window to see her bent over just outside the doors, plastic bags clutched in the hands that grasped her knees.

Drat.

He walked as fast as his aching, pounding body allowed, out into the afternoon sunlight. He winced as heard her strangled heaves, the blanket of humidity wrapping around him again.

"Trina."

She was throwing up, the puppy on some kind of makeshift tether she held, but nothing was coming out of her mouth. Dry heaves.

"Trina." He tried again, placed his hand on her shoulder. "I think you're dehydrated. You need water." The puppy jumped and tried to get to their faces, as if this were a game.

"I thought you were gone." Her tortured whisper reached him, even though she was bent over. Hell. He'd already put her through it once, and she thought he'd done it again after only an hour or two together. Guilt dug its long claws into his conscience, and he had to bite the inside of his mouth to keep from spilling his guts.

"I'm right here, Trina."

Her body stopped convulsing within seconds of him touching her. She slowly straightened, her face as white as the ice freezer behind them. Her eyes blazed with an intensity of emotion he'd thought was reserved for wartime.

"You mother—" To her credit she stopped herself, straightened her spine fully and gulped in large breaths. She reached down for the puppy and hugged him to her chest.

"Just hitting you, huh?" Obviously the trauma of seeing him again had cost her more than she'd let on. He was still trying to process the fact that she'd barely blinked as they outran Vasin. And she had to have recognized him almost immediately. A pain deep in his chest lit a flame of compassion. Now that was an emotion he hadn't allowed himself to feel in a long time. Trina was shaking with her suffering. And he hated himself, knowing he'd caused it.

"You've been here all along. Capable of finding me." She spat out the last, her anger building from a boil to vaporizing steam. And he knew whom she'd like to zap off the planet. He reached out to her as a large horn blare from an eighteen-wheeler ripped through the sultry air, startling both of them.

Damn it, he'd forgotten that they were both still targets of ROC. He never allowed anything to keep him off his mission. He'd never cared for anyone as he had Trina, either. He'd have to go over it later, mentally. How, no matter how many women he'd casually dated off and on since Trina, he'd never forgotten her. No one compared.

"Get in the car, Rob." Her demand cut through his pangs of regret, and she stalked off. No offer to help him as he half ran, half limped back to the tiny car. She waited for him next to the open back door. "Hold the dog." Once inside he held the squirming pup on his lap but otherwise took Trina's lead. Save for noisily gulping the bottle of water she handed to him, then sharing it with the clumsy puppy, he remained silent.

Within twenty minutes of leaving the filling station, Trina turned into the parking lot of an auto rental place where she exchanged the economy model for a huge, honkin' SUV.

She spoke not a single word to him, her only acknowledgment of his presence when she held the front passenger door of the SUV open, motioning for him and the dog to get in. It wasn't fun, climbing into the large bucket seat with his battered bones, but he did it. To show her or himself he could, he wasn't sure. He found himself more than willing to take out any punishment she'd give him. Which was downright stupid. No amount of abuse from Trina would ever make up for what his presumed death had obviously done to her. The pup curled up on the back seat, as if the emotionally charged day had worn him out, too.

They continued their silent journey on a less-traveled highway that paralleled the main routes. Rob went along with Trina's zero communications policy until she turned on the radio and played a country station at full blast. The Garth Brooks tune he could deal with, as well as the Miranda Lambert ode to all the bastards she'd ever dated. But when a melancholy, I'll-never-love-anyone-else ballad began, he pushed the power button and cut the artist off midtwang.

"Just hitting you, Rob?" Her words cut like a bayonet, eliminating any doubt that she'd been as slain by their forced breakup as he had.

"Baby cakes, it hit me the minute I saw you with your new man and baby." Shoot. Double crap. Holy counterintelligence. He'd just spilled his guts to her. Maybe it was time to get out of covert ops, after all.

"You spied on me?" Her tan hands, naturally olive by birth and deepened by the sun's kisses, gripped the wheel of the large vehicle, and he was so damned grateful they were busy. Because he had no doubt she'd wrap them around his throat if she could, and he wasn't sure he'd stop her. Or if he wanted to stop her.

Because he felt lower than dirt. He didn't deserve her in the desert, and didn't deserve her when he'd gone to find her the first time.

"It wasn't spying. I intended to talk to you."

Unexpected tears burned like Mace against Trina's eyeballs, and she damned them to hell. She'd shed more than her share of tears over a man she'd thought dead and buried.

"Wait—I visited your grave at Arlington. Who's in there?"

He looked straight ahead for once, a relief since he hadn't stopped staring at her since they'd driven from the rental place. "No one. It was a cover-up."

"Cover-up for what?"

"I worked for the Agency right after. It was the perfect time to do so."

"The CIA? But that's not such a secret that you couldn't come find me, tell me that you were using a pseudonym."

"I did find you. You were otherwise involved."

His explanation was making no sense.

"Where did you find me?"

"Norfolk. You were still living there—on shore duty."

"That was almost two years after, after…"

"After I was 'killed'?" He made air quotes around the word, and she almost laughed. Then remembered how pissed she was at him, how ugly this whole situation was. Not including that they were hiding out, on the run from ROC's top members.

"Go on."

"I was detained for a while, and then had some physical rehab to contend with." What he didn't say, the obvious mental anguish he must have faced, concerned her more. But he wasn't volunteering, and she wasn't admitting she cared.

"And?"

"And I was on your street, across from your town house, waiting for you to get home from work. It was a beautiful day, the sun shining, the wind cold as the North Pole. You pulled in your driveway and got out, and lifted your kid out of the back seat." He shook his head stiffly, and she thought the little gasps he was letting out through his bruised face were laughter. Until she risked a quick sideways glance and saw the single tear, pointed like a knife, sliding down over his enlarged, purpled cheek. This tear wasn't from tear gas.

"You didn't like seeing me with a child?" It could have been anyone's; how did he know it was hers? He clearly didn't know the real truth of it. That the baby was his. Theirs.

"The kid wasn't the problem. It was the man you handed it over to."

"The man I…" She thought about her time assigned to Commander, Naval Surface Forces Atlantic, a staff in Norfolk, Virginia. It had been a horrendous juggling act to deal with her grief while adjusting to life as a new single mom. There had been only two men who'd been close enough to help her at the time. Craig, another naval officer who worked on the same staff, and her brother Nolan, who'd just completed law school and was working as a lawyer in Virginia Beach. Nolan had also been a SEAL, and had gotten out of the Navy two years ahead of Trina. He had been as certain as she that Justin was dead. Killed in a raid some of her brother's colleagues had participated in and survived.

"Not so smug now, are you?" His sharp words belied the stricken expression stamped on his face.

"There's nothing to be smug about, you arrogant jerk." She turned into the parking lot of a suite hotel and drove around to the back, out of sight of any main roads. As soon as she put the gearshift into Park, she faced him.

"I was with one of two men during that time. One was my brother, Nolan."

She waited for him to turn, not giving a flying fish how much it hurt him. Because she'd hurt for so long, had finally moved on past her loss, and here he was, telling her he'd seen her and their child but had done nothing to broach the divide? Had not wanted to tell her he'd survived? Had picked his adrenaline-seeking career over her and the child he had to have known was his?

He turned, and she saw the glimmer of fear in his eyes. Fear? It couldn't be.

"The other man—did you marry him?" His voice was a croak.

"He was, and is, one of my dearest, best friends. As a matter of fact, I was at his wedding this past spring. To his husband. He's gay. I never married, and even if I'd wanted to, that was what, only eighteen, twenty months since you'd died? Scratch that, I mean *went missing*, right? Because you were alive all along." She shook her head, followed by a single harsh laugh. "You know, a big part of me never believed it, that you were dead. As if I could feel you still alive on the planet. But my brother, my family, they all told me I had to move on. To get past what had happened."

"Did you?"

"Did I what?"

"Move on."

She didn't answer him right away. Couldn't. Because the man next to her, Rob, wasn't Justin anymore. He was a stranger to her. And she had no idea what a man who hadn't told her he'd survived would do once he discovered he had a son. "There's no one in my life right now, if that's what you're asking."

Trina was single. Available, but not to him. Rob hated the spark of light in his heart when she admitted she was solo at the moment.

He watched Trina as she coordinated their hotel room reservation, checked them in, fed the dog with food from the convenience store and continued to stay in touch with her US Marshals boss the entire time. She was the whirlwind of energy he remembered, and more. And because she was keeping her chain of command informed, he knew that Claudia was receiving the same information. All of the LEA chiefs in an area where a TH op was being conducted were alerted to report anything TH needed to know.

"Have you thought about getting some rest? We don't know if we'll have to move again, and it could come with no warning." Rob stood at the kitchenette counter across from where she was perched on a barstool. The dog was still on his leash but Trina had tied it to her wrist, giving the puppy the security it needed while allowing it to sniff and roll about the strange room. Rob was grateful to be on his feet again. Standing was far less painful than sitting, and to get to and from a seated or reclining position was pure hell. The counter was the right height to lean against for support, too.

Trina didn't respond right away as her fingers flew over her phone's touch screen.

"Corey texted me that a medical professional will be here shortly to take care of your wounds." She looked up from her phone. "I don't understand why we can't go to a regular hospital. I get that we're hiding from the East Coast ROC and that you've pissed off the top dudes there, but what aren't you telling me? Who do you really work for?"

"I can't talk about it." Let her assume it was CIA, as she had before.

"Hmph." Her grunt dismissed him, as if he were

playing a game with her. As grim ferociousness bloomed on her face, anger rose in his gut until he couldn't cork his ire.

"What are you so upset about, Trina? Because I'm not seeing your view here. What difference does it make who I work for, what I do? You've made it clear you don't want anything to do with me either way."

"What do you expect me to say, Rob? If we hadn't run into each other on this failed apprehension, I'd be taking flowers out to your grave at Arlington the next time I was in DC."

Pow. Right to the solar plexus of his emotions.

Trina glared at him for several heartbeats. With a roll of her eyes, she shoved away from the counter and walked to the sofa, where she sat down, deliberately ignoring him.

"I took the job with TH, my current employer, so that I would be closer to you. Believe it or not, I finally realized after five years of dreaming of you that I needed to have closure. Face-to-face."

"Uh-huh. How long have you been with them?" Her stubborn countenance hadn't changed, for which he was simultaneously grateful and perturbed. He left the comfort of the counter and slowly walked to the easy chair opposite her position on the sofa. It was a pullout and where he'd sleep the next night or two while they waited for ROC to stop searching for them.

"A few months. Well, six, but I decided to move to Silver Valley three months ago. Until then I commuted from DC for each mission. A lot of my work is overseas, as well. But the only reason I rented a place in Silver Valley was so that I could see you." To find her, face her and allow himself to move on with his life.

"I'll give you the grace of your commuting time. So that leaves three months where you never approached me. Wait, make that five years and three months." Her bitterness tore at him, but he couldn't dwell on it. He had to make her see he'd come here for the right reasons.

"You don't have the edge on everything, Trina. Put yourself in my shoes. It's not so easy going to the woman you once cared deeply about and revealing that not only are you still alive, you need her help to put your demons to rest." He loved being able to say her name aloud. To her, with her, in her presence. As angry as she was, he still felt the soothing waves of Trina's essence pulsing off her, wrapping him in a cocoon of peace.

It was one true thing that hadn't changed in five years.

"So fill me in, Rob. Tell me what you're thinking." At least she wasn't sneering anymore.

He couldn't help the grunts and groan as he lowered himself into the too-soft chair.

Trina was on her feet and at his side in a flash. "Wait—maybe you'd be more comfortable in one of the dining table chairs?" Her hand was on his forearm, and he'd do anything to keep it there. The point of contact was preferable as a focus point to the damned pain radiating from his ribs and arm.

He gritted his teeth and kept sinking until his ass hit the chair. "I'm. Okay. Help. Me. Situate." She stayed with him as he folded himself into ninety-degree angles, bent at the waist and knees. Trina placed throw pillows between his back and the chair to keep him as upright as possible, with the least amount of pressure on his frame.

"Thank you." His gratitude came out on a relieved exhale.

"I've been there." She was squatting next to him, her hand on his thigh near his knee. As her face turned up to meet his gaze, he was stunned by the ferocity of emotion revealed in her eyes. Anger, yes, but also compassion and maybe even trust. After all of their history, much of it a blank page to Trina, she trusted him. Physically at least, or she wouldn't risk being alone with him. She'd have told her boss to have the other marshal take him in, the one who'd been called off the case. Rob would take her trust in any amount available. As a trained killer, it meant more to him than if she'd miraculously healed his battered body with a wave of her feminine hands.

She leaned over to readjust a pillow and her T-shirt sagged open, revealing the tops of her beautiful breasts and the lacy fringe of her pink bra. So the US marshal still had her penchant for sexy lingerie. He involuntarily smiled, the reflex stretching his skin over the bruises Vasin had dealt. A flash of gold just above her cleavage caught his eye. A charm suspended on a thin gold chain hovered between them. It was a camel. He'd bought her a twenty-four-karat camel charm when they'd taken a quick break and gone into the souk that was just off base. And she was still wearing it, five years later.

"How's that?" She asked about the pillows, his comfort level. He responded to the tiny flicker of hope that had been lit deep inside him.

"As good as could be expected. Maybe even a bit better."

Chapter 5

Trina looked into Rob's eyes and knew he wanted distraction from his pain. She reacted instinctively, making sure he was as comfortable as possible on the motel furniture.

"After you…disappeared, I wasn't myself. The grief, it was unbearable, and I was unable to focus on my job. I didn't tell anyone about us, not then, because it seemed too self-serving. As if I was looking for attention when all the focus needed to be on you and the other SEALs who were lost, and the ones who'd survived."

She knew he understood; it was something only a veteran would. They'd kept their relationship quiet to be able to keep their professional bearings intact. There was nothing preventing them from dating, as they'd been from different units and both officers. They didn't share the same chain of command. What they had shared was still sacred to her, she realized. He deserved to know her experience. All of it. Including Jake.

At Rob's silence, she stood up and sat on the coffee table directly across from him. Their knees were almost touching. The dog crawled under the table and curled up as she stroked him. "I insisted on staying in the seat, flying the next mission. The P-8 isn't like a fighter jet, as you know. We have lots of options when it comes to crew and pilots within a mission's time frame." She referred to the dozen or so crew members to include at least two pilots on every flight. "We got shot at while I was in the seat. Shoulder-launched antiaircraft missile. Normally we fly too high for it to be a concern, but we were low, conducting surveillance on what we thought was land in the middle of nowhere, with no civilian occupation. We were wrong, and more importantly, I was wrong. Intel had mentioned there could be a resistance unit in the mountains but I dismissed it. It nearly cost me my crew. And the plane." Trina could smell the inside of the plane's cabin as if she were back there and not in the hotel room with Rob. She looked at him and saw he was listening intently. Like he used to do when they'd talk for hours on end after a hot lovemaking session in her quarters. Communication had always been their strength, physical and verbal. And that unseen yet tangible spiritual connection.

"Did it hit you? The missile?"

She hated this question, even five years out. "No, I evaded. I was the PPC." She'd been the patrol plane commander, flying the aircraft and in charge of the crew. "But the maneuvers coincided with losing an engine, and we had to ditch. We took a belly landing on a dirt road in the middle of Iraq. I'm lucky our folks got to us before the bad guys did."

"You were injured?"

"The plane broke apart a bit on the landing, let's say." She wasn't going to go into specifics and in fact couldn't. How the plane bore the stress of the ditch was classified. "The copilot and I each had a few broken ribs, collapsed lungs, you know, the usual." She shrugged. "The worst thing was that everyone back at the base tried to make it out that we were heroes. We all got back alive and the classified material was saved or destroyed, to include the airframe. No enemy learned anything from one of our newer military platforms."

"You are a hero, Trina." Quiet words.

"No, no I'm not. A hero would have listened to intel and never been anywhere near that enemy encampment. Certainly not flying at one thousand feet." A true heroine would have told her flight surgeon she thought she might be pregnant, and grounded herself from the op. She stood up, ending the intimacy created by sharing her story with Rob. "That was my last flight. I requested a transfer to shore duty. The squadron was coming home the next week, so it didn't hurt the operations that I grounded myself." Since she'd also begun to suspect she was pregnant, she didn't want to do anything to harm her child. Their child. Holy hell, she was going to have to tell Rob the truth.

"It sounds like you might need some closure, too." His voice soothed, but she fought against it. She didn't want his compassion.

"I have my closure, Rob. At least, I did."

"And then I walked into your gin joint." His attempt

to lighten the mood by referring to her favorite movie only fueled her regret.

"You remember." They'd watched *Casablanca* on her tablet computer, huddled next to each other on her twin-size cot. A wartime desert date.

"I never forgot." The fierceness of his statement gave her pause. The tiny part of her that desperately wanted to believe him, wanted to think he'd never stopped caring for her, was growing. She couldn't let it become the biggest part of her, though. Her heart wouldn't survive it this time.

After the doctor had checked Rob over, declaring he was severely bruised but most likely had no broken bones, Rob's hunger made an appearance.

"Where's sandwiches?"

Trina straightened from setting down a bowl of water for the dog. She pulled a bright yellow plastic bag from the mini refrigerator and handed a wrapped bundle to Rob. "Here you go. Chicken Caesar wrap."

She'd remembered his favorite salad from the military canteen. It could be coincidence, but when she unwrapped a tuna sandwich for herself he knew it was more.

"You still like tuna, huh?"

A small smile painted her lips. "Yes."

They ate at the tiny kitchenette counter. Rob stood as it was simply less painful. He was constantly aware of Trina next to him.

"We can order takeout later if you want." She bunched the paper from her sandwich and tossed it into the garbage bin in a perfect arc.

"My appetite's not as strong since I took the acet-

aminophen. But maybe by then I'll be hungry again."
It was a miracle he was hungry now, with the pain still
throbbing at several points on his frame.

"I still don't get why you didn't take the stronger
meds the doctor offered. There's not a whole lot that's
more painful than bruised ribs. And I don't care what
he said, I'll bet you have a small fracture in that arm."

"They're manageable. And my arm's not broken,
which is a plus. I've had more success using non-opioids
and ice, frankly." Besides, his head needed to stay clear
in case they had to make a run for it again. His interior
radar was pinging, and he had to fight his urge to flee.
It was probably having the object of his dreams sitting
right next to him. After five long years.

"Suit yourself. But if you change your mind, I can
go to a quick drive-through pharmacy."

"I think we're going to do everything drive-through
or delivery, at least until we're back in Silver Valley."

She gave him an odd look. "How did you know you'd
find me, taking a job in Silver Valley? It's a big enough
town, and close to a good-sized city, but still…"

"I looked you up. You haven't remained off the grid
as much as a lot of our former colleagues have. I saw
you were working in Harrisburg. I didn't know you
were a US marshal, though, until I took this recent job."

"You're telling me that the CIA resources didn't tell
you where I was and whom I worked for?"

Score one for Trina. "Maybe they could have. But I
wasn't one to abuse my privileges. And I wasn't ready
to come find you again until I realized I was done working for the Agency. It was time to come clean and do
something a little different. I took five months off between the CIA and this current agency. That's when I

did the hard counseling work I probably should have done at least four years ago if not sooner."

"I've learned that beating myself up about the past doesn't work." She was still holding something back. He'd wait her out. "It doesn't strike me that you're doing anything different. You're still some kind of undercover agent, for what? A CIA contractor?"

"Something like that." He couldn't divulge Trail Hikers' existence. Wouldn't. He'd signed a nondisclosure agreement that was just as binding if not more so than the one he'd signed for the US government on other occasions.

She got up from the counter and moved into the small U-shaped kitchen area. "Coffee or tea?" She filled a mug with water as she spoke.

"I'll have a coffee. Full strength is fine. Nothing keeps me awake, except…"

Their eyes met, and he watched her absorb and process his words. At one point he thought she'd laugh, but she quenched it by biting her lower lip with teeth as pearly as they were even. Her smile had only grown lovelier over the time they'd been apart. Time he suddenly felt had slipped through his fingers like the finest dust. Never to be captured and relived.

"Lucky you. I can't have caffeine after three in the afternoon." The microwave beeped, and she pulled out the mug and placed a tea bag in the steaming liquid. His cup was next, and in short order they each had a steaming hot beverage.

"You never drank anything but coffee when I knew you." He deliberately nodded at the mesh bag of herbs she steeped in her prepared water.

"No, I was pretty much a live wire in those days. I

uh, had some, some health issues that forced me to evaluate my nutrition and caffeine intake. Nothing major, just enough to find out what does and doesn't work for me and my body type."

"Define 'body type.'" Because if she couldn't, he could. Without hesitation. He deliberately intoned the demand so she'd know exactly what he meant.

A hard glare was his reward for pushing her past her comfort zone. His dick got the message in a different way, and he wished he could take back the tease. A relationship with Trina was not happening. It would spell disaster for both of them. If he wanted to stay in Silver Valley, work with TH for the long term, he didn't want to always be concerned about running into her. At work or out in town. Friendship was the best option.

"By 'type' I mean fast or slow metabolism, more of a muscular frame versus a more slight, fragile set of bones." Her words were carefully neutral.

"Makes sense to me. My metabolism hit the skids when I left the SEALs." He sipped his coffee.

She looked him over, and he wanted to strut around like a peacock, fanning his tail and turning in a circle. It'd never been this way with another woman. He was a guy; he liked knowing he turned a woman on. With Trina it went to a primal level, this elation at her approval.

"You don't look any worse for the wear." Spoken like the compliment it wasn't—sincere but with a grudge. He got it. Someone who came back from the dead should look like they had died. Not all strong and healthy.

"Don't be fooled. Sure, I'm a little broader, stronger. But I can lean toward a beer belly since I'm not burning it all off like I used to. I'm not a SEAL. Staying in shape is one thing, but that kind of conditioning is for the very young. They say it gets worse as we age."

"My mom says that all the time. But she tells me to enjoy the extra cookies now, before my metabolism shuts down."

"I don't remember you having a sweet tooth."

She sighed. "I've always adored my mom's home-made baked goods. And it's true. It is harder, much harder, in fact, to lose weight. Especially after—" She stopped dead cold.

"Especially after what, Trina?"

The Trina moat was fully flooded again, her draw-bridge pulled up and away. He wasn't going to glean any new information from her. And they'd only been talking about metabolism. It wasn't as if it was anything personal.

She didn't budge on the drawbridge. "Nothing. Hey, we're each five years older. It's to be expected. I'm going to hit the shower. Do you mind keeping an eye on the dog? You okay waiting out here?"

"Where will I go without you?" He tried to be humorous, but it fell flat, as had every emotion he'd tried to express to her. It killed him to admit if only to himself that how Trina felt, how she viewed the world, was as important to him today as it had been all those years ago.

Her eyes narrowed. "Exactly. You can try to take off, but trust me, Bristol, I have eyes in the back of my head and I'm not afraid to use them." She flashed him a bright smile. "If you need me, holler. I can be dressed and holstered in a minute."

He'd really like a variation of that—maybe Trina

holstered and undressed. But he remained silent. Timing was everything, not only in covert ops.

Trina took her time in the shower, as if by lingering under the hot spray she'd somehow gain back her peace of mind.

A US marshal wasn't guaranteed serenity of any sort, but knowing she could still work in a role supporting the government after she resigned from the Navy had been a godsend. As a new mother her priority was completely Jake, and remained so. But as he grew up and needed her less for the physical routines of the day and more for his emotional and mental support, she found herself wondering if there wasn't another job she should be looking for. Something that would keep her closer to home, able to pick him up after school and see all of his athletic events.

Being a local cop had crossed her mind, and she'd even mentioned it to Corey, but he'd waved his hand and said "no way" enough times that she'd started to believe him, accept that his assessment of her talents and capabilities was spot-on. Being a marshal was the best fit for her and Jake. Besides, he was only five. She had time to figure it all out.

She'd left a voice mail with her brother and save for the brief two-word text reply, Got him!, she hadn't discussed her situation with Nolan. How could she tell anyone she was with her son's father when she hadn't told Rob yet? The anger and betrayal at finding out he was alive and had been this whole time would take a long while to work out in her mind. And yet she knew she couldn't keep his son from him. Rob deserved to know he had a son. And Jake deserved to know his father.

The bottle of body wash she'd had with her in her backpack whistled out its last drops. She looked at the bar of soap that sat on the shower's tiny shelf. There was only one, and sharing it with Rob felt too intimate, too much like something a real boyfriend and girlfriend, or husband and wife as they'd posed as in the lobby, would do.

She was overthinking everything. A side effect of the adrenaline rush.

She rinsed off the sudsy shampoo in the shower stall and thought of his hands on her. God, she wanted to run to his arms, allow him to comfort her as she accepted he was still alive. He was *alive*. Her body had no reason to defend itself against Rob, apparently as her attraction to him was still incredibly hot, over-the-top.

Vibrations shook the shower glass as the bathroom door banged open, followed by Rob's deep baritone.

"Trina!" She'd never heard such a strident tone from him before, and her fingers shook as she shut off the water.

"Yeah?"

"We've got trouble. Get dressed and get ready to climb out that window over your head."

She blinked away the last of the suds and stared at the small sliding opening. "You're kidding. That can't be more than twelve by twelve inches big." One square foot was not enough for either of them to squeeze through.

"Get out and dressed. Hurry!" His demand was punctuated by pounding on the room door and shouts of "room service!" Since the motel didn't have room service and they hadn't asked for anything, she knew Rob was correct. They were about to be ambushed. Trina wiped at her skin with the towel she'd thrown over the stall door.

"I called 911, and I'm sure as soon as they hear the sirens they'll take off, but we can't count on it." He didn't have to say what they both knew. ROC didn't care if the local LEAs found both of them with a bullet between their eyes. And they'd make it look like it had been a murder-suicide.

"Fine." She shoved open the shower door to face him, the puppy clutched to his chest, his face a map of painful injury. Save for his eyes, which heated at her nakedness. "Stop being a perv and hand me my clothes. And put the dog down—he'll be okay. We'll carry him when we have to." She'd hung them on the hooks on the back of the door, her weapon on the sink's minuscule counter. Silently he held out her panties, bra, jeans and T-shirt, followed by her body armor and holster. She put her gun in its place while still barefoot.

"You need body armor, Rob. Can you move quickly? Where are my boots?" The pounding was louder and they both tensed, looking to each other for what the next move should be. "Crap. We've got to go now." She turned back around and looked at the window, which wasn't looking so bad. "But we're on the second floor. You'll never make the fall."

"That's why you're going to jump first." Rob looked like he was about to push her through the window, bruised skeleton be damned. He still held the dog, at whose comfort she couldn't guess.

"And leave you and the puppy here? Never."

Rob bit back the harsh order on his lips. Trina wasn't a Trail Hikers operative and had never done deep undercover ops. Her loyalty to him was misplaced, but he'd have to address that with her later.

When they were both safe.

She'd literally shoved her soaking wet body into her clothing and now stomped her bare feet into her boots. A distant siren pierced the spell of silence in between their pursuers rapping on the door and their own heavy breathing.

Trina stood up fully and held her hand up. "Is it…"

A second, shriller siren sounded, followed quickly by the echo of footsteps running away from their room.

She looked up at him, her expression triumphant. "Score! Thank God you called emergency right away." She arched her brow, its smooth shape in sharp contrast to her tangled hair. Her eyes, the deepest shade of gray, framed by her clumped lashes, drew him in.

"Trina." Slowly, he put the dog down. There was so much to say, and nothing. Words escaped him as quickly as his pulse shifted into overdrive and the erection he'd been fighting came on hard and insistent. Her lips were moist, plump, parted.

She placed her hand lightly on his chest. "Rob, no. You said that Justin was dead. So is the woman you knew. So—so are we."

Her words would cut later, when he replayed them in his mind. All he could sense was his body's need for her. He allowed her to maintain the space between their upper bodies with her hand as he grasped her hips and pulled her up against his cock. And God help him, he ground into her pelvis, unable to stop the bliss-inducing movement. He closed his eyes to the pain from his ribs and focused on the sensation of her hot center rubbing against his erection.

"Are you sure about that, Trina?"

She looked at his mouth, and her pupils dilated as her breath hitched. When her eyelids lowered, he took it as the invitation it would have been five years ago.

He kissed her.

Rob expected Trina to pull back, push him away or endure a few seconds of lip-to-lip contact. As a courtesy to a dead man come back to life. What he never envisioned was how quickly her arms would wind around his neck, her breasts press against his chest, how their staccato breathing and soft sucking noises would be the only audible elements in the tiny bathroom. The biggest surprise was how forcefully she kissed him back, her tongue demanding all he had to give her.

Rob had everything to give Trina. If she'd let him.

It was a kiss of loss, regret, sorrow. Affirmation that they were together again, in the same place, not separated by war or death.

Distantly he heard a siren, close enough to cause alarm. "Trina." He hated to pull back, to end the moment that felt frozen in the timeline of their relationship with each other. *A relationship that's over.* He'd be better off if he kept that in mind.

"I know." She groaned as she pulled away and took a step back. "We have to meet the cops, tell them what's going on. I can have Corey call their supervisor. What county are we in? Did you see the township?"

He grasped her shoulders. "No, we absolutely cannot see the police—or rather, they can't see us. I'm an undercover agent and you're being chased by ROC. Their connections are far and wide and we don't know who these officers are."

Her stunned expression shook him. Trina might be

a US marshal, but she obviously still wanted to believe all cops were good, on the right side. "Trina, we have to get out of here."

"Right. They're still not on this floor—we can walk out of here." He was touched and annoyed by her concern for him. But she was right—if he jumped out the window, normally an easy move for him, he'd risk blowing everything, as he might not be able to stand back up from the ground.

"We have to move now. Get the dog. And follow my lead." This was his turf, staying clandestine in a fully connected world.

Chapter 6

Trina's lips still quivered from Rob's kiss when he stopped short in the parking lot behind the hotel and pulled her to him. The puppy in her arms wiggled between them. She'd put up no argument as they ran together to the hotel room's door, cleared the hallway and made their way down the cement steps to the back parking lot.

"Act like we're long-lost lovers."

His lips were on hers again, but this time it was for show. She could be professional at this. She opened her eyes a slit to see the police cars pulling up to the hotel, sirens blaring and lights flashing in the dimming light. Sometime between the totally unplanned kiss in the bathroom and this strategic gesture, day had faded into dusk.

"Don't look at them." He moved his hand over her waist, her hips, to the fullest part of her ass.

"Really?" She spoke against his mouth, her lips acting of their own volition, as well as her tongue. Dang, she'd missed how it felt to have Rob's mouth on hers, their breath one motion in the midst of their raging desire. And it was theirs, for sure. This was something she'd never experienced with another man, no matter how good the sex was. Rob was special, their tie to each other inexplicable.

He buried his head in her neck and gave her a deliciously moist kiss, his tongue tracing the sensitive skin with exquisite pressure. "Really. They'll think we're having a sordid affair. As soon as they're inside, we'll take off."

Her mind was frantically trying to keep hold of what needed to happen to make the mission successful. But her hormones and emotions were at war with reason, and heat rushed into her cheeks when Rob said "inside."

Trina knew there wouldn't be another kiss after this; she wouldn't allow it. So why not go along for a bit longer?

Rob's lips were on hers again, but after only a second or two he lifted his head, looking past her. "Okay, the coast is clear." He turned his focus to her. "You all right?"

"Of course." She wrenched herself away from him and placed the dog on a patch of grass to relieve himself. Part of her hoped Rob would collapse on the asphalt. How could he kiss her like that and maintain any kind of logical thought process?

He's a trained operative. And he was the same man who'd allowed her to think he'd been killed. She wanted to add the fact that he was the father of her son, a son she was raising as a single mother. But as unfair as the entire situation was, she couldn't accuse Rob of being a derelict dad. He didn't even know he was a dad.

"You're awfully quiet." He spoke from the passenger seat as she drove them to a hotel twenty minutes away, in the opposite direction of where the ROC thought they were headed. The darned dog was on his lap, curled up as if he was the one fighting the bad guys and mentally exhausted.

"It's been a full day. And I'm freezing." Shivers had started to rack her and she pushed the buttons for the heater. "I'm sorry to need heat in the hottest part of the summer."

"Hypothermia can set in on the hottest of days. We need to get to the hotel and get your wet clothes off."

"Not happening." Even through her chattering teeth, the tone of her statement was sharper than she'd meant. "I mean, something between us. After the kiss. The kisses. I don't want to lead you on."

"Trust me, that's the last thing I'd ever expect from you. The leading me on part. As for kissing you, hell, Trina, it's been five years. We had amazing chemistry when we were together, and that's not gone away."

"We had more than chemistry." She wasn't letting him off so easily. "If it was only a physical attraction, you going off the radar by allowing Justin to officially die wouldn't be such a big deal."

"I thought you were married, Trina." His quiet words weighed heavy with what sounded an awful like pain. Regret.

"Not good enough, Rob. Even if I'd remarried, was still married, whatever. What we shared deserved more than you walking away when you saw me again." She fought to keep her words aboveboard, fair. Her heart screamed at her conscience that if she were really fair she'd tell him about their son, how she'd really felt about Rob. How she hadn't been able to let go for so long.

"You seem really angry, Trina."

"You don't know the half of it." She spotted the hotel sign and maneuvered to make the left into the parking lot. "You're correct in that I need to get these clothes off, and into another hot shower. Wait here while I check in." She mustered as much dignity as one could in soaking-wet clothes and dripping hair and slid out of the SUV. She felt his gaze on her back as she walked into the hotel lobby. Hollywood and sometimes real life allowed for over-the-top, joyous reunions of lovers thought lost or dead. But in her case, seeing that Rob was still alive and as attractive as he'd ever been was pure agony. The sooner she was able to get them both back to Silver Valley, the better.

Rob stared at the muted television from one of two double beds in the much older, run-down hotel. Trina was talking in low murmurs to someone he thought might be her brother. She'd made it clear she wasn't married, but hadn't said she'd never gotten married or hooked up with anyone since him. And he hated the part of himself that burned to know if she'd fallen in love with another man.

"Hey, buddy!" Trina's voice lifted into pure happiness, and he couldn't help taking a surreptitious look at her. She was wrapped up under her blankets, her hair dry thanks to the yellowed but still functional wall hair dryer unit in the bathroom. He'd found an extra comforter in the closet and placed it over her. She'd uttered a quick "thanks" and busied herself with calling whomever she was still on the line with.

"Mommy has to work on something for the next few days. Uncle Nolan and Grandma and Grandpa are going to take care of you. Are you okay with that?"

Rob though it odd that she asked the kid if he was okay with something that he had no control over. Who did that? *A mother who loved her kid is who.* Nothing he'd know about, as his years in foster care hadn't given him a good model of a healthy parent-child bond. His gut soured over the realization that another man had fathered a baby with her. Their relationship when they were both Navy hadn't progressed to the point of discussing a future that entailed family, but he'd hoped it would. Hell, he'd expected it would. When he and Trina had started seeing each other, during the war, it had changed him. He'd begun to think about life in a totally different way. It was a certainty that he'd have wanted a family with her.

"Sorry about that. You can turn the volume up if you want." She stared at the ceiling as she spoke. He clicked the television off.

"Nothing to apologize for. I take it that was your kid?"

Silence. He'd wait as long as it took.

"Yes. Childcare is always tricky, but I've been so lucky. My brother got out of the Navy a year or so before me, and my parents are still in Williamsport. Not far from here, actually. Maybe an hour or two west, only two hours from Silver Valley. When I landed the job with the Marshals I was lucky to get one tour in Philadelphia and then moved to this one in Harrisburg. It's allowed both me and—and my child to settle down. My hours are usually pretty conventional, as I don't do as much in the field as I used to."

"When we worked together I never thought you'd leave flying."

"Yeah, well, priorities change once you have a kid to think about. And I can't blame motherhood for it—I would be bored flying commercial airlines. I need something that's a little more different on a day-to-day basis. I'm applying for an administrative position with the Marshals, as soon as one opens up in our local office. I don't want to move again. Not while my son is in school."

"Settling down has its benefits, I'm sure." He wanted to say anything to keep her talking. He loved her voice but even more, any little glimpse into the woman she was today. Regret hammered at his insides more than the pain in his bruised ribs. He'd been so damned inconsolable after he'd seen her in Norfolk.

"What about you, Rob? Why haven't you settled down?" She was on her side, facing him. Still hunkered down under layers of blankets, incongruous with the air-conditioning that blasted over his bare chest and barely kept him cool in the hot night. The puppy curled next to her, fast asleep. She'd fed him more of the kibble. They were going to have to do something about that dog. It couldn't stay with them—it was too risky. It could bark at the wrong moment and give their position away.

"That's a good question. I hate to admit it, but I think my head was messed up for a while after the explosion." He wasn't going to tell her that memories of her got him through. "I was still in the mode of doing whatever I could to serve my country."

"It looks to me like you still are."

"Yeah." He let out a laugh that sounded like a grunt. "But it's more on my terms. Part-time, if you will."

"What do you do when you're not working?"

"That's a good question." One he wasn't going to answer, for now. Part of being a Trail Hiker was finding a civilian identity in the community of Silver Valley, so that no suspicion would arise on how an agent earned a living, or where they went when they disappeared on global missions. Rob had pursued a career that would help foster kids and other at-risk youth find their way at a community center for kids with no parental support. He'd earned his master's degree in social work part-time over the last several years. He wasn't ready to tell Trina this, though.

They lay in silence for several minutes, each lost in their own thoughts. Although Rob's dick seemed to have a mind of its own, with Trina so close. The separate beds and small space between them may as well be a concrete prison wall, though. He sensed she'd created a safe space for her thoughts to inhabit, just as he had. Military training on compartmentalization had its benefits.

Rob's phone woke him from a deep slumber in which he'd dreamed he had a chance to either work with Trina on a mission or go work with a scary, deadly dude who wouldn't say what his missions were. The insistent vibration of the device broke through the dream's cobwebs and he strained to see who was calling at 0415. Claudia Michele, director of Trail Hikers.

"Claudia." He lay on his back, prepared to listen.

"Rob, glad you're okay. From your GPS and phone I

see you're safely ensconced with Trina Lopez." There was nothing invisible or unreachable for Trail Hikers. The super secret shadow agency had every technological capability available to any nation on the planet.

"Yes, ma'am."

"We've had a development. I hate to ask you to participate with your injuries, but I need you to go in and get one of our agents. She's stuck up there, with the ROC group you've evaded."

Rob sat up and swung his legs over the bed. "Do I know her?"

"No. She's newer than you, and her background is human trafficking. There's a corridor of trafficking between New Jersey and Silver Valley, straight through the Poconos. That's why Vasin was holed up there. We have reason to believe Ivanov is in the vicinity, ensuring this latest effort goes off without a hitch."

"I could have told you that." He didn't want to say too much within earshot of Trina. He trusted her implicitly but this was about mission integrity—operational security. Other agents' lives were at stake.

"Our agent has been posing as the solicitor for underage girls who will be sent to work in strip clubs. They have jobs during the day as domestic help, mostly housekeepers. What ROC hasn't figured out is that we've kept these girls out of the bars. A onetime payment is made to ROC for them, and they don't follow up."

"That's unusual for them, isn't it?"

"In the past, yes. But with the weight of law enforcement coming at them from all angles, they can't afford to maintain ties to any shipment—be it drugs, weapons, underage girls. They take their cut and take off."

"What do you need me to do?"

"Take Trina Lopez to the nearest bus stop—she'll get back to Harrisburg on her own. Use the SUV you've rented and go back to Vasin's hideout. There's a trailer park on the premises."

"I saw it." But it had looked abandoned even to his trained eyes.

"They moved the girls there three hours ago. Our agent was supposed to pick them up last night but with the recent events Ivanov pulled up all his feelers and ordered the young women and our agent into the park. We've overheard conversations that indicated he's going to issue an order to kill them all."

"How many captured and how much time do I have?"

"Twelve, and you're already behind by an hour. But don't go in there until I send the word. Situate yourself within fifteen minutes of the location I'm going to text to you and sit tight." Claudia ended the connection. She wasn't one for small talk during an op.

"What's the plan?" Trina's sleepy voice made him pause before he replied.

"We're splitting up. I've got to report somewhere ASAP. You're on the next bus to Harrisburg."

Trina let out a string of obscenities that made him smile in the early-morning darkness. You could take the woman out of the Navy, apparently, but her Navy vocabulary remained intact.

"What, you don't like buses?" He was already putting on his cargo pants, his adrenaline surge masking the pain he knew was still there.

"There is no bus, Rob. I'm going with you."

"Like hell you are." As he spoke her phone rang.

"Corey, what's going on?" He watched her silhouette by the fuzzy light of the bathroom night-light. She nodded, gave one-word responses. Relief mingled with dismay in his gut. Relief that she'd have to listen to her boss, who was obviously telling her what Claudia had just told him. Dismay that he might not see her again. If he was smart, he'd let go of his plan for any more closure, his hours with the counselor be damned. This was about all the closure he could handle.

"What you don't get, Corey, is that I'm here, on the ground, and with a man who was with the fugitive I was supposed to pick up. And this man, Rob Bristol, is in no condition to go into an ROC vipers' nest on his own. We've helped with ROC cases before, why not this time?"

A short pause as Trina listened, then her shocking reply.

"Fine, Corey. Put me on an official leave status starting now." She put her phone down and clicked on her nightstand light. Rob was struck by her stunning beauty, but kept it to himself out of self-preservation. He didn't want her phone slamming against his skull.

"I'm going with you, Rob. Either we both go rescue the girls, or they get hurt or worse. Your choice."

"Your boss told you the whole story, then?"

"Enough to know that this is time-sensitive and we're the closest, most capably trained law enforcement—" she snorted "—or whatever the hell you are, nearby."

He stared at her, knowing that if he agreed to allow her to accompany him, he was putting her life on the line, too. To let her go put his heart on the line, but it might not be life-saving for Trina. Because he knew ROC, and they didn't give up easily. At the first sign of Trina they'd be all over her like rain in April. Ivanov had to know by now who she was, what she'd been doing on his compound. The security system on the storage building was directly connected to the ROC's systems headquarters, which meant Trina's face was plastered probably in a text message to every ROC bad guy within a thousand miles.

Trina's life was at stake no matter what Rob did.

"It's my mission, my orders." He'd never forgive himself if anything happened to her. She had a kid now, for heaven's sake.

"I can help you with the girls, Rob. Corey said there's a dozen or more, smuggled from Ukraine, being prepped to go to Harrisburg. We're going to need another SUV or two."

"My orders, Trina." She'd fought him when he was a SEAL, too. She'd been the pilot in charge of a support mission and wanted to give him suggestions that he didn't have time for—his team had already considered all options. Not something he'd expect a non-SEAL to completely comprehend. It'd turned out her concerns had saved the lives of his men during that deadly raid.

"But—"

"My orders. Or the bus stop."

"Aye, aye, sir."

She'd relented. Now Rob had fourteen women to save—twelve young girls, a Trail Hikers agent, and Trina.

"You never thought I was going to get on a bus, did you?" Trina sipped hot coffee with cream from a foam cup as Rob drove back through winding roads and heavily treed countryside. She'd agreed that since it was his mission, he should drive. She understood—it was a way of letting your brain and body know that you were in charge and in need of top performance.

"No." All of their conversation since they'd left the hotel had been clipped on his part. Trina got why Rob didn't want an extra body tagging along on his op, but she knew that his ribs were still hurting and at risk of complete fracture. She'd be his backup if he collapsed a lung. "The dog, Trina. We need to do something about the dog."

"He's a good little puppy. He can stay in the car— we'll leave the windows open. My guess is he'll be happy to smell us, and stay put. It'll be cooler than being outside, especially if you park this under a tree."

"I've got a better idea." Without fanfare, he turned off the highway and onto a winding country road. After about a mile he pulled off onto a farmhouse drive, and she saw the Paradise Creatures sign. "We're taking him to a kennel?"

"Until you are able to come back for him, yes. I've already reached out to the owner and they've agreed to open for us."

She smiled inwardly, inexplicably buoyed by his concern for the tiny dog. "Thank you."

Rob grunted his acknowledgment as he put the SUV in Park. "If you don't mind, could you take the dog in?"

"Of course."

Trina signed the papers for the puppy, and when the attendant asked her his name, she thought a minute. "Renegade. His name is Renegade."

She returned to the car, where the motor was still running and the air-conditioning divine.

"How is your arm feeling?"

He shrugged. "Fine. Sore, like I pounded out too

many reps in the gym. If it had been broken, we'd both be on a bus right now."

"I know."

"I don't think you do, Trina. You've single-handedly decided that you're going to get in on this mission when you've never worked something like this before. You usually apprehend one person at a time, right?"

"Not always. It depends. And no, I have no clue whom you're working for or what you're doing, except that Corey mentioned young girls being trafficked and I had to help. They're being sent to my neck of the woods. Have you spent a lot of time in Silver Valley in between your missions? It's peaceful, a rolling green-and-blue horizon atop woods and farm fields. Not usual for a place so close to three major cities." She referred to Philadelphia, New York City, and Washington, DC.

"I've recently become acquainted with Silver Valley, yes." He'd lived right in her backyard for three months. And she was furious with herself for caring, for wanting to know where he lived and how long he planned to stay.

"Then you know it's worth fighting for, to keep these evil bastards out."

"I don't think that ROC is interested in settling in there anytime soon. They only want their cut for the girls."

"Maybe." She didn't know what he did, and wasn't trying to pretend to.

"What I want to know, Trina, is why aren't you more concerned about your kid?"

"I'm very concerned about my child." She bit her lower lip. It was so very difficult to not just spill it all, tell Rob that Jake was his. But not like this, not in the midst of an op that could go south at any point. "I'm also lucky to have supportive family."

"Yes, you are." His judgment couldn't be clearer. It stung that he thought her career was a threat to her child. She'd asked herself the same question, and it always came back to accepting that law enforcement was a calling for her. And so was being Jake's mother.

"What should I know about what we're walking into?" She had training, but knowledge was the best weapon in any op. And an open mind.

"Have you ever worked any kind of SWAT?"

"Only training. I've been pretty lucky as far as ops go—most of my apprehensions have been textbook. If there's any chance something is going to get risky, we go in pairs and ask for backup when needed."

"Great. So you forced yourself on this without the skills to be of any help."

"Excuse me. I have plenty of skills. And it won't be just the two of us, will it?" She'd assumed they'd be going in on the tip of a large spear of LEAs. "We're wasting time talking. Let's go."

He shook his head. "We can't do one thing, make a single move, until we get the go-ahead from my boss. I'll drive to our waiting point and we could be there five minutes or five days until the call comes. It's how these things go. We won't have backup at the start. We're going in clandestine. The ROC group won't hesitate to kill these girls in order to keep how they got them this far into the States from being revealed. Until the girls are placed where they're being sold, and the money is in ROC hands, they're a liability. I have no desire to have the deaths of these young women on my conscience."

Cold dread made her blood feel as though it was thickening, pumping too slowly through her body.

"You okay?" She heard Rob's voice, but her vision blurred as she remembered the cold stone basement, the hours that she'd been certain would turn into days. "Trina."

His forceful tone shook her from the hell that had been the first major turning point in her life. "I'm fine."

"You're thinking about the time in high school, aren't you?"

"Yes." She placed the empty coffee cup into the holder on her door. "I'm in this for whatever it takes."

"I forgot about it until you got so quiet. Look, Trina, this is not the mission for you to prove yourself on. It's not a hill worth your blood." His twist on the military adage about whether a hill was worth dying on wasn't missed. He was trying to get her back to herself.

"I'm good. That was a long time ago. I've been through wartime ops since then." And had birthed a baby, his baby.

"You've got a kid, Trina. I get that you've changed, you're not the same woman I knew, but you're still *you*. You'll never forgive yourself if you get hurt, or worse." He shifted onto a new road and started the long twisting way into the deepest part of the Poconos.

"J—he's fine."

"You have a son."

"Yes."

"His father—are you with him?"

"No. He—he's never been in the picture." Crap. The flashback to when two male high school classmates had grabbed her off the abandoned path between the girls' locker room and the track, locked her in the football storage garage, promising to come back later for the "real" action, had left her raw. It felt like Rob was ambushing her with everything she'd worked so hard to leave in her past. Including him.

"Did you do in-vitro or adopt?" His curiosity was sincere, his expression open. Fury flashed hot and potent, making her turn in her seat and look at him as he drove.

"Damn it, Rob, you can't come back to life and interrogate me about what I've been doing for the past five years that I thought you were dead. It's not your business anymore!"

He matched her previous litany of profanity as he slowed the SUV and drove off the road into the space between two copses of trees. They'd be invisible to any passersby, but she wasn't concerned. In this remote part of the mountains they'd be lucky to see one other vehicle per hour if at all.

The SUV was shielded from the bright sun by the evergreen forest, which provided a better canopy than any stretch of canvas. Rob rolled down the windows to allow for airflow, and to Trina's surprise, goose bumps appeared on her forearms. It had to be ten, maybe fifteen degrees cooler out of the blazing sun. The early-morning dew still glinted from the tiny green plants that grew at the base of the tree trunks.

"Trina. Look at me."

Damn it, she was trembling again.

"Please."

She wanted to ignore his demands, his arrogance, his sheer ignorance of the hell she'd been through, believing he'd been killed. Rob's gentle persuasion, however, had always been her Achilles' heel. She sucked in the pine-scented air and faced him.

Rob's initial fury that Trina refused to take orders and go back to her office in Harrisburg had been pierced by the stricken expression that he could only attribute to what he remembered as the scariest time of her life. She'd told him the story of the two teens who'd terrorized her in high school, and he'd wanted to go back in time and kill them. As her story unfolded under the desert stars, he'd put his arm around her and listened, giving her all the comfort a SEAL on deployment could. And he'd thanked God that her school had a security system that prevented her captors from doing any physical harm to her. The security guards had caught them and freed Trina.

Her life's purpose had changed, though. Once on track to become a doctor, she'd decided to do something more physical to help others. And, Rob suspected, to make her feel more empowered. The US Navy beckoned. He understood, because his desire to become a SEAL had been born out of wanting to get out of the chaos that had been his childhood.

Now as he looked into her eyes, eyes that had haunted him since he'd said his private goodbye to her five years ago, he saw the woman he'd made love to in the midst of the highest operational tempo both of them had ever experienced before now.

"I'm sorry if I'm coming across like a tank. But I want to make it perfectly clear, Trina. I moved to Silver Valley, took the job with my current employer, to be closer to you. Even if we only met for coffee once, had one conversation where I'd told you I was still alive and wished you well in your current life, it would be worth it to me. We shared something when we were deployed that few ever do. Forgive me if it's been too long, and you've buried the memories too deeply."

"I didn't bury the memories, Rob. I relived them every damned day. For a long time. And I'm still not understanding why you didn't reach out sooner." Tears were forming and leaking out of the corners of her eyes, trailing down her cheeks. He couldn't stop his hand, and his fingers brushed away the sign that he'd hurt Trina far more than he'd imagined. They'd both needed closure.

"I wanted to, babe, but it wasn't possible." He hadn't thought enough of himself to do it for him, but he should have done it for her. Walked across the street and—

His gut clenched in the certainty that a person had less than a handful of times in life. When he was a kid and saw his first SEAL movie and knew that was his path. When a bombing raid had gone terribly wrong and he'd ended up severely injured, only to be captured, tortured as a POW, and once back in friendly hands had endured the most excruciating pain yet—rehabilitation. Knowing his SEAL days were over, and that he'd be able to keep up the good fight in the CIA, but only if he had no shot with Trina.

He'd thought he'd had no chance, but this moment of clarity pierced through everything. His thoughts and planning for what they were going to accomplish once at the ROC Poconos compound took a back seat, and Rob had never allowed a mission to take a back seat.

He didn't care that she had a child, either. Usually he'd dated only single women without kids, not wanting to involve another potential casualty in his very fluid lifestyle. An adult woman understood "no permanent ties," but a juvenile didn't. He paused. If the toddler he saw Trina with had been around two, then he'd be what, five by now?

A bolt of truth pierced him.

"Trina. How old did you say your child is?"

Her eyes widened, and she moved her upper body back, away from him. But she didn't break eye contact. In that moment, he knew.

"I didn't. He—he's five."

"Five. Years. Old." Rob let the words hang there as he struggled with the denial exploding inside him, the pure angst that he might have missed the most important thing that ever happened to him.

Trina knew he knew. He saw the regret, the sorrow, the truth in her eyes.

"Yes. He's five, and his name is Jake. Justin 'Jake' Berger Lopez. I call him Jake because, because it's easier."

Her proclamation was a hand grenade to his gut. He couldn't breathe, couldn't do anything but stare at Trina. She was his only anchor to the present.

"Rob, I know this is a shock, and trust me, I understand." She let a nervous laugh bubble out, filling the front seat. "How do you think I felt when I saw you walking out of that storage building? And I had my weapon trained on you. God, I could have blown you away, if I'd thought you were Vasin."

"He's mine, your kid."

"No, he was fathered by one of the next half dozen men I slept with after you died. I only named him after you for the hell of it." She pulled a face of pure disgust. "Of course he's yours. He looks just like you. Except he has my gray eyes." Her face reflected a mother's satisfaction. "You saw us, saw him, when you found me in Norfolk. And as I said, my brother was there, helping me out. He'd come over for dinner a lot of nights when he wasn't studying for law school. I was on shore duty, biding my time until I served out my time and could resign. All I wanted was for Jake to be safe and for me to have a normal nine-to-five job so that he'd grow up protected and in a happy environment. It made sense to come back to central Pennsylvania. You had no family, as far as I knew, and since we'd never been officially married, there was no way I could seek financial support from the Navy for your son." She stopped, and he felt her hand on his arm, her slight squeeze.

He looked at her hand, then up at her. A man could dive into her eyes and never come out. "I'm so, so sorry, Rob. If I'd known…"

"If you'd known what? You'd have taken me back, started up where we left off? I was a broken man, Trina. It took me almost two years to come back from my injuries." Physically. His mental and emotional healing had yet to be finished, if it ever would. "And you knew that not one, but two fathers had failed me, miserably so. The second one was my foster dad, so that was pure circumstance. But my biological father was a drug addict who never was able to get sober. What kind of example is that? Worse, what if it's in my DNA to be a lousy parent?"

Trina remained silent, but her eyes shone with compassion and regret. *She* had regrets?

Elation, joy, anger, anguish. The emotional cocktail hit him without warning, making speech impossible. He wanted to run around shouting that he had a son! He was a father! But he'd missed the boy's first five years. Five. Years. Did his son wonder about him? Did he know he existed? Pain worse than any broken rib squeezed the air out of his lungs. If his son had suffered at all due to his absence, he wouldn't be able to live with his decision to not walk across that street three and a half years ago.

He and Trina had just reunited, started to tiptoe around their emotions. And now he had to accept that he'd missed the first five years of his child's life. He hated being at the mercy of fate, but to realize his own actions may have caused more harm than good was devastating. But he couldn't change the past, no matter how much it hurt. Today was what mattered.

Trina hated that Rob hurt so much. If she could play the last five years back and have him know Jake from the time he'd been in her womb, she would. Even as she thought about it, though, she knew that wasn't entirely true. Rob was right. They'd been very different people back then.

"Rob, this isn't how I imagined telling you that you have a son. " And she had imagined it countless times. Hoped for this exact situation, that he'd somehow come back to her, the KIA report a mistake.

"You never pictured it. You thought I was dead."

"Stop blaming yourself for this. It is what it is. You said yourself that you weren't over what you'd been through. That you're still faced with the hell you survived."

He shook his head, the rest of his body still as he looked out the windshield. She shifted to face forward, giving him at least the illusion of space from her, from her desire for him to let it all go. Nothing in this was simple or black-and-white, and it had all started with the first day they'd worked together in the Navy, on the preparation meeting that led up to the fateful mission that had torn them apart.

"I have a son." He was saying aloud what his heart wanted to believe but his mind couldn't yet wrap around. This, Trina understood. She'd had the opposite problem in that her heart had refused to believe Rob, then Justin, was dead, that he'd miraculously appear and be thrilled they'd made a baby during their brief but intense affair. Her mind told her otherwise, as had the headstone in Arlington National Cemetery.

"I still can't believe that I laid flowers at your grave."

"You never sought any kind of compensation for our son, you said?"

"How could I? You and I were only—" she waved her hand "—what, lovers? Boyfriend and girlfriend? You know how the military works. If you're not a dependent, if you're not marked down on page two of the member's service record, you don't exist."

"You could have searched for my family. My brother." He'd told her about him, where he lived.

"I've already told you why I didn't." She watched as a herd of deer appeared to the right of the vehicle. A huge stag with a full rack of antlers stood amid several does, and she spotted a fawn.

"It's not fair of me to ask you about any of it, Trina. I wasn't there for you. And not for our son, either."

"You didn't know you had a son. And who knows? If you'd shown up as soon as you could have, it might have been a disaster. I was so protective of Jake, and you say you were really messed up. I'm not sure I would have been the partner you needed at that point."

"You'd have been perfect."

"Um, no. I swear I called my mom twenty times a day when I didn't demand she be right there with me."

"What's he like?" Rob spoke as if in a trance.

"He's the most enthusiastic person I've ever met. I mean, that boy gets excited about going for a walk in the woods as much as he does about Santa Claus. He's also very bright, scarily so." She laughed at a memory. "When he was in preschool, his teacher asked the kids to draw a picture of a triangle. Jake drew what looked like a scribble. I could see a tiny triangle in the middle of it, but the teachers were looking for just a triangle on the page. It was so him. He probably drew the triangle and then improvised until they had to turn it in."

"I don't think I knew what a circle was, much less a triangle, when I was in preschool."

"I know, same here. And I told the teacher as much." At least Rob was perking up, coming back from the dark place his thoughts must have taken him. That she understood, too. The years of wondering how he'd died, if he'd suffered in the blast or slowly died before help could reach him, if the enemy had captured him. Finally she knew most of it, and all she cared about was that he was alive.

"Rob, this is too soon, too much, for both of us. But you have to know that I'm glad you're here. And I know Jake is going to be happy to meet you."

"He can never meet me, Trina. He'll think it's his fault I didn't show up until now. That's how kids' minds work. I know he's not in the same situation I was in as a foster kid, but he's been without a father. And you said he's smart—he'll put two and two together. What have you told him about me?"

"I told him his dad was a brave man who gave the ultimate sacrifice for his country."

"More like a coward who couldn't walk across the damn street. Let's face it—I didn't have a father, so how can I be one?"

She let his words lie. She couldn't take him through the mental and emotional processes he needed to travel to fully absorb what he'd discovered today. That he was a father.

"That was then, Rob. This is now. We're both different people. As odd as it felt to call you by a different name, other than your core self, I don't see you as Justin any longer. You're still you, I feel that, but…"

"This is the crux of it, Trina. Can you live with who I've become? More importantly, will Jake accept me as his father? Hell, I don't even know if it's safe to tell him about me. I don't want to screw him up for life. And my work, it could bring some really bad guys to our doorstep."

Trina had gone over the same thoughts, the same mental path. She had so much she wanted to say, so much she wanted to share with him about Jake, his son.

Had *she* fully accepted that he was here, alive?

"When I saw you yesterday, standing there with your pistol on me, I couldn't have defended myself if I'd wanted to. It was like you'd dropped out of the sky."

She offered a smile. "Maybe we're overanalyzing this. It's the twenty-first century and we're used to instant communications, knowing everything in real time. During past wars, take the Civil War or World War II, family members went for years not knowing anything about what was going on with one another. Lots of cases of sailors or soldiers gone missing occurred, and those folks picked up and kept going. It was a mere blip in their life. They focused on the positive."

"I get where you're going with this, Trina, and forgive me but I just can't handle your positive affirmation baloney right now."

Like a physical slap, his words stopped her cold. This side of Rob was what she'd written off as the warrior part of his SEAL personality. It was what all military folks understood—the mission had to be the top priority. And it had never reared its head between them like this before. Of course, they'd never gone on an op together as parents to the same child.

Trina retreated inside herself, forcing all the acidic comebacks aside. They'd only spent two days together. After five years apart, what did any of this really mean?

Chapter 7

Trina's insides shook, but this wasn't the place to tell Rob the thoughts running through her mind. Worse, she couldn't begin to describe what his harsh words had unleashed—memories of her time with him, knowing she'd seen the best in him while also dealing with his most primitive side. As he had hers. They'd been in battle where all rules boiled down to one: complete the mission.

She shot a quick look at him, and he was as still as a statue, his chest's exaggerated movement the only indication he wasn't carved from the limestone that lay under the forest floor. He was in battle mode, all right. As was she.

"You know, I've imagined how I'd find you again, let you know I was alive, a thousand times. It was going to be a shock no matter how it went down, but I never wanted you to suffer one minute more, Trina. Now I can see in your eyes, your tears, that you've suffered as much as I have. More—you didn't know I was alive. At least I had the knowledge that you were still walking around, that I could reach out if I chose to. I can't see a way that you'll ever be able to forgive me, but I promise I won't make anything harder for you than it has to be."

"It's too much, too fast, Rob. We're both only human, even though we both seem to still like to participate in extraordinary professions." She reached over and rubbed his shoulder, as much for his comfort as for her reassurance that he wasn't a mirage. An apparition her mind had conjured.

He turned to her, and the air in the car went from muggy due to the humidity to sultry as their attraction hit another flash point. Rob's nostrils flared and his mouth lifted in a lopsided grin. "Chemistry hasn't left, has it?"

"No." Her reply was a whisper, adding to the sexy ambience. A giggle erupted. "We're both maxed out on adrenaline, waiting for the order to come, and oh, by the way, you've come back from the dead and found out you have a son. And we're looking at each other like this."

"Let's stop the watching and get to the good stuff, baby cakes." Heat flared in her center at his use of her nickname, and she leaned in, eager to meet his lips. It wouldn't be a kiss that sneaked up on them like the one at the hotel, in the cramped bathroom. It would be like the heat they'd enjoyed in the desert together: sizzling and a good place to escape to as a reminder they were both human amid what could become a hellhole in a blink.

"That's it. Come here, babe." His lips curved and his breath led her the rest of the way.

A sharp *rap rap rap* hit the driver's-side window, and Trina cried out in surprise.

"Son of a—" Rob didn't finish and his hand went to his weapon as he looked out the glass at the intruder. Trina quickly scanned the area around the SUV.

"All clear around us. I don't see another vehicle." She spoke quietly, for Rob's ears only as he dealt with the uniformed man standing outside.

"Officer." Rob had rolled down the window, and Trina saw a man in what looked like a police uniform but that wasn't quite right. She let out a sigh of relief. They'd run into the local constable, for heaven's sake. And she knew him. He hadn't recognized her yet, though.

"I'm Constable Weeks. Can I ask you folks what you're doing in my neck of the woods, parked like you're hiding from the law?"

Trina wanted to sneer at the man; she'd had her fair share of run-ins with constables. By Pennsylvania law they were community civilian law enforcement positions that were often held by military veterans or former LEA. And they did a good job for the state, helping to keep things in line when the local police departments were stretched thin or in fact nonexistent.

"US Marshal Lopez, Constable Weeks." She held up her badge and credentials, and the man peered past Rob to her.

"That you, Ms. Trina? Well, why didn't you say so?" He spat on the ground, the juice of his chewing tobacco dribbling on his chin. Just as she'd remembered.

"Yes, it is, Constable Weeks. This is my colleague

Rob. He's going through some training, and I wanted to familiarize him with the area."

"No one told me there was going to be any kind of military training up here today."

Trina gritted her teeth. "It's ad hoc training, Buddy." She used his first name and her friendliest tone. She'd had to deal with him when she'd come up to get Vasin yesterday, running into Constable Buddy Weeks at the local diner when she'd stopped to use the restroom.

"Anything I can help with, Ms. Lopez?"

"No, no threat to the peace here, Buddy. We'll be out of here shortly."

Buddy wasn't convinced. "I've got my truck up on the highway. We could run through some drills if you'd like."

Crap, crap, slap-your-momma crap. That was all they needed, a huge honking constables vehicle sitting on the main road in this area. She'd been careful, as had Rob, obviously, to keep them off the main highways, but it wasn't a guarantee that Vasin's men and even Ivanov weren't going to pass through. And she wasn't convinced that Buddy wasn't somehow complicit in the activities that went on in "his" forest, as he'd put it.

"Thanks, Buddy, I'll keep that in mind for our next exercise. If you don't mind, Rob and I need to get on with it."

"Okay. Just trying to be helpful." Buddy slapped the steel frame right next to Rob's door. She saw the tic in Rob's temple moving like a dogwood in a rainstorm and stifled a chuckle.

"Thank you, sir." Rob nodded, playing the eager US marshal intern to a T.

As soon as the windows were up, Rob started the

engine and put the AC on full blast. "You and Buddy go way back?"

"It's an odd thing, the constable deal in Pennsylvania, but it's all part of the civic system here. They're elected for six years, and for the most part I haven't had any issues with them. Buddy, however, he's just a weird dude."

"That's comforting. His last name isn't Russian, is it?"

"Weeks? No. It's okay, Rob. We can drive up a little farther and hunker down until we get the okay to move in."

"I do not want to see the likes of that man for the rest of our time on this mountain."

"He's out of our hair for now. Buddy needs to feel he's part of the solution, is all. Even when there isn't a problem."

Her phone ringtone cut in, and Corey's voice echoed around them; the SUV had synced to her phone when she'd rented it, not Rob's.

"Trina, you were supposed to be back already. I understand from Claudia Michele that you've decided to spend some extra time in the Poconos?"

"I'm sorry about that, Corey. Yes. I'm here with Rob, who also works for Claudia, as you know." Trina shook her head. How the hell was it that she was working with Rob like this but had no idea who he worked for?

"You can't do this, Trina. Not as a marshal."

Panic threatened as she envisioned Rob going into the compound on his own. "That's why I requested leave. I'm off the clock. Corey, you told me yourself, there's a group of young women, girls, underage, waiting to be shipped down to our area. Most of them are headed for Bill's Broads out on the Pike." She referred to the strip joint that had opened in Silver Valley and, much to the chagrin of the locals, raked in the bucks. It had gotten its business license in a sleight of hand that the Silver Valley City Council was ferociously trying to rescind. No one was shocked by a strip club but they didn't want any kind of bar or club that had rumors of drug dealing or human trafficking. And there had been both with Bill's Broads but nothing enough to make arrests.

"It's not US Marshal business, Trina. You know the deal. I'm sorry you weren't able to get your man, but you got Agent Bristol out of there, and that's the end of US Marshal involvement."

"I'm on leave."

"Trina." Corey's exasperation was familiar. She often pushed her duty to the limit of its legal boundaries, if it meant they caught the bad guy.

"It's okay, Corey. I've got all those days held over from last fiscal year, and I'll go to my new place and set it up all next week as planned."

"Fine. But Trina?"

"Yes?"

"Cover your ass out there."

"Thanks, boss." The line cut off, and she felt the warmth of Rob's gaze on her but refused to look at him. She didn't have the answers as to why she'd still chosen to be with him through this, knowing the risks and knowing Jake waited at home for her. All she knew was that if she didn't do her best to help out the virtually enslaved women, she wouldn't be able to look her son in the eye. She believed in always working for justice.

"He's right. You should be on that bus, Trina."

"Just get us out of here, Rob. Before Constable Buddy shows up again."

Rob drove but didn't let up on their previous conversation. "I'm not asking you for anything here, Trina. I mean with us. All I want is a chance for me to know my son, if you'll agree to it. It's pretty clear that whatever we shared is over—we're two different people, living very different lives."

"I don't have to be reminded of that, Rob. Your name used to be Justin, remember?" She knew it would hurt, tossing that grenade out there. Rob had been clear that he was no longer Justin and wanted, needed, her to not call him by that name. A tiny part of her wanted him to feel the pain she'd gone through when she'd believed he'd died. It wasn't a part of herself she was proud of.

"You haven't lost your touch for cruelty, Trina."

"You don't know the half of it." She stared at the road as they passed by the constable's vehicle, good old Buddy sitting inside sipping from a thermos. "And for the record, I'd never keep you from your son. My only concern is how we'll present it to him, but kids are pretty resilient—it's not a cliché for no reason."

"I appreciate that. We can discuss it more after we're back in Silver Valley."

"Did you buy a place in town?" Her stomach was so tight as she verbalized what she'd wondered since she learned he had returned to Silver Valley.

"No. I'm renting a small house on a much larger farm. It used to be the owners' in-laws' house, but now the owners need the cash."

"That's a common way to make ends meet around here. Rather, there." She took in the slope of the mountain they were climbing. "This is only two hours out, maybe three, and yet the scenery is so different."

Rob remained silent. He'd never been the small-talk type.

"What about you, Trina? You own a place in Harrisburg?"

She squirmed on the leather seat. "Actually, I've recently purchased a home on the west shore of the Susquehanna, in Silver Valley. It's a farmette of sorts. I wanted a place where I could have chickens if I wanted to, and for Jake to have a bigger yard."

"He's in kindergarten?"

"Starting in September, yes. It's full day out by us."

"What kind of school?"

"Public. There are many options, but the public schools are excellent." As evidenced by the higher tax rate, but she'd do anything to ensure Jake's education.

"What about bullying?"

"What is this, Rob, the Inquisition? You haven't even met him yet." As soon as the words were out, she realized how harsh they'd sound to the man who'd missed the first five years of his son's life. Rob was right; she hadn't lost her streak of cruelty.

"True." He looked like he was going to say something but his lips were clamped tight and he focused entirely on his driving. As if, like her, he didn't want to prolong any illusion that there was anything left to salvage between them. Physical attraction was one thing, but to commit to the very person who had caused so much hurt? That was impossible.

They weren't on the secondary road for five minutes before Rob's phone vibrated so loudly they both jumped. It was Claudia.

"Read it out to me." His hands on the wheel, his mind out of reach for now, he didn't move to pick up his phone.

Trina picked up the heavy black cell that was obviously capable of a lot more than her phone, from its weight to the extra app-like programs on the opening screen.

Move in. Backup on the way, thirty minutes out. She watched his reaction. "Sounds like our go-ahead." Trina spoke clearly, as though they hadn't just dropped the equivalent of a relationship nuclear bomb between them.

"It is. Let's use the next ten miles to go over our plan." Rob started to list various situations, and Trina gave her response in rapid-fire style, the way they'd handled operational preparations in Iraq. It had been highly unusual for Trina as a P-8 pilot to become deeply involved in SEAL ops, but she and Rob had met during a particularly intense op tempo that had required all hands on deck. Meaning she'd caught tiny glimpses into what Rob and his team were facing. They'd never worked this closely together, however.

"Trina, I'm not happy about both of us going into an op that could turn deadly in a heartbeat. If something happened to both of us, where would that leave Jake?" Rob spoke as though he'd always thought of his son first. A pang deep in her chest threatened to break through Trina's professional poise.

"First, we're going to handle this without any trouble, and if there's trouble, we'll deal. Second, I made my brother Jake's guardian in the event of anything happening to me. Between him and my parents, Jake will want for nothing."

"Except for his mother, and now a father he doesn't even know is alive!"

"I know it's been a lot for you to take in, Rob. And I'm sorry about that. But if you can focus on meeting Jake, having the opportunity to know your son, I think you'll feel a bit better." She found it so odd to be the one comforting Rob. Usually her brother had to talk her down from worrying too much about Jake. She missed her little boy fiercely. The longest she'd ever had to be away from him was three months, for a short overseas assignment while she was on shore duty. Since she'd been in the US Marshals, they'd only experienced a few weeks of separation here and there.

"We didn't have a kid to worry about in the war zone." Rob was like a guard dog, and he wasn't letting go of this bone. "How can you work as a US marshal when you have a kid?"

A flash of anger made her composure disintegrate. "Let's get something straight. I owe you no explanations for any of my choices. You're the one who died, the one who chose to remain dead! You gave me no choice in the matter. So don't come waltzing back into my life and think you can start throwing your judgment around." She might not be the perfect mother, but Jake was the perfect little boy. Happy and healthy, which was all that mattered to her most days. He was growing up with a good dose of appreciation for hard work, too. Trina had scrimped and saved over the past five years for their new home in a top school district. The sprawling farmhouse and surrounding property gave Jake room to explore. It was going to be the best place to raise him through high school.

No, she'd said nothing wrong. Rob needed to get a

grip on where their boundaries were, ASAP. Or risk another excoriating verbal attack.

Maybe she was the one who needed to be certain of *her* boundaries.

Trina's words were more bracing than menthol lotion hitting his skin right after he'd shaved his deployment beard. Because they rang all too true.

Her words sounded harsh, but were an accurate assessment of what had happened. He'd been declared dead, found and brought back to a functioning human being, then he sought Trina out and seen her with what he now knew was his child, but at the time he hadn't made the connection. And he'd chosen what he thought was the noble path—to allow Trina and her family to go forward without the complication of him showing up again.

He hadn't questioned his motives for walking away, always chalked them up to duty. But had they been deeper?

"My country needed me for the CIA back then, too. I can't go into specifics, and won't, not on our way back into ROC territory. But there are some things you're not aware of that I'll eventually tell you."

"Oh, goody." She deadpanned her reply, and he couldn't stifle his grin.

"I knew I could count on you to keep things light before we get into the thick of this op."

"Trust me, it's not on purpose." She leaned forward in her seat. "Enough of our history—it's time to earn our paychecks. There's the building the truck trailer is supposed to be parked near. Up there through the trees, do you see it?" She pointed at the long shipping container, the same kind used on cargo ships and trains. They were driven all over the eastern seaboard, pulled by powerful diesel engine rigs that exchanged one standard module for another with ease.

He nodded. "I sure do. Are you ready for this, Trina?"

"Damn straight."

He parked the car and they got out; the forest floor was blanketed with dry leaves. It was peak fire season as no rain had fallen for over two months, highly unusual for the past century but typical of the warming weather patterns.

"Ready." She put on her earpiece under a US Marshal ball cap and tested to ensure she and Rob were synced.

"We're good to go." He handed her the rental ring of two keys and a fob, and his fingers brushed her upturned palm. It zapped a zinger of attraction straight to his dick. Exactly what he didn't need for this operation to be a success.

"Above all else, stay low and safe. Wait for my signal to come out and help me with the girls. Do not under any circumstance reveal yourself before then. Are we clear?"

"Crystal." She met his eyes, and he knew he read her perfectly. She was prepared for whatever this faction of ROC threw at them.

"So that puts you right about here." He motioned toward a group of low bushes at the edge of the clearing. Only twenty-five yards ahead was a corrugated metal building, similar to the one where he'd been held captive.

Trina didn't respond verbally as she crouched low and prepared a tiny hideout area in the deciduous shrubs. Forsythia, he thought, that had passed its bloom a few months ago and was now a tangled mass of vining branches, the mint-green leaves starting to shrivel in the drought.

"You can take a clipping of it if you'd like." Rob couldn't help noticing how much she adored the local flora.

"I'm good, thanks. Don't forget to call in when you need me." On her haunches and posed like a mean badger, Trina was ready to strike anything that came her way. He'd best remember that.

Rob headed for the building that looked like the one from which he'd barely escaped with his life only two days ago, wondering where his common sense had fled. He trusted Claudia's intelligence that told him about the risks, and on paper it looked like a fairly methodical takedown for human traffickers. At all costs he had to act as if he knew what he was doing, in the likely event he ran into Vasin or even Ivanov.

The air was heavier than yesterday, the bright, hot sun giving way to heavy, thunderous clouds. They'd be lucky to rescue the girls before it rained down buckets.

It was difficult to watch Rob walk away and out of sight. Logically Trina knew that he had to; the trailer where the girls were being held was around the other side of the building. And she had to stay here—she was his backup if things got ugly before they got the young women safely out.

She checked her surroundings repeatedly as she'd been trained. It was second nature to her. A crack of a twig and she spotted a herd of deer; rustling in the leaves helped her identify a groundhog. The forest was a cacophony of animal noises, from the constant chatter of squirrels to birdsong that swelled as the day grew longer. The heat had refused to let up, and her T-shirt and pants were stuck to places she didn't want to think about. Her shower in her new house's master bedroom was tiny but would be pure bliss once she finally got back to Silver Valley. Home.

Jake. Thinking of home immediately brought him to mind, and she could almost smell the sweet scent of his hair after he'd played out in the sun. *Soon, son, soon. I'll be home before you know it.*

If all went as planned, she could be home tonight.

Nothing from Rob either on her earpiece or via text. It'd only been a few minutes; she wasn't supposed to check in until after fifteen.

At ten minutes, her calves needed a stretch, and she did so by doing forward bends, straightening and moving her knees in long, slow movements. As always she was careful to remain as quiet as possible. Just in case.

The sound of a door opening had her crouching back down, and she watched as Vasin walked out of the storage facility as if it were any other day and he was any other man looking for sunshine. He had a cigarette in one hand and a semiautomatic rifle in the other, its strap slung over his shoulder. As if he were a Russian soldier and not the hardened criminal that he was. It was beyond frustrating to be unable to do anything in the moment. Her fingers twitched as if they wanted to cuff him on the spot. If she spoke into her comms unit, she'd risk being heard. She didn't want to text Rob as her movements, even hidden in the brush, could be detected by Vasin. As she observed, he walked around, taking a smoke break. He'd eluded capture yesterday, and she realized that it was almost certain that Ivanov was in the facility, too. Vasin wouldn't come out of that building slinging such a powerful weapon unless there was something, or someone, inside to protect.

A shout from the open door, in Russian. Vasin answered in a guttural low stream of words Trina had no chance of translating. She'd been studying conversational Russian over the past two years as ROC became more of an issue for her job, but Vasin was too far away to catch the actual words. From his body language, he was annoyed at being bothered but went back into the building after smashing his cigarette with his heel. Even ROC heeded the fire season warnings.

As soon as the slam of the door cracked through the otherwise silent area, Trina noticed movement to her far right, alongside the edge of the forest clearing. Two men, not in uniform, walking in slow steps around a parking area for ATVs and small commercial trailers. Two of the three ATVs from yesterday were there; she'd memorized their license plates. Satisfaction curled in her belly, knowing that one was still missing because she and Rob had stolen it and left it on the side of the road, in the woods.

Trina heard a shout in Russian directly behind her and she flattened to the ground on her belly, her heartbeat reaching into her throat. *Please don't see me.* She longed for her P-8 flying days, when she'd be able to watch an op like this from thousands of feet above. Her pistol was in her hand, the safety off.

The sound of footsteps grew closer, and she held her breath in the dense bush, knowing that if the interlopers saw her booted feet she was dead.

Jake. Her baby.

When she thought she couldn't take one more second without oxygen, two bulky men walked within feet of her, past her hiding location and toward the building. As soon as their footsteps were out of earshot she carefully retrieved her phone and texted Rob. He had to know that they were far outnumbered, at least until backup arrived.

As she tapped in her message, she'd never felt more torn between mission and personal needs. Namely, Jake's needs as a young boy. Rob was right. Jake deserved a mother who could be there for him 100 percent. What the hell was she doing out here?

It's the operational exhaustion talking.

It wasn't uncommon to think you never wanted to do a mission again when faced with danger. Trina shook her head, slightly. She had to knock off the negative thoughts. She and Rob were a good team and would do what they needed to do. What came afterward for them wasn't her concern. *Right.*

At least four men with AR-15s circling perimeter. Vasin appeared with AR-15 during a smoke break. Someone inside bldg called him back in. Too far away to make out words.

Rob read Trina's text, and a shot of fear cleared his mind of anything but figuring out how to get the young women out of the eighteen-wheeler trailer four hundred yards in front of him. It was parked behind the building he suspected Ivanov was in, half of it shoved back into the woods. At least there was some shade on it. But the cries of the women still reached his ears, as did the reprimands the lone guard gave them. ROC had stationed the skinny bastard at the open back of the trailer. Rob had watched two pairs of women be allowed down the ramp and out into the woods, the guard ordering them in Russian to "hurry up and piss" in front of him. They were beyond sobbing, but he heard the women cry out as they stepped, barefoot, onto the dry, heat-baked pine needles. It was so typical of ROC to have these women totally at their mercy. The lack of shoes was deliberate, as was the refusal to allow them the use of a normal bathroom facility. Nothing would be left to chance, not when the Russian crime ring was getting tens of thousands of dollars per woman.

Another text came in, this one from Claudia.

FBI within ten minutes

Ten minutes. He had ten minutes to neutralize the guard and then take on the trolls that Trina had reported. If they were very lucky, they'd handle it all without anyone in the building finding out until it was too late. The FBI would take care of the rest—take out Vasin and whomever he was protecting in the warehouse building.

As the minutes passed, he shot off a text to Trina. She didn't reply right away, but depending upon where the guards were, she might not be able to. That didn't stop the heavy creep of fear from sliding across his gut and up his spine. *Stay here. Stay with the mission.* His combat mantras usually helped, but he'd figured out that in the brief thirty-six hours since he'd come face-to-face with Trina again, nothing in his life could be classified as "usual."

He watched the trailer guard harass the latest pair of girls as they scurried to relieve themselves in the forest. The guard was speaking loudly and Rob's Russian was very good, so he heard the guard tell the girls that their first taste of American opportunity was going to come in the shape of his anatomy. Rob allowed the initial flash of anger to fuel his dedication to duty as he assessed how to take the guard down. A clean shot would be easy, but then there wouldn't be a suspect to question. The more junior the ROC member was, like this guard, the easier it was for them to be turned. They weren't hardened like Vasin and certainly not Ivanov, who had the power of the entire ROC behind him. No, this guard would have to be restrained, quickly and quietly enough to not alert Vasin. Rob had to keep the guard alive.

But the perimeter guards were another problem. Trina couldn't be expected to take out four guards. It was too dangerous. As the minutes ticked down and he still didn't hear back from her, he was going to have to make a decision: Complete the mission or save Trina.

Trina watched from the safety of a low tree branch as the other two men circled around toward her location. Would she be as lucky this time, that they'd be chatting away about tits and ass enough to overlook her as the previous guards had? Her Russian wasn't perfect but she kept it proficient enough to use as needed in the field. She'd arrested several ROC members and had always been grateful for the language ability.

Crouched in the low branches of a bushy tree in a Pocono campground was never how she'd anticipated using her skill. But it was reassuring to know what the guards were talking about.

Single guard on unhitched 18-wheeler trailer full of girls. They go out in 2s to use forest as toilet. I have to take out guard, get captives into forest. You move them to safer ground and wait for backup.

She read Rob's text again and knew that if these bad guys walking around her heard one sound from the trailer they'd be over there in a flash. Rob was a former SEAL, and CIA operative. He was an organized crime thug's worst nightmare. But even with Rob's capabilities, she didn't like the odds.

It was going to be up to her. She deliberately did not respond to Rob right away. She'd rather be able to tell him she'd neutralized her area. Four guards. It was a matter of which two she'd take out first.

As the two men drew closer, she heard the dreaded words. Thank God for her Russian training. "What the hell is that?"

"What?"

"There, under the bush, idiot." The one guard lowered his voice, realizing they weren't alone. Trina watched as they neared the bush, the one in front motioning for the other to follow at a distance. They zeroed in on her boots, only two or three yards away.

"Come out of there." The guard spoke in excellent English, his rifle pointed at the bush.

Trina knew it was now or never.

She jumped down from the low tree branch she'd climbed. A quick hit to one guard's head with her pistol had him unconscious on the ground. She was ready for the second man when he turned around, searching for her. Trina made short work of aiming her pistol and shooting in defense at his shoulder. He dropped to his knees, his screams echoing around her. She grabbed his AR-15 by yanking its strap over his head as he crashed to the ground.

The noise alerted the other two men, and they ran at her. They were only yards away. One stopped and aimed his rifle at her. Trina acted on operational instinct as she grabbed the first man's AR-15 from the ground and ran for the back of the building. She flung the extra weapon into the brush as she ran, ensuring the other two men wouldn't find it easily. As shots hit the ground around her feet, she zigzagged until she heard the pounding steps behind her. A man emerged in front of her, and she prepared to take him out until she recognized it was Rob. He motioned with one swift up-and-down swipe of his left hand for her to hit the deck. She complied, and within a split second the sound of two bullets whizzing overhead was followed by two quick *oomphs* and thuds as her pursuers hit the ground. Rob had taken them out.

She was back on her knees, getting up as Rob's hand closed around her upper arm and pulled her to a standing position. His eyes blazed from the adrenaline, and she knew hers did, too.

"You okay? Any more?" He looked her over.

"Okay. We got them all, except Vasin and whoever he's guarding in there. One's unconscious, and I shot the other in the shoulder. The trailer guard?"

Rob nodded. "Got him. Tied up to a tree, out of sight. Our backup team will find him. Come on. We've got to get the girls out of here."

She followed him, noticing that his stiff posture wasn't as pronounced as it had been yesterday or even a few hours ago. Like her, Rob thrived on the thrill of a mission's execution. Although Trina preferred to bring in fugitives. She'd never fired her weapon as a marshal before.

They ran around the back of the building, and it reminded her of casing the other building. Had it only been *yesterday*? She felt a decade older.

As they drew around to the other side, she looked for the trailer, anxious to help the young women to safety.

Rob halted, and she almost smashed into his back.

"Holy hell." Rob's words, low and meant for her only, alerted her to the sight in front of them.

"This what you came here for, Marshal Lopez? Robert Bristol?" Vasin underscored the ROC's power by using her name. He'd known she was at the other hideout, probably from the camera feed, and ROC intelligence had tracked her identity. She didn't have time to worry about it as Vasin waved his rifle at the trailer, holding one of the girls by her hair. She whimpered as Vasin tugged on her locks. He spat on the ground.

Trina swallowed and stepped out from behind Rob. "No. I came for you. Backup is on the way, and you're never going to survive it. Come in with me now or take your chances with dozens of trained SWAT team members." She didn't want to reveal the FBI's presence. It wasn't Vasin's business.

Vasin laughed. "You mean like Robert told us yesterday? Your backup didn't get me then. Why now?" He continued to reply with profanity in Russian, and she smiled.

"No, unfortunately I'm not one to do that to myself. Take my orders or else." She stared at him, speaking in Russian.

"So the US marshal knows Russian? Then you understand." He repeated his previous sentiment, this time in colloquial Russian.

Rob hadn't moved the entire time, and when he ran in a flurry of movement toward the nearest copse of trees, Vasin dropped the girl and fired. Trina used the nanosecond to aim and fire at Vasin. She saw his arm jerk, but he jumped from the ramp and disappeared into the woods.

Rob's voice reached her before she saw him. "Get to the girls. I'm going for him." His large form moved like an Olympic athlete, bruised bones and tissue be damned. Trina looked around, seeing no other ROC criminals and no backup. The girl Vasin had held was still huddled on the ramp of the trailer, whimpering. Trina ran up to her, and as she comforted the teenager she looked up into the truck trailer and into at least fifteen pairs of eyes, staring at her in shock.

She held up her hand in a wave. "It's okay. You're safe. I am US Marshal Trina Lopez. We're going to wait for help to arrive, and you will be taken to safety."

Her simple Russian elicited a mixture of relieved shouts, an onslaught of words of thanks and a few laughs of relief. After she urged the women to remain calm, she looked over toward the main building and wondered if Ivanov was in there. Before she could think any more about it, she saw a helicopter come out of the sky and land for the briefest moment in the largest part of the clearing. The building blocked her view, and she was unable to see if anyone got off or boarded the helo before it rose back up and headed north. Trina couldn't see if anyone got into the chopper, but she'd be willing to bet it had been Ivanov.

Disappointment made her stomach churn but all she

had to do was look at the group of girls she and Rob had freed. Ivanov's escape would be temporary—the effect of saving their lives was lasting. As she watched the helicopter disappear, déjà vu struck. She'd felt this same sense of accomplishment, of a job well done, when she'd worked alongside Rob during the war.

No matter what had passed between them, no matter what their future held, they still were a great team.

Chapter 8

"It's done, Corey. Vasin is in custody with the FBI, and we're watching the girls board a passenger bus. They'll all go to the hospital to be checked over." Trina caught her boss up on the ops success before she admitted the one failure. "Ivanov was nowhere to be found. They captured all of his men that we knew were in the area, but no sign of him."

"Sounds like your theory about the helicopter is correct." Corey paused. "I'm not saying this officially, Lopez, but I'm damned proud of what you did. Even if it was incredibly reckless and stupid."

"Thanks, boss. You can put me back on the clock if you want, but if I can have the weekend with Jake I'd appreciate it."

"You got it. See you Monday morning."

She disconnected and didn't hesitate to call her brother.

"Hey, Trina. You're still alive."

"Yes. How's Jake?"

"Great. Ate two huge blueberry pancakes at breakfast this morning. Mom let him put as much syrup on them as he wanted."

"Of course she did." Trina loved her mother for many reasons, but how she acted as a grandmother was tops on the list. "I hope that camp keeps them hydrated."

"Relax, they do. Jake's having a blast there." Nolan grew silent, the way he did when he needed to talk about something serious. An attorney, he was adept at drawing out the truth. "You okay, Trin? This work job seemed to come up awfully quick."

"Hey, I can't dictate the needs of the US Marshals." She gave a nod to the slogan of how everything depended upon the needs of the Navy. She knew he'd understand this.

"No, but you're usually ahead of your schedule. I can't remember the last time you had to ask us to fill in on short notice. And you've been talking about getting a desk job." He didn't press her, but she knew what he wouldn't say, wouldn't ask. He wanted her to be happy as much as he wanted his nephew to have his mom around for a long time.

"I could ask you the same, in terms of running for judge." Nolan had served as a juvenile defender in Silver Valley for the last two years. He often talked about running for county judge.

His sigh was audible. "Yeah, about that—we've got such a heavy caseload here that I'd be a prick if I quit now."

"Can you say what kind of cases?"

"More serious drug dealing than we've experienced. These kids are being backed by organized crime."

"That's exactly what I've run up against here. I'll fill you in when I'm back tonight. Want to come over for pizza?"

"Sure thing. I'll let Mom know that Jake will be back at your place tonight."

"Thanks, bro. See you then." She leaned against the rental SUV, under the shade of an overgrown oak tree. She wanted to tell Nolan about Rob, formerly Justin, but it wasn't something you handled on the phone.

Rob walked over from the group of FBI agents he'd been talking to and stopped a couple of feet from her, his eyes unreadable under the ball cap he'd picked up. It had FBI emblazoned on it.

"How are you holding up?"

"I'm good. Hot and thirsty, and I think my shoulder's going to be sore tomorrow. Pretty damned good, considering what we did today." She shielded her eyes from the sun that had broken through the storm clouds.

He nodded. "You're as good as you ever were, Trina."

"Same to you. Although the helicopter. It's going to haunt me that I didn't run after it." Or try to shoot it down.

"You couldn't. We saved the girls, and the FBI has Vasin, the man we both were going in for. We can't ask for more." Rob seemed almost cheerful in his demeanor.

"I can't ask for more, you're right. I'm not the one who's responsible for taking down Ivanov or ROC. But I'd have loved a shot at it."

"Believe it or not, neither am I." He looked up at the sky, where two red-tailed hawks made slow, wide circles atop the late-afternoon hot air streams. "It takes all the agencies working together to bring down something like a ROC group. Look how long it takes to dismantle any of the Mafia groups."

"True." She wiped the sweat off her brow, dragging her palms against her pants.

"What are you going to do with this?" Rob slapped the side of the SUV.

"Drive it back home for tonight, turn it in to the local rental place in Harrisburg in the morning."

"I've got a better deal for Uncle Sam." She saw far enough beneath the brim of his hat to see the glint in his eyes.

"Oh?"

"I'll follow you back to where we picked this up, and then you can ride back to Silver Valley with me. Unless you need to get your car from the Marshal office downtown? I can take you to either place."

She contemplated him. Rob's entire six-foot length was lean and sexy. Funny how quickly she'd adapted to calling him anything other than Justin. As if they were living an entirely new life together. Scratch the *together* part.

"I should go back to the office, but frankly I want to get home to Jake as soon as possible."

He winced, and his reaction was so physical she winced, too. "I'm sorry, Rob. Of course you don't want to do that, not tonight. I'm tired, on the adrenaline rush comedown."

"Nothing to apologize for. I get it, remember?" He lifted the cap off his head and ran his fingers through his tufted blond crew cut. "We can talk about it on the drive back. Let's get out of here." He knocked on the

car frame and headed toward the Jeep she'd seen him
drive up in an hour ago, after the FBI had declared the
area safe to move about. He'd left the Jeep buried in
the woods yesterday when he'd begun his surveillance.

Trina got in the car, turned the key in the ignition
and immediately blasted the air-conditioning. Better to
get cooled down before spending the next three hours
in the same car as the man she'd had the hottest sex of
her life with, a long time ago during a Navy deployment far, far away.

Rob told himself repeatedly that he wasn't going
to say or do anything stupid during the drive back to
Harrisburg. Trina was his son's mother, and as much
as it hurt to think he might not see Jake yet, he'd have
to play this by Trina's rule book.

He followed a decent distance behind her on the
highway, ignoring the desire to speed up and drive next
to her, hooting and hollering like a teenager. It was as if
they'd never been apart, the way they'd worked together
the last twenty-four hours. The entire op had gone like
clockwork with a few expected-*unexpected* challenges
thrown in. Perfect work for a former SEAL and a bit
of a stretch for a former naval aviator. But Trina knew
what she was doing. The Marshals had trained her well.

Pulling into the rental office parking lot behind her,
he parked off to the side, out of sight of the other cus-
tomers. He knew they were safe from any ROC members for the moment, but couldn't shake the feeling this
wasn't done. Ivanov had escaped, if indeed he'd been in
that building. Rob didn't doubt he'd been holed up there.

The agent he'd been while CIA would have taken
out Vasin and all the guards and gone in the building

to get Ivanov. Before he saw Trina again. And found out he was a father.

He had a son he wanted to meet. That made the risks higher. He stilled for a split second. If the mere knowledge that he had a child affected him like this, made him want to finish the mission safely, what was it going to be like after he met his son? After he looked into his eyes and connected at a soul level? Wondering how his parents had left him to the foster care system had always been a question, one he didn't expect an answer to. But now he was a father. His enthusiasm to meet his child gave him new insight. His mother and father must have been suffering themselves, be it from addiction or other equally devastating emotional wounds, to give up the fight to be his parents. He knew with unwavering commitment that he'd never give up on the son he hadn't even met yet. They had to get through this mission, and he had to get to Jake.

"Hey, stranger. Care to give a girl a lift?" Trina opened the passenger door and didn't wait for his answer as she placed her luscious ass in the seat. He gave himself a moment to take her in, away from the constant tension of an ongoing, high profile op. Her dark cargo pants were dusted up, but he couldn't care less—he couldn't stop staring at how they hugged her sexy-as-hell legs, her strong thighs well defined under the thin material. Where said thighs met, his perusal stopped, and he wished he had X-ray vision as a skill, as his memory of Trina naked and willing wasn't enough anymore.

"Rob?" Curiosity lit her eyes and brought out a peony pink flush on her cheekbones.

"Give me a minute here, Trina."

He didn't allow her to rush him as he continued his inspection up to her waist, where he knew creamy skin covered her toned muscles under her torn and dirty T-shirt. When he got to her breasts, his head felt like it might explode, so he continued to her lips. Wet lips that she must have just licked. When he met her gaze, he knew what he'd known since yesterday.

Rob knew with the understanding only previous lovers shared that Trina still wanted him. Maybe not for a friend or to go on a date with, and certainly not for any kind of commitment. She wanted him as he did her—in bed, on a sofa, on the forest floor, in this Jeep. Connected in the most primal way.

"I want you, Trina. Tell me you weren't lying when you said you weren't married. Are you with anyone right now?"

"No." Her voice was thick, and he watched her nipples pucker under her cotton top. He saw the motion of her throat as she swallowed, and he knew she was going to give him an excuse, maybe even a good reason why they shouldn't be together as lovers at least one more time.

Rob was tired of excuses. He hauled her to him, and she didn't fight him but leaned in, her hands around his skull, in his hair, pulling her to him as her mouth opened for his.

"Hell, Trina." He reveled in her reciprocal desire. They continued to kiss, and he took advantage of her being pressed up against him, running one hand up her spine to between her shoulders while cupping her breast with the other. "I've missed this." He gently squeezed through the fabric, damning her bra for being another added layer in the way of her nakedness. At least she'd stripped off her body armor.

"Me, too." She dragged her mouth down his neck, digging her teeth into his shoulder with just the right pressure. Rob thought his erection was going to split his pants and groaned when her hand touched his length, stroked him. "We've got too many clothes on, Rob."

He pulled back, recognizing her need.

"Not here." He looked around the asphalt lot. "But I know where we can be alone, and fast. Buckle up."

He put the Jeep in gear and drove without thinking to the campsite he'd stayed in the night before his surveillance of Vasin. If he stopped to allow for rational thought, this moment would shatter the way their affair had. He couldn't handle that, not after what they'd just been through. Not after finding out they'd made a baby together.

Rob needed to make love to Trina, if only once more.

Trina refused to listen to the logical side of her brain. She all but told it to shut the freak up as Rob drove a few miles down the highway to an exit that was marked with a camping sign. He pulled up to the guard shack and held up a tag, and the guard walked around to the back of the Jeep to verify that it matched the vehicle's sticker.

"Good to go. Enjoy."

"Thanks." Rob's hands looked steady, his demeanor calm and controlled, but she remembered how he'd looked right before he'd taken her into his barracks room the first time they'd made love. All professional and collected until his door clicked shut. Then the primal animal she loved came out.

No other man since Rob had drawn out her deepest

passion as only he could, and she had to admit, it was
going to be fun to see if it was the same between them.
If that kiss in the hotel room, and this incredibly lusty
foreplay were any indication, it was going to be better.

"There are private tent lots farther up." He spoke low
and controlled, as if afraid to break the mood. Since
it was a weeknight, the place wasn't as crowded as it
would starting tomorrow, Friday.

Rob passed several campers and kept going until
they didn't see anyone in sight.

"Are you sure we won't be interrupted?" When she'd
taken Jake camping, they'd hiked all over the grounds.

"Do you care?" He ground out his reply, letting her
know that he was as primed as she was. Knowing that a
man wanted her was always a turn-on, but when it was
the man who'd fathered her son, who'd loved her as no
other, it took *turned on* to a new level. "Sorry. No, we'll
be alone here—see how there's a long, private drive to
each site?" He navigated through the forest, until they
reached a slight clearing that was surrounded by trees
and bushes.

He parked on a graveled area, meant for motor vehicles. "Meet me outside."

She got out, and the air in the depth of the forest was
so much cooler, a relief from the relentless sun they'd
dealt with all day. And to her surprise, there weren't
any bugs.

"I don't see any mosquitoes—"

Then he had her in his arms and kissed her words
away, reminding her why they'd taken this detour. Giving in to the attraction that simmered between them
since she'd gotten past the initial shock that he was
still alive was as inevitable as ice cream melting on hot

pavement. Still here—to kiss her, caress her, make love to her like she was the only woman on earth for him.

They made short work of their clothing, stripping down to nothing and both standing fully up to take each other in. Rob's gaze feasted on her, and she'd never felt more beautiful or more powerful in a lover's presence. The sight of him so fully aroused for her slaked the deep thirst she'd had for him since the day she thought he'd died. Trina didn't want to think about the past any more. This moment was the most powerful of her life, save for when Jake was born.

Trina didn't try to break the intensity of the moment with words. It would be fruitless. All there was was Rob, her and this incredible chemistry.

She ran the last two steps to him and allowed him to hold her ass as she wrapped a leg over his hip, urging his erection to press against her.

He'd laid a blanket out on the ground, and they half fell, half rolled onto it. He gently put her down on the fabric, the move incongruous with the ferocity of their hunger. She saw a flash of discomfort on his face and froze.

"Your ribs."

"To hell with them." He lowered his mouth to hers and Trina stopped thinking. Gave in to the deep kisses, the caresses, the expert strokes. Rob lingered at her breasts, sucking on each nipple until she thought she'd climax before they got to what she craved: Total connection with Rob.

He let out a slow exhale. "I'm good, but with these ribs I'll have to be on top. I wanted to take the ground for you—"

It was her turn to stop his words with her mouth, her

tongue. And not only on his mouth, but over his entire body, as much as he'd allow her to reach before putting on the condom that had appeared like a quarter in a magician's hand. "Where did you have that?"

"No. Words." He closed his eyes as he leaned over her, and it was obvious to her that the pain in his cracked ribs was warring with his desire for her. Thank God his lust won out.

Trina opened her legs, her center, her soul to him. And Rob took full advantage, thrusting into her in the slowest increments, half inch by half inch, until she began to spasm around his length. And they'd only just begun. She let the orgasm take her, but Rob wasn't done—and neither was she. As he continued to move under her, the swell of a second, more powerful climax propelled her to keep moving, too.

"That's it, Trina, let go, babe." And she did, her cry matching the sheer magic he elicited from her. Before her second orgasm ended, Rob was moving with her in the cadence she thought she'd never feel again. He held on to himself so tightly that to see the carnal expression on his face, as if he were claiming her, sent her to the edge again.

She nipped his throat, licked where her teeth marks were. "Your turn, Rob. Let go."

He stiffened for an infinitely long moment before he reached his climax, his guttural shout making the instant that much more primal. But Trina had no time to think about it as she came again, her sensitized body at his mercy. Their bodies were slick with sweat as Rob eased away and rested on his heels, his eyes on her. She stared back, unable to speak just yet. Slowly her thoughts floated back to her, until she realized she was lying completely naked in a public campground. A private part of the campground, but still. She sat up. A flash of light on the ground caught her eye—her camel necklace. She moved to retrieve it, but Rob beat her to it, held the chain in his fingers, the charm dangling in the early-evening air.

"You still wear this."

"It's an old habit." She went to take it, and he held it just out of reach.

"We broke the chain." He gave it to her.

Trina accepted the necklace in her outstretched palm. The familiar weight of the camel stirred emotions she didn't want to address. Sadness. Nostalgia. Finality.

"It's the charm that matters. Your poor ribs." Her fingers lightly touched his rib cage, not wanting to cause him further pain.

"They'll survive. Are you all right?"

"Are you kidding me? Is my hair standing straight up? Because it feels like it should be. You gave me three incredible orgasms!"

"Trina." He kissed her firmly on the lips before he stood up and unselfconsciously walked to the back of the Jeep, where he leaned as he put on his shirt.

"Let me help you."

"I've got it." She ignored him and helped him get into his briefs and pants.

"Bruised and cracked ribs are awful. I've been there. I always thought getting dressed and undressed were the most difficult parts." She blushed, and Rob didn't miss it.

"I always loved how you would get all modest after being a complete animal in bed."

She looked up into his eyes and searched for what

she knew would be there. Their connection. Familiarity. It wasn't familiar as much as a sense of being right. Which was fair, as they were both different people, no matter what their names were.

"What deep thoughts are you wrestling with, Trina?"

She moved away from him and started to get dressed. The frogs were chirping and the cicadas thrumming as late afternoon turned to dusk.

"It's as if we've always been together, but at the same time, incredibly new. I mean, we made l—had sex, you know, like we know each other. But it was different than before." She shrugged into her T-shirt, hating putting dirty clothes back on, but her shower was waiting in Silver Valley. "Let's face it. I don't know you anymore, Rob. Your name has changed, and so have you."

His head tilted as he listened. "That's fair. You've changed, too, Trina."

"Not really. I'm older—I'm a mother. But I feel the same as I always have."

"You're not, babe. You're a woman who knows what she wants, and you're not afraid to go for it. You always had that quality, of course, or you wouldn't have made it in naval aviation. But you're tougher, more certain of yourself."

His words struck a raw nerve, and she decided on the spot to wait until she was alone to process why. The sad truth that had started to sing its mournful tune from the minute she'd accepted he was still alive was growing into a full aria. She and the man she'd known were done. Rob might find a relationship with his son, and she sincerely hoped he did.

Rob and she, however, didn't have a future together. They'd both moved on.

* * *

Rob was grateful that Trina disappeared into the woods to either find public facilities or use the forest as her restroom. He needed a little time to get his head screwed back on straight. It had been sweet of her to help him dress but he didn't want Trina's help. He wanted Trina.

And here was his problem, not much different from where he'd found himself over three years ago. Wanting a woman who was out of reach. They still shared phenomenal chemistry, and they worked well together in the field. That hadn't changed. In fact, he was certain what they'd just shared was only a taste of what they'd find if they explored being together.

But it wouldn't work. Trina had made it clear they'd both changed. He sure had, and while she looked and spoke like the younger Trina he'd known during the war, Trina had completely evolved into the powerful woman he'd caught glimpses of in the cockpit as she'd flown her plane. She no longer trusted so readily and was a ferocious advocate for her child. Their son.

Like the fully realized, powerful woman she was, Trina deserved a life partner who'd be there for her through thick and thin. Rob had a job to do as an undercover agent. It was his calling as much as being a SEAL or CIA operative had been. And it was another job that didn't mesh with family life. Not the kind that Trina needed or was entitled to.

He still wanted to meet Jake and he prayed they'd forge a bond, that he'd develop a solid relationship with his son. But for his heart's sake and Trina's best interests, he had to keep it at that. He and Trina weren't meant to be more than parents together.

Trina's soft steps sounded and he saw her emerge from the trees, her hair still tousled, her cheeks flushed. A new ache settled, this one under his ribs. She was off limits.

"Talk about drive-through servicing." Trina thought her quip as they left the campground was pretty funny. According to her phone they'd only been "camping" for fifty-three minutes.

Rob cast her a quick glance as he looked to the right and left for other cars on the road. Turning left, he shook his head. "Wow. You *have* changed, Trina. You never would have joked about sex like this before."

"Yeah, I was more uptight then, I grant you that. We've both changed. This was our way of saying good-bye to the past, don't you think?"

She watched his profile as he drove. Definitely more relaxed than when they'd left the ROC compound, but she also detected a note of resignation in his demeanor.

"Maybe. Probably." He passed a trailer hauling horses, going up the last major hill before the road flattened out as they neared the Susquehanna Valley.

"Don't forget we have to stop back at the kennel."

"I haven't. You said you named the dog Renegade?"

"It seemed natural. He fit in with us incredibly well for such a tiny guy. This is the turnoff, right?" She nodded at a green exit sign.

"Yes. Then a right turn at the end of the ramp."

Thirty minutes later Renegade was snuggled in her lap as they sped back to Silver Valley. "He smells a lot better after a bath." She stroked his soft puppy fur.

"Any idea how big he'll get?"

"No. That's okay, isn't it, buddy?" She held up his

face to hers. The puppy licked her, and she set him back down. "My son—I mean, Jake—is going to be thrilled. I know I should take Renegade to the vet first, to make sure he doesn't have any health issues, but I'm going to throw caution to the wind."

Nervous energy made her skin feel transparent, as if the wind that blew through their cracked windows was streaming into her center. "Rob, we need to figure out how to handle Jake."

"Handle him? He's not a mission to accomplish."

"You know what I mean. When, or do, you want to meet him? Because if you aren't up for this, I under-stand." And she did. Because she'd raised Jake to this point, she knew she'd survive if Rob didn't want to be-come a full-time parent.

"What the f—" Rob cut his expletive off, his face red and his eyes glued to the road. Not looking at her.

"It's been a long time. You said yourself you're dedi-cated to your career. Being an undercover operative is not conducive to stable parenting."

"And being a US marshal, hauling in the dregs of society, is?" Like her brother Nolan, Rob cut to the heart of what she'd been considering for the past year. Unlike Nolan, Rob didn't know this part of her, didn't have the years of helping her with Jake to understand her decision-making process. But the fact was that Rob knew her better than her brother did. Rob knew her on a soul level. He always had. And that was what made all of this so damned hard.

"Why couldn't this have been a disaster?"

"What, Trina?" She felt his gaze on her like a caress. "Do you mean when we just made love?" Rob shook his head. "It's never a disaster when we're together. What we shared at Camp Serenity proves that."

"More like camp screw-your-brains-out." She couldn't help it—she reverted to lousy attempts at humor whenever confronted by the most serious issues in her life. And it wasn't lost on her that he'd said "made love." It had to have been an expression. It didn't, couldn't, mean anything more.

"What we just shared wasn't screwing, Trina. Don't even try that route with me. As for my son, our son, of course I'm going to meet him and be involved with his upbringing. I have five years to make up for. The real questions are whether you're going to make it easy or difficult for me to do so, and what kind of relationship you and I are going to have moving forward. I think you've already answered the second question." His neutral tone gave nothing away. She had no clue if he was disappointed that she didn't want a further romantic relationship with him or not.

Romantic—the very word seemed so weak, so insipid compared to what she felt with Rob. Their bond was beyond description, beyond comparison. And it was cemented at the very least with the child they'd made.

Her instinct was to shut Rob down, close off any chance of him meeting Jake. It would be easier; there would be no hard feelings to deal with on her side. Except, knowing what joy and love Jake had brought to her life, could she possibly deprive Rob of any of it? No matter that it had been his choice to walk away over three years ago.

He'd had no idea the boy you were holding was his.

She expelled a long breath and watched the land whip by. As the sky darkened it released brilliant splashes of fuchsia and amethyst. Twinkling lights glimmered to the west, and she longed for home. To have Jake in her arms, to read him his bedtime story, to take a long, hot shower after he was asleep. Sip a cup of herbal tea and try to knit the scarf she'd started last Saturday in the Silver Valley knitting shop. Knitting was a new hobby for her, and she loved how she could sit on the back patio while Jake ran around the yard, a completely uninhibited five-year-old boy. He was as content with toads and crickets as he was with a handheld video game.

Jake deserved to know his father.

"Trina?" Rob didn't like how still she sat, her face turned toward the passenger window, away from him. Was she going to tell him he'd never meet his kid? That she didn't want to ever see him again, either?

And the sex they'd just had—it was life-changing. Not from the mind-blowing orgasm he'd had, or the three she'd had. He'd been damn careful, even in his frenzied need, that she had pleasure, too. It was about how readily they'd come together again, no matter that he'd bared all when he'd told her he'd made an attempt to see her again three and a half years ago. And he'd walked away.

"Hmmm. I think that maybe you meeting Jake tonight, if he's still up, is okay. Making a big deal out of it doesn't seem right to me." She fluttered her hands in front of her, her giveaway that she was unsettled. "I've only ever told him that his daddy was a hero, and that he'd given the ultimate sacrifice."

"You told him I was dead, though?" Rob couldn't imagine keeping that from a kid.

"Yes, but it's not something he's grasped yet. I've

been preparing myself for a barrage of questions once he starts kindergarten in the fall. Until now he's been in a smaller, private Montessori school, and with my brother so active in his life, he doesn't seem to miss a male role model." She looked at him as she trailed off. "I'm sorry, Rob. I don't mean he doesn't need a father in his life."

"I get it. I'm the interloper." And he was. He would have been three years ago, too, but less so. Fierce regret welled in his chest, making his breathing shallow. He couldn't change the past but he sure did mourn it. To be able to get back Jake's first five years...

"It's not going to be easy for either of us, Rob." She fiddled with the wrapping from a straw. "To be honest, I have no idea how Jake is going to react. But there's a good chance he'll take this better than you or I."

"Kids are supposed to be more adaptable than we are, right?" He'd have to find some books, read up on it. Rob was confident that he could escape from just about any man-made contraption, survive anywhere on the planet with the right gear, but had no idea what it took to be a good parent. A father. It wasn't something he'd experienced. That darn pain under his ribcage, that had nothing to do with the fractured bones, and it wouldn't let go. He was sad he'd missed so much with Jake. And not a little apprehensive about how he'd measure up to the young boy. Would Jake take one look at him and proclaim he didn't need a dad?

"They are beyond adaptable. It's a little scary to realize how accepting they are, how open." A longer pause this time. He knew her well enough to know she was getting ready to drop a bomb. "I'll do anything to keep him safe, Rob. I've never spanked him. Time-out is the harshest punishment he's ever needed. Sometimes I take away his toys if he's being stubborn."

He heard the unspoken order at the same time he felt the visceral punch to his gut. She knew about his foster families, his biological family's history of substance abuse, which had often led to his physical abuse as a child. It was the reason he and his brother had been put in the foster system. Her statement was reasonable; he'd be surprised if she felt otherwise. It still smarted more than he'd like, however. His gut tightened into a coil of barbed wire. A defensiveness, no, *protectiveness* toward Jake. It was how he'd felt in the foster system, when his brother had been threatened. And before their foster family, when their biological father had gone after them in a drug-induced rage. Rob had always fought for his little brother. But what he felt for Jake was much deeper, more primal. It was a depth of emotion he never encountered before. He sighed. He had a lot to learn about being a dad.

"I'm not going to harm my own kid, Trina." Couldn't she give him some credit here?

"I don't want you to think I'm expecting that, Rob. It's what I never expected once I had a child. First, I had no clue how much I'd love him. No one tells you that— they all warn about how tired you'll be, how stressful the teenage years are, how some kids turn out bad no matter what you do. But no one told me how very much I'd fall for the little guy, the tiny baby who's turned into a sweet, full-of-mischief little boy. I'd die for him, Rob. In the military we knew we could be killed with any mission, at the drop of a hat. We accepted it. It was easier to take it as part of the job description before I had Jake. I knew my parents and my brother would be devastated if I died defending our freedoms, but I also knew they'd survive. Jake needs me as much as I need to know he's safe and sound each night, tucked in his little race car bed."

"He has a race car bed? I would have loved that!"

"Yes. He loves trains, and there was a locomotive bed frame I thought he'd pick, but when he saw the racing car with all the decals on it he was beyond ecstatic. He's outgrowing it and needs a twin bed, but I'm afraid to tell him. He'll be heartbroken."

"I'm going to pay you child support for the last five years. Whatever my fair share would have been." He didn't say it as a form of manipulation to make sure she'd introduce Jake to her, or as a way to assuage his own guilt at not pressing forward and making sure that the baby in Trina's arms wasn't his. It hadn't even occurred to him, as he'd figured with both of them using contraception while on deployment the chance of pregnancy was nil.

How wrong he'd been.

Her sharp intake of breath was his only warning before she launched into a classic Trina tirade.

"No, you are not. There's nothing to pay for. You weren't here. Whether it was your choice or not, that's debatable, but Jake has been cared for."

"You couldn't even go after any medical or Social Security benefits for him. We weren't married—you weren't my dependent."

"No, but Jake was my dependent while I was on active duty. And he's fine. My parents and Nolan and I have all been contributing to a college fund, and I have excellent health insurance. We don't need your money, Rob."

Maybe not. But he needed to contribute in all ways possible. "Can't I at least put something into his college fund, then?"

"Sure, that's always available. Why don't you slow down here and focus on meeting him first?"

"He's not a damned puppy, Trina. I'm not going to take him back if we don't connect right away."

"I didn't mean it that way."

"We're both tired. I'm not so sure meeting Jake when we're both this worn out is such a good idea."

"It's the best idea, Rob, because it's real life." She laughed as she resettled herself in the bucket seat, legs folded in front of her yoga-style. "I hadn't slept for two days when I delivered Jake. The labor had kept me up through two nights, and I was so excited that he was on the way I couldn't rest like they told me to in the hospital. And of course those first couple of weeks are whoppers—he was always hungry, always crying to either eat or be changed."

"I hate that I wasn't there for you, Trina."

"I hate that you weren't, too. Not so much for me but to watch him as he grew. I have a lot of photos that will fill in the blanks for you. My mother caught some good ones of me nursing him, where I fell asleep with him in my arms. Don't worry—I was sitting on the floor with my back against the sofa. I used a bumper pillow that went around my waist so that he was always supported. I never dropped him. The picture I'm thinking about is hilarious—it shows his greedy little hands clutching at my boob and bra and my head is back, mouth open, clearly snoring."

He remained silent. He'd missed so much. When was it too much? When did it cross the line of being an anomaly that other families had experienced—a parent gone for an extended period due to military operations or a medical situation—into irreparable damage?

"It's okay, Rob. I'm sad for you that you've missed the first several years, but look at it this way." She held up her hand as if she were presenting him with a precious gem or solid gold gift. "There are still thirteen years until he's eighteen. You haven't even missed a third of his upbringing. My mother always says that boys need their mothers early on and their fathers more as they turn into teenagers. I'd say that's right, because while Jake loves his uncle Nolan, he's a momma's boy all the way. He calls me his best friend. You know that's going to change by the time he's twelve!"

"We'll see how it goes, then. If at any time you're uncomfortable or think it's going too fast for him, you have to tell me. I'm new at this parenting thing." Normally it pained him to admit he needed help or was short on any type of training. Because frankly he rarely needed assistance with anything on a day-to-day basis. Being around Trina again had opened up something in his heart, the part that reminded him he was human. And needy. He rubbed his chest, wondering if the ache he felt every time he thought of his son was every going to be appeased.

If it was anything like his desire for Trina, he knew the answer.

They pulled into her paved driveway and parked in the large area in front of the triple garage. She had one car and used the other two vehicle bays for the gardening and livestock equipment she was collecting.

"Nice place. How long have you been here?"

"Less than a month. I wanted to get Jake settled long before school started. I hate to say it, but that was a mistake—he doesn't know anyone around here yet, and there aren't any school functions until the last week in August."

"You did say he went to a different preschool." Rob asked the kind of questions that showed he was interested in Jake's education, but she saw how his eyes reflected exhaustion. She'd bet it wasn't from the last two days, either. Rob was stressed. The former SEAL who was invincible expected to be slain by an almost-six-year-old.

Once they were out of the Jeep and standing in front of the house, she squeezed his forearm for a brief moment. "It's okay, Rob. You're saying hi to a little boy who's tired from spending all day at a kids' camp. He'll be excited to see me, but don't expect a lot. He hates it when his grandmother has to leave. And this puppy is going to knock his socks off."

"Got it."

She dropped her arm and nodded at the front door. "Let's go. I usually go in through the garage, but without my car and my garage door opener, we'll go in this way."

He walked with her up the concrete steps and across the worn wooden porch to the front door. A matching pair of door lights were on, and insects flickered all about, despite the bulbs being yellow. Trina waved her hand in front of her face, shooing away the flying insects. "Damned stinkbugs. They're the ones that look like primitive tanks. Don't squish them or it'll smell to high heaven out here and in the house, too."

He didn't reply, and she wondered if he thought she

was nuts, buying such a beat-up old house. Once the door opened and the living room light poured out into the night, she noticed that his eyes scoured the room in front of him for any sign of his child.

His son.

The room was empty, and Trina saw the kitchen light down the dim hallway that connected the front and back of the house, a classic hardwood-and-white-painted staircase in the center to the right. "Hey, I'm home!"

An excited shout followed by the certain stamp of little feet on the linoleum kitchen floor made her heart catch midbeat. She looked at Rob. And tried not to laugh at how frightened he appeared.

"Relax, Rob, it's a five-year-old boy, not a python."

"Right." He stood rooted to the spot, unable to take deep breaths, and it had nothing to do with his cracked ribs. He narrowed his gaze on the light at the end of the hall, waiting, waiting. His breath hitched higher as a short figure ran around the corner and barreled toward them. Pounding feet that sounded light on the hardwood, then Trina's admonition to "slow down, buddy!" A brief glimpse of cropped hair that was definitely more blond than brown. A flash of eyes as deeply hued as Trina's. And the same exact shape.

"Mommy!" Jake launched himself at Trina. Trina was ahead of him, on her knees and scooping the small but sturdy boy up into her arms and hugging him to her.

"Hi, sweetie pie. Oh, I've missed you!"

"Me, too, Momma. Uncle Nolan said you had 'portent busyness to do and that you'd be back. Guess what? We did art today and I made a pottery for you. It's going to be painted but it has to cook in the kiln first. A kiln is a, a high-temp'shure oven for ceramics. Hey, what's this? Oh man, Mommy, did you get a puppy? We have enough to take care of." God, he never took a breath. Not unlike his mother.

"Here, sit on the floor and I'll put Renegade in your lap."

Jake complied with comic swiftness, and his peals of laughter hit Rob in his heart. "Mommy, he's licking me!"

Jake's exuberant tone of voice had magical healing powers. As Rob watched him and listened to him, he swore he felt the ache in the center of his chest lessen. Instead of regret, which he knew could probably return, he felt a warm rush of joy filling all of the cracks that had addled his heart.

"That's how puppies kiss, silly."

"He needs to know who the boss is." Jake's stern voice was a perfect imitation of Trina's.

Rob looked at Trina's expression for a clue as to how to respond. He wanted to laugh but didn't want to be that kind of friend who encouraged bad behavior.

Friend—he wasn't a *friend*. He was Jake's father.

"Hey, sweetie pie, I've got a friend for you to meet. Put Renegade down and let him check out the house." She lifted the boy up as easily as if he was a bag of flour. "Jake, this is Rob."

"Hey." Jake looked at him from the safety of his mother's arms, his little face even with her shoulders.

"How do you do?" God, was that all he could think of to say? This kid probably never heard anyone talk like that, except maybe his grandparents.

Jake held out his small hand, reaching across from

his mother's hug to where Rob stood, feeling like a this-tle among orchids. "Nice to meetcha, Mr. Rob."

Rob accepted his son's hand in his, and the lightning bolt of warmth that streaked up his arm went straight to his heart. This was his son, his child. He blinked, clearing his eyes, as he'd accept not an iota of blurri-ness during this first meeting.

"Same here." He allowed Jake to hang on to his hand as long as the little guy wanted. If it were up to Rob he'd gather the boy to him, hug him, tell him how very, very sorry he was for missing so much. He'd never had hugs like that. Wait—did he want to hug Jake to make up for his own childhood losses, or to simply express this new sense of love and connection he shared with the little boy? As he looked at Jake's smiling face, he had no doubt. He wanted to shower Jake with unadul-terated love and affection.

His chest was itching again.

"Tell you what, why don't we invite Rob in for a quick drink of water and you can tell me what hap-pened at camp today."

"Great!" He wriggled out of his mother's embrace and slid down to the floor, where he immediately took off for the kitchen.

"See? It wasn't so bad, was it?" Trina's eyes widened as she took in his expression. Her cool hands wiped tears from his cheeks, and he shook his head. He hadn't known he was crying like a big baby.

"He's incredible."

She grinned, her mother's pride unbeatable. "Just wait. Come on, let me treat you to a glass of ice water. Unless you want something stronger?"

"No, no—water is just fine." No blurry tears and no spirits to keep him from experiencing this once-in-a-lifetime reunion. No, sir.

Chapter 9

Trina watched her mother's eyes grow round when she walked into the hallway to see what was taking Trina so long to come into the kitchen. No doubt Carmen Lopez had heard Rob's deep voice, too.

"Mom, this is Rob Bristol. We work together."

"Oh, well, hello, Rob." She gave Trina a hug and kiss. "You okay? Nolan said..." She trailed off, probably not wanting to say too much. Having two children in the military and now both in government service positions had trained her to be careful with what she said. Trina couldn't love her mother more than she did in this moment. Her mother was faced with Trina bringing home a strange man and yet didn't play Twenty Questions with her. Carmen Lopez had trusted her children to make their own decisions since Trina was a girl. It was something Trina strived to instill in Jake—to know that his mom had faith in his judgment. Now it would be both her and Rob working together on this, and all facets of parenting.

Instead of the loss of control she thought she'd feel, she enjoyed a sense of calm and...relief. Rob would be a great dad and it was going to be a pleasure to co-parent with him.

"It's okay, Mom. Yes, I had to work an extra job, but it's all okay now."

Carmen looked at her daughter and nodded, then turned her attention to Rob.

"Are either of you hungry?"

"No, ma'am. I'm good."

"I'm just getting Rob a glass of water. We're dehydrated a bit. We've been out in the sun all day." All three of them walked into the kitchen, and Trina motioned for Rob and her mother to sit with Jake at the battered farm table that was left by the previous owner. Even though she planned to seriously rehab the place with modern conveniences, she appreciated the more rustic touches, too. Trina knew the historical roots of all she did, including purchasing a dilapidated farmhouse that sat on three of the farm's original two hundred acres. It had been in the same family for generations, since the Revolutionary War era, until the last had decided to let go of the farm. Roots were important to her; it was why she'd left the Navy, so that Jake would grow up close to his extended family, especially his grandparents.

"Mom, we made plants in camp today." Jake spoke with crystal-clear certainty, his hair mussed from her hug and his cheeks rosy from the sun.

"You mean you potted plants?"

"Yes! We did cactuses and ivy."

"Cacti and ivy. Did you put your sunscreen on?" She cracked open an ice tray and filled three glasses to the brim with cubes. Trina didn't have to look to know Jake was rolling his eyes. So she was conscientious about grammar and the risk of skin cancer. Jake needed to see this side of parenting, too. The more practical, day-to-day parts that could wear her down, make her forget to relax and enjoy Jake. He'd only be five once.

"*Moooom.* Uncle Nolan put sunscreen on me, and then the teacher reminded us to do a touch-up before we went outside."

"Okay, that's good." She slid the glasses onto the table and noted her mother was staring at Rob. Hard. Crap! She wasn't putting two and two together, was she? Trina had told both Nolan and her mother that Jake's father had been killed in action. She had shown them each photos of Rob, then-Justin, mostly selfies and candids from deployment. The only time they'd spent not in a battle zone had been a quick R & R to Istanbul, Turkey. Those photos she'd kept for her eyes only. It was too painful to remember how happy she'd been.

And now the cause of that joy was sitting at her kitchen table. Alive, not a figment of her grief, which she'd thought she'd closed the door on almost two years ago. It had taken three full years to let him go.

"Trina." Rob's low voice shook her out of herself and she looked between him, her mother and Jake.

"I'm sorry, did I miss something?"

"Mom, I'm telling about the bug collecting trip."

"You're talking about the trip, or you're telling a story about it."

"Yeah, that's it, I'm telling the bug story. We had to

be very quiet and pay close attention to the grass and the leaves."

"Why was that?" Rob asked the question with hesitation and reverence in his tone, as if Justin held the secret directions to the Holy Grail.

Her mother didn't miss Rob's rapt attention on Jake, as if he were afraid Jake would disappear with a blink. As Trina watched, Carmen's gaze went from Rob to Jake, Jake to Rob.

Damn it. Her mother was the smartest person she knew, and right now Trina didn't have the wherewithal to deal with an inquisition. Which she saw coming.

"Rob, are you a marshal, too?"

"No—I work for a private security firm. Trina and I were working together on the same case and ended up spending more time on it than either of us planned." Trina bit back a grin. Undercover agents were adept at providing alibis and fake employment. Rob was no exception.

"It was complicated, but I can tell you we kept a significant number of young girls from being exploited." Trina spoke quietly and without any drama, so as to not draw Jake's attention.

"What's 'splotated?" Jake had missed nothing.

"It's when someone hurts someone else," Rob answered, and Trina glared at him. Really? He'd been in the presence of his son for all of fifteen minutes and he was deciding what to tell him?

"Some girls got hurt?" Jake's little face scrunched up in concern. "That's wrong."

"No, they didn't get hurt. That's what Mommy's job is about, remember? To keep everyone safe."

"Keepin' it safe for democracy!" Jake yelled the way

he did when he was up past his bedtime. She looked at the clock.

"It's the weekend, and you know what that means, Jake!" Trina never tired of how his face lit up from the mere mention of "weekend" and his favorite breakfast.

"Waffles!" But his face immediately fell as he processed where Trina was going with her reasoning. "I don't want to go to bed, Mom. I want to talk to this guy."

"It's Rob." Rob had told him his name but Trina wanted to correct him, to tell him to call his father 'dad.' That was plain silly—it was too soon to tell Jake who Rob really was, and certainly not in front of Carmen, who was now staring at Rob with wide eyes.

"Mother, I'll explain more tomorrow. Let me get Jake ready for bed." Trina couldn't blame her mother for looking so shocked. She'd shown her as well as Nolan the several photos she had of Rob, and he hadn't changed, except for his blond hair sprouting some silver strands here and there.

"If you're sure—" Carmen's hair, the same dark chocolate color as Trina's but sprinkled with long silver threads, framed her face, which was wrinkled in concern at her only daughter.

"I'm certain, Mother." Trina gave her mother her best listen-to-me-I'll-tell-you-later look. Fortunately, being slow on the draw wasn't one of Carmen's traits.

"Okay, well, I'll be going. I've got my Saturday knitting group in the morning, down at Silver Threads." Carmen referred to Silver Valley's local yarn shop, located in a converted Victorian home.

"You're going to knit in this heat?"

"Unlike your new house, the yarn shop is air-conditioned."

"I have air-conditioning. Weren't you able to fiddle with it?"

"Fiddle? I asked Nolan to bring your daddy's biggest plumbing wrench over to slam that puppy into functioning." Carmen reached down and patted Renegade's head. "No offense, doggy. The air's blowing but there's not a lot of 'cool' to it."

"At least it's cooler outside than it's been over the past few days." Trina felt fine in the house but knew the upstairs could become stifling with each heat wave. The central air was inefficient, and it would be one of her first investment repairs.

"Okay. See you on Sunday?" Carmen picked up her purse and car keys and kissed Trina's cheek.

"Yes. We'll be there."

"Nice to meet you, Rob." Her mother leaned in and stage-whispered, "Bring him with you on Sunday if you want."

"Bye, Mom." Trina did all she could to not make a face.

"Come here and give Grandma a kiss, Jake."

He shuffled over to his beloved grandmother and hugged her with all his might, the sound of his kiss a loud smack in the small kitchen. Carmen laughed. "That's my boy. See you Sunday."

"Bye, Grandma."

She left out the back kitchen door. The door stuck and she pulled on it extra hard, which made the shade on the door sway.

"That door needs to be fit to the frame." Rob's observation set off Trina's radar-like defenses.

"It's hot and humid—it's only swollen. It'll be fine in the cooler months."

"More like freezing. It'll shrink and let a draft in." He stood up and walked to the door, ran his hands around the edge.

Jake hopped over to Rob, peering at the battered door as if it held the secrets to his five-year-old universe. "Yeah, it's got cracks, Mom."

Trina's breathing hitched somewhere between her gut and her heart.

"It's time for you to go to bed, mister."

"Mom. I'm helping Mr. Rob with the door." He folded his little arms over his puffed-out chest, his glare at its most powerful.

"Don't even try it, Jake. We can have Rob read you your story if you'd like, but you can't be pulling any nonsense about bedtime." She'd worked hard to establish regular routines with Jake. It helped both of their sanities.

"What are we reading?" Rob slipped right into their routine, and again Trina had a mess of emotions swamping her. Her protective urge toward Jake was the strongest, but not as dominant as she'd expected. She trusted Rob, and she trusted him to be here with Jake.

But if he wasn't going to be here as a permanent fixture in Jake's life, she didn't want to put the little boy's heart at risk.

As Jake ran upstairs to his room to pick out a book, or more likely a stack of books, Trina faced Rob on the stairwell. "You don't have to do this. You only just found out that you have a child." She kept her voice low, almost a whisper.

His eyes were intent upon her. For the first time in a long while it was deeper than the sexual energy he normally radiated. It was something more overarching, bigger. "I'm never where I don't want to be, Trina."

Rob's inner GPS felt as though it was permanently programmed to the little boy. Jake. His son. Before tonight he would have admitted he'd never stopped thinking about Trina, and in fact still cared deeply for her. It had been a tremendous relief to find out she was single and even better, had never found a man to settle down with. He still couldn't believe she wasn't married.

But Jake…

The little being who nestled so naturally between him and Trina on the race car bed was a live wire. As Jake sat on his knees and held the book, Rob read the story of some bears figuring out the difference between healthy and junk food. Trina had selected the book from the stack Jake presented, most of which were train- or dinosaur-centric. Rob did his best to act out each voice, booming it out when he did the Papa Bear parts. "The end." Jake let out a whine of regret next to him and Rob couldn't help but laugh. "I agree, buddy, it ended too soon."

Jake threw his arms around Rob's neck and gave him a hard, quick hug. "I like you, Rob."

Rob blinked, unable to process the emotions that made his throat feel raw and his chest three sizes bigger. He didn't even care that Jake had knocked up against his sore ribs. The injury was no match for the love he was getting from his son.

His son.

"I'll put it back." Jake took the book and slid off his lap. "Mom, can Renegade sleep with me?" The dog was in the hallway in a crate Trina had found in the house basement. The little pup had collapsed into sleep after playing so hard with Jake.

"No, not until we get him checked by the vet. Then we'll talk about it."

Rob looked at Trina. Her eyes were teary and he hoped it was from happiness. "Was that your book?"

She nodded and motioned at a shelf chock-full of kid's books. "All of those were Nolan's and mine. The agreement is that Jake gets to have them until Nolan finds someone to have kids with."

"Yeah, Uncle Nolan needs a woman." Jake's tone and expression perfectly mimicked Trina's mother's, and Rob laughed. When Jake made him laugh, it wasn't a simple reaction to humor. It was a sense of well-being and happiness that radiated from the center of his chest. *This is pure joy.*

And he'd missed the first five years of it due to his own stupidity.

"Okay, lights out."

"Can I have the stars and planets night-light?"

"Of course. Let's say our prayers." Trina didn't make a move for Rob to join them, though he wouldn't have dared intrude on something so private. Jake took matters into his own hand, literally, when he reached one hand to hold Rob's, while he held Tina's with the other. The nighttime prayers were said and Jake tucked under his sheets—the hot night proving too much for the superhero comforter—in under two minutes.

He silently followed Trina back downstairs to the kitchen.

"Is he always that easy to go to sleep?"

"No way. He can have a good-size fit if he wants to. Some nights he's turned on his overhead light and read on his own. I find him sprawled out on his bed, the lights still on and books everywhere, when I wake up." Her dimples appeared in her smooth cheeks. "One night he got up and played with his train set. He has one of those wooden ones and he'd laid tracks down the hall and the stairs. All of the cars were in a pile at the bottom of them, on the braided rug."

"I'm surprised he didn't wake you up."

She sighed. "Yeah, I'm a solid sleeper. I'd like to think that mother's intuition would wake me up if anything was wrong, and in fact it has."

Rob's anxiety peaked. "Like when?"

Trina looked at him sharply and placed a hand on his arm. "Relax. Nothing horrible, just the kind of childhood stuff we all go through. Crying out during a bad dream, waking up sick. Jake gets really high fevers, but I think he's mostly outgrown them. The doctor said it was genetic, but my mother says I never had fevers like Jake got as a toddler. Neither did Nolan."

"I did." Memories of his mother screaming at his father to help her get him into a cold tub assaulted him. "I had them when I was very young."

"That solves where he gets them from, then." She spoke quietly, and he saw the tears in her eyes, the way her hands trembled.

He covered them with his, needing to reassure her. Seeing her suffering because of him cut like a steel knife through butter. "Trina, I'm never going to be able to apologize enough for walking away three and a half years ago. But I'd like to think that maybe I can make it up to you. And Jake."

"You didn't walk away in the classic sense, Rob. And like you said, you weren't in a place to be a father or a partner." She shut her mouth and shook her head, red stains on her cheeks. "I didn't mean that last part. I don't expect you to be my partner. I don't need someone to help me, or even to raise Jake. Jake could use a dad, and I'd never keep him from you. But this isn't an experiment to see if you and he get along, Rob. This isn't a temporary deal where you meet Jake, decided to tell him you're his father, and then disappear again. I won't have it. Do what you need to do, but don't for one minute think it's okay to do one damn thing that will hurt Jake."

He watched the tears spill down her cheeks, and she swiped at them. His fingers itched to help her, but she had her shoulders hunched in a defensive posture. Protecting herself from further heartbreak.

"I couldn't agree more."

His phone buzzed, and he would have ignored it but it was on the table in front of them. As Claudia's number appeared, he picked up.

"Rob here."

"I trust you're back in Silver Valley?"

"Yes. I'm with US Marshal Lopez."

He heard Claudia pause, not usual for the Trail Hikers' director. "Glad you're together, because this applies to both of you."

He gripped the phone tighter and turned away from Trina. "Yeah?"

"Intelligence reports confirm that Ivanov was the man in the helicopter. We're getting testimony from Vasin, and he's not veering from the risk to you and Marshal Lopez." Claudia's voice rang clear. "I understand she has a child. He's at risk, too."

"What can we do?" Immediately plans of escape with

Trina and Jake, stowing them in a safe house, raced around his mind.

"Nothing for now. This is just preliminary, and I've got two agents on it. The FBI has dozens. Go about your usual business, but be extra aware of being trailed. Tell Lopez the same. If it at all looks like Ivanov's team is near Silver Valley, I'll have you disappear with Lopez and your boy."

His heartbeat sped up when Claudia said "your boy." So Claudia had known, somehow. And he had no doubt she'd put Trina in his path. This wasn't the time for that conversation, however.

"Are you still there, Rob?"

"I'm here." And ready to punch the walls. Why had he been the last to know about his son?

"Stay focused on the next step. Like I said, if you need to evacuate, we'll do it. I'll see you in the morning." She disconnected, and Rob set his phone back down.

"Bad news?"

He couldn't say everything; Trina wasn't a Trail Hiker. "Vasin is making a lot of noise that we're in danger from Ivanov for splitting up their operation."

"What kind of danger? Do you mean you and me specifically, or the Marshals, law enforcement in general?"

"More direct than that. Ivanov may seek restitution for losing those girls. He's done some heinous things in the past." He watched Trina's face go from flushed to waxy pale.

"He—he wouldn't…" She wouldn't say the words. Rob put his arms around her as they sat in chairs next to each other.

"No, he's not going to hurt you or Jake. No one is going to. If we get word that he's sent anyone in, we'll get you and Jake far away and for as long as it takes to make sure it's all clear. But it probably won't come even close to that. ROC is powerful and evil to the core, but they like to keep their life easier. Going after US government agents and their families isn't part of the deal, not usually." As he said the words he prayed that what he believed, that Trina and Jake would be safe, was true.

Trina didn't have a hard time falling asleep after Rob left for his apartment, as the past forty-eight hours finally hit her exhausted body and as soon as her cheek landed on her high threaded pillowcase she was out. But she was up at four thirty, an hour before usual, wide-awake. A full moon spilled light onto her—she'd forgotten to shut the drapes in her bedroom again. Truth was, she liked waking up to the sunrise, or seeing the stars if it was a long winter's night. With the oppressive heat and practically nonfunctional air-conditioning in the house, she'd left all the upstairs windows cracked, screens installed to keep Jake safe.

All that mattered in her world since the moment the midwife had placed Jake in her arms, still wet from birth and rooting for her breast, was her little boy's safety. She'd accepted he'd never know his biological father, and as the years sped by she faced the reality that she might never connect closely enough with another man to be willing to risk bringing him into their family. Because it was a risk. As a marshal she knew firsthand how incredibly devastating the wrong man in a home could be to a woman and her children. She'd read enough reports on incest and child abuse, and had arrested pedophiles. Sexual abusers preyed on single mothers as it made their access to victims easier.

Rob's not a criminal. You know Rob.

She'd known Rob, yes. When his name had been Justin Berger and he'd been entrenched in doing whatever was needed in the pursuit of liberty, justice and peace. Which oftentimes meant going into a war zone and laying his life on the line, time after time. Since he'd left the Navy he'd done similarly risky jobs. If she opened up their home, and Jake, to Rob's reality, it meant that Jake could end up orphaned. Of course, she was always at risk in her job, too. But two LEA parents was different. It seemed like a double threat —shouldn't at least one parent be doing something that was without such high risk?

She'd faced the risks and decided that while they were worth it to a point, she'd fast reached the place where she was going to make a decision to go to a desk job. Jake deserved that much from her.

How could she expect Rob to do the same?

And what he'd said about Ivanov chilled her. Would ROC really come after her and her family because of her involvement in the case, brief though it had been?

Trina threw off her sheets and got up to knit. It was the one sure thing she'd found comforted her in the darkness of early mornings like these. The puppy whimpered to remind her he was in the crate just outside her door. "Come on, Renegade. I'll take you out."

After they came back inside and the puppy was safely back in his crate, she couldn't sleep. A cup of chamomile lavender tea steamed on the end table as she sat on the worn sofa and worked on a light, lacy shawl she'd started in the spring. She remembered when she and Jake had come out and explored this house and surrounding few acres to see if it could work for them. She'd never forget how his laughter had tinkled across the farm fields, how the dirt and grass were cold underfoot but there was the promise of warmer weather on the soft breeze.

As she wound her needles with alpaca yarn, her phone lit up, indicating a text.

You up?

Rob. Chills ran down her spine, and she didn't want to analyze if they were from receiving a text at such an ungodly hour or if they were a repeat of the physical reaction that had led to her total surrender in the Poconos campground.

I'm up.

Almost as soon as she sent her reply, Rob called. "Let me guess. You're up this early every day. Or is it the SEAL training—you only need two hours of sleep per night?"

His short laugh sounded ragged. Like she felt. "I wish. No, I'm calling because we have a problem."

The way he said "problem" made her stomach drop, and she swore she felt her adrenals kick out adrenaline in response.

"Is it Ivanov?"

"No. Yes. No—he's not an issue right now. Trust me, if he was I'd already be over there and you and Jake would be on a trip far away."

"I can handle Jake's safety."

"God, Trina, I'm not saying you can't. Of course you can. And that's not why I called."

"So what's the problem?"

"I can't explain it, and I'm sure you know more about this than I do as you've been a parent, known you're a parent, longer. But there's no way I'm leaving Jake, Trina. I get that you and I had something before, and whether we ever have something between us again has nothing to do with this. I want to be in Jake's life. For good. I have to be."

She placed earbuds in and picked her needles back up as she spoke. "That's a good thing, Rob." She wasn't really sure that it was for her, but for Jake, yes. "I'd never keep you from him, not for any petty reasons."

"Thank you. What are you doing up?"

"Couldn't get back to sleep. My body's aching, and I know I'll want to crawl back under the covers the minute Jake wakes up, but my mind is racing. I haven't felt like this since the war."

"I hear you. It usually takes me two days to come down from a mission."

"Are sleepless nights part of your regular life, then?"

"Only when the op goes longer than expected or gets more complicated, like what we were dealing with. You handled everything fantastically, by the way."

"Ah, thank you? You know I'm a trained law enforcement agent, right?"

"Yeah, you mentioned that a time or two. Let's face it, though, Trina. You usually go in, get your suspect or fugitive, and bring them in. Am I right or off base here?"

"You're right." She started a new row of the shawl,

the rhythmic motion of the stitches and Rob's voice easing the tension out of her muscles.

"Then take the damn compliment, Lopez."

"Thank you." This time she said it with sincerity. "You weren't so bad yourself, Agent Bristol."

"Do you mean during or after?" His baritone scraped across the connection and her skin flamed.

"No comment."

His silence was companionable. What could he say to that, really?

"Rob?"

"Hmm." He was still thinking about it, she knew it in her center. Images of them together, skin on skin, moving to their unique beat, made her wish he were in the same room with her.

"I've gotta go."

"What, something cooking on the stove?"

"No. Actually, I'm knitting."

"As in the thing my grandmother did?"

"It's quite the relaxing exercise. I'm not a yoga person. I needed something to help me chill out after I put Jake to bed, and this has done the trick."

"Does Jake sleep over at your mom's or brother's when you have to travel for work?" Rob's interest turned back in Jake as if by a switch.

"Sometimes, but now that he'll be in school full time, taking the bus, I think Mom will stay here if needed. Like I told you, I've been thinking about transitioning to a desk job."

"I can't see you in a cubicle."

"Neither can I, not totally. But the constant worry about what could happen to me isn't worth it anymore."

"You're incredibly competent at what you do."

"Thanks, but you only saw me in the most unusual circumstance. My job is routine to a point, until it isn't, if that makes sense."

"I hear you." She loved his voice.

"You'd never consider changing the kind of work you do, would you?"

A long pause. "I wouldn't, no, but my body's talking a different story. My joints are pretty much shot to hell, with the maximum amount of surgery having been done on my shoulders and knees. My hips have steel in them since my active duty time." He referred to his POW time without mentioning it. Was he still in denial about it, or was this how he managed the atrocity of it?

"What is your body telling you?"

"That I need to talk to my boss and see what other kinds of work I can do for my agency. For instance, taking down Vasin could have been straightforward—apprehend him or take him out if he proved unwilling or dangerous. But as you experienced firsthand, it didn't go as expected or planned. A younger, stronger man without my prior injuries might have been able to get himself out of that building sooner than I did. Or not caught in the first place."

"Maybe, if he had magic powers and could disable half a dozen men with semiautomatic rifles in hand." She dropped the sarcasm. "Your experience played out flawlessly in how you got out of the building without being killed."

"But if you hadn't been there, hoping to catch Vasin for yourself, I could have been killed while I was still trying to get away on the ATV. Remember, while I could have hot-wired them if I had to, I would have been hard-pressed to drive one with my rib and arm injuries."

"We always did work well together." Did he remember the way they'd briefed the admiral and generals in their chain of command during the war, and then executed each mission? She'd never felt more in sync with her fellow sailors and Marines than when she'd worked on the missions that had involved Rob's SEAL team.

"And apparently we still do." Gruff but not grudgingly. He remembered.

"I'm going to have to do a debrief Monday morning. Besides what I'll tell Corey, my boss, in the next few hours."

"He won't have you come in on a Saturday?"

"Normally, yes, but since I had to be out overnight he'll let me stay home until Monday." It was what she liked about the smaller units. All US marshals worked as a team, but the more closely knit offices provided more of a familial support system that she needed as a single parent.

"I'll call you soon." He disconnected, and she kept knitting, not wanting to stop and think about how she felt too deeply. It was better this way. If she could somehow manage a little emotional distance from Rob, it would be better for Jake. She'd be able to tell how stressed he was or wasn't around Rob. Especially after they told him Rob was his father.

She put down her needles and laughed softly to herself. The time for emotional detachment would have been about ten miles before the turnoff into the Poconos campground.

Chapter 10

"I appreciate you coming in to talk with us, Marshal Lopez." Colt Todd, chief of the Silver Valley Police Department, spoke from across the conference table at SVPD headquarters.

"Thanks for having me."

Trina sat next to Detective Rio Ortego, with whom she'd worked in the past. Rio was the official Silver Valley PD contact between the US Marshals office and Todd. Trina hadn't had much prior interface with Chief Todd, but it was clear from how Rio spoke about him and how the department hummed with positive activity that he ran a solid outfit and was respected by his officers.

"I understand that you had a routine apprehension that went sour up in the Poconos." Colt eased back in the leather chair. "We've been tracking more Russian

organized crime activity here over the last six months.
Just when we thought we'd rooted out the remaining
perpetrators in a human trafficking scheme, one of my
detectives was called out to the home of a Silver Valley
resident. His neighbors reported unusual activity. Turns
out he had all the makings of a weapons storage facility in his garage. But by the time we got there, along
with the ATF, his building and basement were empty,
and he'd disappeared."

"'Disappeared' as in, took off and you haven't been
able to locate him, or as in you think someone kid-
napped or killed him?"

Colt shook his head once. "We don't know. It makes
sense to me that he's still around, just off the grid, so to
speak. ROC has unlimited funds at its disposal. If an
active member wants to disappear for their own protection, it can easily be done. And since the neighbor
didn't have any family members living with him, he'd
be the perfect candidate to have taken off. Odds are he's
set up shop in a new city, biding his time until he can
move whatever his limits are on weaponry."

"I've read a lot of reports on ROC lately, but what
kinds of weapons are we talking about?" Trina couldn't
keep up with all the law enforcement developments in
the area any longer. She focused on her assignments
and what she needed to know for each one. Most officers and agents did the same.

"Handhelds. Pistols, rifles, a few specialty knives
thrown in. The ammunition is very dirty, as well. Always the hollow point bullets. Not armor piercing, but
they explode upon impact, doing way more bodily
damage than a normal bullet. They make head or limb

wounds more likely to be lethal." Rio spoke in his usual professional manner.

"You had help from ATF and the county, from what you said."

"Yes, but we can always use more." Colt leaned forward. "I've asked your boss if I could speak to you about a couple of things. First, we've had a rash of heroin overdoses."

"Who hasn't?" Trina didn't want to sound unsympathetic, but the opioid epidemic showed no signs of slowing down and had reached all corners of American life.

"True. We think the most recent shipments have come from ROC. The last one was tainted, killing eight in our county in one weekend. Silver Valley had two deaths."

The math gave Trina pause. Silver Valley was a medium-size town that was classified as a suburb of Harrisburg. Two deaths in Silver Valley and three times as many in the surrounding county was significant.

"What do you want the Marshals to do for you, Chief?"

"Pick up the phone when we call. One of my officers was in the middle of a routine traffic stop when he realized he had pulled over a suspected ROC member. We couldn't get through to anyone in your office quickly enough to verify for your apprehension." Colt looked annoyed, and Trina didn't blame him.

"That doesn't sound right, Chief. There's always someone available 24/7."

"Right. So what I want to know is if ROC is also hacking our systems. Is it possible they already had the coding in place to reroute our calls, or any calls, for that matter, that came into your office?"

"I'll find out. But it wouldn't be surprising, would it?" She'd ask Corey, who would talk to IT, but whatever the outcome it would most likely be something she'd never be able to reveal to a local law enforcement entity. But the thought of ROC even trying to meddle in official communications made her see red.

"No, it wouldn't be a surprise, unfortunately. Thanks for checking, though. I appreciate it." Colt looked at his phone. "We've got something else to talk about. It appears our other meeting attendees are here. Rio, will you bring them in?"

"Sure thing, Chief." Rio was out the door and back in under ten seconds. Trina didn't recognize the woman who followed him. She was tall and trim, with a chic silver bob. Her smooth skin and the light in her eyes belied the age her hair indicated. She was immediately followed by a very familiar figure. Rob.

"Marshal Lopez, this is Claudia Michele, the social media director for SVPD. And I believe you know Rob Bristol."

Trina shook Claudia's hand and nodded at Rob, who sat next to Rio, directly across from her. She noticed that Colt and Claudia exchanged warm smiles, more than what she'd expect from usual LEA colleagues. Rob's gaze was on her, his mouth neutral but his eyes warm and intent.

"Hello, everyone." Claudia looked at Trina. "Marshal Lopez, I've spoken to your supervisor, Corey, and he's aware of what we're about to brief you on."

This was all news to Trina. Rob's presence indicated that maybe Claudia had something to do with what or whom Rob really worked for, but Trina wasn't going to ask. The obvious elephant in the room was something all LEAs knew to stay silent about, in case there was a chance of breaking another officer's cover.

If Rob had one cover, he probably had dozens. This should frighten her, or at the very least make her concerned. A man who could change identities like she changed her clothes wasn't necessarily the best father material. But this was Rob, and she had no doubt about his sincerity. He wanted to be the best father for Jake.

"Go ahead." Trina worked hard to stay composed. Had Rob sold her out somehow? Was this all a ruse to tell her she was completely off the case since Vasin was behind bars and Ivanov had escaped?

"Trina, Rob and I work for a clandestine agency whose headquarters happens to be here in Silver Valley. Rio and Colt have been read into our program, as has your boss, Corey. He knows the rudimentary functions of our agency, but not any details. What I'm asking from you is if you're willing to come in to our offices and allow us to read you in, and give you full access to our ROC files."

Trina knew what "read in" meant. She'd sign an agreement and take an oath to never divulge what she learned or saw while in contact with whatever this super secret agency was.

"I have no problem participating in whatever programs you need me to, Claudia, but the obvious question is, why? And why me? I did my job in the Poconos. I'm not used to remaining on a case for any extended length of time. You know our job description, I'd imagine. We apprehend and then leave the rest to other experts." Trina referred to intelligence, stakeouts and other regular enforcement activity. "I'm trained to do just about anything, but it's not a US marshal's style to infringe on another office's territory."

"Copy that." Claudia's crisp reply was very familiar.

"Have you served, Claudia?"

"Claudia's a decorated combat Marine, retired major general." Colt spoke up as though he took personal pride in Claudia's past achievements.

"Thank you for your service, ma'am. I'm a former Navy pilot myself."

"Yes, Rob told me. And I'm aware of the work you two did together overseas. That's why I'd like you to consider working with Rob more permanently on the ROC issue. I've spoken to Corey and he's in agreement with me that between the two of you we'd stand a better chance of getting ROC out of Silver Valley. I know your history, all of it, and I trust that you'll both keep business, business. Whatever is going on between you two personally is exactly that. If you find it's interfering in your ability to do your job, I expect you to let me know ASAP."

Trina appreciated Claudia's candor but it was still a bit of a shock to realize there were truly no secrets that Trail Hikers didn't uncover.

"It'll take a lot longer than a short-term op, Claudia. I know you understand this. And this isn't what I do—I'm a marshal. Why me?" Concern over Jake's safety made her pulse pound in her head.

"As I said, it's your proven ability to work well with Rob that we want. Rob's asked repeatedly to take a broader role in our anti-gang and organized crime mission, and he needs a partner."

"I guess it would help to know who exactly you and Rob work for before I make any commitments."

Claudia smiled. "That's fair." She turned to Rob. "Would you mind bringing Trina in to our office?"

"Not at all." Rob stood. "Trina?"

Rob's Jeep felt too familiar, and Trina couldn't help thinking about the last time she'd been in it with him, and what they'd done when he'd driven them into the campground. What had she been thinking? In the harsh glare of daylight and in the middle of her normal workday, she questioned her judgment. Until she remembered how exquisite their lovemaking had been.

You acted with your heart.

"Thanks for agreeing to this." Rob started the engine.

"I don't feel I've agreed to anything, Rob." In fact she felt she'd been bamboozled into something bigger than herself. "I should have said no to Corey when he told me to go to SVPD instead of the office this morning."

"He let you think it was your decision, but if you ask me, Claudia had already requested your presence. Did you ever get any rest this weekend?" Rob eased around a huge semitruck, a common sight in Silver Valley as the town sat in the crossroads of logistical operations for all of the eastern seaboard of the United States. Three major highways converged from points north and west, and fed into southern routes that went all the way to Key West, Florida. Silver Valley was set in a beautiful rolling countryside, bordered by mountains that the Appalachian Trail cut through. Since Silver Valley was also bordered by the Susquehanna River, it was an ideal location for distribution centers, countless numbers popping up over the region as more and more manufacturers and online businesses discovered the need to be close to the country's main highways.

"Rest in terms of a break from work, yes. Sleep, not so much."

"Is it the ROC op that's keeping you up?" Rob shot her a concerned glance as he idled at a red traffic light. They were at the largest intersection in town, where a country highway crossed the main pike that twisted through the commercial area. Silver Valley's more quaint, historical district was a mile away, far from the noise where two six-lane highways intersected.

"Partly."

"Am I the other part of that?"

"No. Yes, no." Dang it, she didn't want to talk to him about any of this. Not until she had it straight in her head.

"How's Jake?" He drove onto the main thoroughfare.

"He's great. I know other parents struggle to get their kids ready for school, but that's never been a problem with him. He's so excited to have his own place to go to. And he really enjoys the other kids, for the most part."

"Funny that we'd have such a social son." Rob's observation made her laugh.

"I know, right? We're lucky we stopped long enough to have a conversation with each other outside of work, back on the base." She wasn't sure if it was her comment or Rob's that made her acutely aware of how damn strange their situation was. They'd once known each other so intimately, every nuance of each other's conversation or body language. What they'd shared on Friday had been physical intimacy and possibly a kind of spiritual cleansing, at least on her part. But the fact remained that they hadn't spent any normal time together for over five years.

"A lot changes in five years, Rob."

"That goes both ways. We've both changed, and yet the most important thing we ever did together is constantly changing."

Jake.

"Your point?"

"We could make a conscious decision to accept where we are today and move forward, for Jake's sake."

"Why do I feel you mean, for *your* sake?" Why was she being argumentative? He wanted to be involved in his son's life. If she were in his shoes, wouldn't she do anything to make that happen?

"Of course I do. I'm not trying to hide my desire to be here for Jake. It'll be your call when we tell him, Trina, but we will tell him. And I'm not going to leave him again." His voice was steady, his hands firm on the wheel but not tense as he pulled off the road and into the parking lot of some kind of corporate building. Trina counted at least seven floors, their uniformly tinted windows all sparkling.

"I thought this was the global headquarters for that online news source." The name escaped her; she'd read about it in the local paper.

"No, that's the building we just passed, about a half mile ago. This is meant to look similar, but we do far different things here." Rob pulled into a parking spot behind the building, under a tree.

Trina wondered why she'd never noticed this before, but in reality there were so many office buildings and corporate headquarters in the Harrisburg area that it was an easy oversight. And from what little she'd put together about this secret agency, it was an oversight it cultivated. She wasn't ignorant to the fact that other law enforcement agencies existed, and that she had no clue what they all did. She didn't have to; her job was to be a US marshal and carry out her duty as such. But she was still taken aback that the headquarters for something so secretive, and probably just as powerful, was located in Silver Valley. Silver Valley was the epitome of an all-American medium-size town: big enough to have all the diverse benefits of a city and small enough so that everyone still said "hello" when they walked past one another on the street. They all held doors open for one another, too.

Rob stood at the entrance, holding the glass door open as he waited for her. Trina smiled and Rob's eyes narrowed. "What's so funny?"

"It's an honor to have the same agent who took on an entire arm of ROC last week be nearly human."

He returned her smile. "I thought I made it clear that I'm very human." His eyes smoldered, and she wanted to turn and run.

"Wait, Trina, I was kidding. If that was inappropriate, I'm sorry."

"Not inappropriate as much as too true." She walked ahead of him into a very ordinary front reception area, where they were immediately ushered back into another waiting lounge. Trina noted that both the escort and Rob provided their retina scans, and she was asked to place her fingers on another scanner. "This is until you get your biometrics completely uploaded." Rob spoke as the escort remained quiet and disappeared back to the entrance.

"Have a seat and the director will be with you shortly." The receptionist spoke to Trina.

"This is where I leave you." Rob's hard tone made her stomach do a jig. Trina couldn't help it—she always

felt a shot of adrenaline course through her veins whenever Rob spoke so definitively, with nothing to soften
the edges. It reminded her of wartime.

"Okay. Will you be the one to give me a lift back to
SVPD to get my car? If you can't, don't worry. I can
call someone to pick me up."

Rob leaned in, speaking quietly even though they
were the only two in the waiting area. "First, you never,
ever bring anyone else here or have someone meet you
here unless it's part of a preplanned deal. Second, of
course I'm the one taking you back to SVPD. Claudia
will let me know when you're ready. I've got a lot to
catch up on, so I'm heading up to my office. Good luck."

They stared at each other for a heartbeat and the skin
on her cheek tightened, her back arched into a slight
lean, as if expecting a kiss. Rob winked and walked
away, around the reception desk to a back hallway.

Trina forced her wobbly legs to walk over to a chair
and sank down, needing the comfort of the soft cush-
ions. Rob had her off her game. As well as she and Rob
worked together, her hormones weren't about to follow
suit. They danced to their own beat—and it was a tempo
set by the incredibly hot chemistry she and Rob shared.

The decor in the waiting area was professional and
incredibly sleek yet still reasonably comfortable. This
wasn't a regular government agency, that was for certain. Trina almost laughed aloud as she compared the
chair she sat in to the steel-framed director-style chairs
in the US Marshals lobby. Not that she'd want it any
different—taxpayer money went to apprehending fel-
ons and preventing man-made disasters. Posh furniture wasn't in the deal. She waited for ten minutes but
it felt like an hour.

"Marshal Lopez? Claudia's ready."

"Thank you." She walked over to where the receptionist stood at a large door that, once opened, revealed it was built more like a bank safe. The inside of the door showed several inches of steel with countless bolts that Trina bet were all connected to encrypted codes.

"Hi again, Trina. Please, have a seat." Claudia looked up briefly from the large computer screen she sat behind, typing on a lower keyboard. She nodded at one of two chairs in front of her massive contemporary desk. Trina watched Claudia work and noted that if the woman's hair hadn't been that striking shade of silver, but instead dyed, she'd be hard-pressed to believe Claudia was old enough to have been a flag officer in the Marine Corps.

Claudia pushed her keyboard tray into her desk with a flourish and stood up. "There! I'm sorry to be so rude but I had to answer some direct comms with our agents. Would you like coffee or tea?" Claudia walked over to a small kitchenette area where she clicked on an electric teakettle.

"Tea's great."

As she waited for the water to boil, Claudia examined Trina with her bright eyes. "You've been through a lot over the past several days, Trina. I appreciate your willingness to come in so readily."

"Yes, ma'am."

"It's Claudia. And you should know that my SVPD title, the social media director, is a cover. I'm the director of Trail Hikers." The kettle clicked off. "Green tea? Herbal? Black?"

"Green is wonderful." She wanted a lift but didn't think her nerves would handle much more stimulation.

It figured that Claudia was the director. The woman struck her as someone who could move mountains. And she knew it.

"Here you go." Claudia placed a mug on the table between the two chairs and sat in the other empty chair instead of going back to her desk. Trina's surprise must have been evident.

"I don't bite, honest." Claudia sat back, relaxed but with the alertness only typical of a war veteran. Always watching for what lurked around the closest corner, or inside the person next to you. "As I said, I know how much you've been through. You should know that I run an agency that has access to anything imaginable, to include personal records. We only use our power as needed to take down our opponents, not to spy on American citizens."

"Claudia, do I need to know all of this?"

"You will, if you agree to what I'm going to propose. What I'm talking about right now, though, is you and Rob. More importantly, you and Justin—before he became Rob."

Claudia knew, just as she'd said at SVPD. And she knew it *all*.

"I'd say your systems are thorough." Trina's voice was steadier than her shaky bearings. Was anything sacred?

"This is why I told you about our abilities, if rather vaguely. I could have found out whatever I needed, but I didn't have to. Rob told us as soon as he reported for duty, after he left the CIA. I take it you know he worked for them for several years?"

"Yes." Would there be any point in lying to this woman?

"Rob needed a change, and my agency offered him that. He's only come here on a mission-by-mission basis. We happen to have several permanent positions available. I'd like to see him directing bigger operations instead of doing the day-to-day ops like what you were involved with last week." Trina forced herself to keep from shaking her head. If coming face-to-face with ROC bad guys was part of what Claudia considered a day-to-day op, she wasn't sure she wanted to know what a major or strategic op entailed.

"Why are you telling me this, Claudia?"

"Actually, I need you to answer a question for me first. Are you willing to be read in to the Trail Hikers?" Claudia's expression and straightforward demeanor signified no manipulation. This was Trina's decision entirely.

"Will it affect my position as a marshal?"

"Not at all. If anything it may help you, as you'll be privy to information and leads on cases you might otherwise not be. Of course you can't reveal it in your daily US Marshal activity. Any information that's proprietary to Trail Hikers is just that, but I think you'll see that it won't be difficult to keep the two paths of data separate."

"I'm in."

"Wonderful. But we'll give you a little more information and time before we make you sign on the dotted line. You'll have to sign a basic nondisclosure agreement now, though." Claudia looked toward her desk. "Jessica, please take Trina to the classrooms."

After several hours of basic indoctrination, Trina was brought back into Claudia's office to sign contracts to agree to keep all she saw at Trail Hikers headquarters secret, and to not involve any uncleared personnel in Trail Hikers business if at all possible. After she placed her signature on the last line of the last page, Claudia held out her hand. "Welcome to Trail Hikers, Trina."

"Thank you. It's an honor to work with you. I know I'm not a full-time TH agent, but anything I can do to help with this mission, and future ops, I'm here."

Trina had to sit through two full days of briefing and some operational drills at the TH offices. Corey knew what she was doing, and the rest of the Marshals office was told she was taking classes. The training explained a lot to her and answered her most pressing question—how much of TH work could she do while still working as a US marshal?

A lot, it turned out. Trina had to admit to herself that this was what she'd been looking for. A way to broaden the challenges of her work without having to leave the area. Settling down in one area with Jake had been her long-term goal, and it was a relief to have the Trail Hikers. Serendipity came to Silver Valley, apparently.

And she'd remain a Trail Hiker, even if for an unforeseen reason she ever left the US Marshals. She'd have to have another job or occupation to serve as her main career, as it was a requisite for all Trail Hikers agents to have a cover job, but it had to be real, as well. Actual Trail Hikers work and missions would occupy only up to a third of her time, but they would pay handsomely. A great way to save up sooner for Jake's college, that was for sure.

Three days after she'd begun her Trail Hikers indoctrination, or "indoc," Claudia called her into the office again.

"I take it your training has gone well?"

"Yes—although maybe you should tell me? We don't seem to get much feedback from the instructors."

"You didn't get much feedback because you've had most of the training. There isn't much you haven't already been exposed to."

"True. Except for all the technology." Trina had noted that where her tools such as handcuffs and comms gear were limited to what the government gave the US Marshals, Trail Hikers didn't seem to have the same budgetary constraints.

"Yes, we have the best and latest. Futuristic, in many cases."

"It'll be fun working here."

Claudia leaned back in her office chair, her expression relaxed. "I hope it's more than fun. My wish is that you're able to grow as much personally as professionally from all that TH offers you." Before Trina responded, Claudia stood up and walked around to the front of the desk, where she leaned as she continued speaking. "Now on to the first mission I need you to do." As if by magic, the door behind Trina opened, and she looked over her shoulder to see Rob walk through. They hadn't spoken to each other in the days she'd been participating in the intensive indoc training, and it was like seeing him for the first time all over again. He was at her side in three long strides, lowering himself into the second chair.

"Claudia, Trina."

"Rob, Trina, I have a mission for you both. I understand that working together may be a bit tense for you at this juncture in reacquainting yourselves, but it can't be helped. You're two of my best Russian speakers and we've got a big problem right here in Silver Valley that needs to be stomped out before ROC thinks it can run this town."

"Is it with the same group we were up against in the Poconos?"

"Yes. It turns out there was another trailer of girls that went unnoticed until they'd been dispersed to several towns in southern Pennsylvania. Five of them are local to Silver Valley, and all working at the Den, as well as making extra money at the truck service station off the main drag."

The Den was labeled as a "gentlemen's club" in Silver Valley, but everyone knew it wasn't just a strip joint. It had come under fire for unlicensed gambling, and there were unsubstantiated reports of prostitution.

"If you know the girls are there, why can't Immigration take them in, for their own safety?"

Claudia's lips pursed as though she, too, was frustrated with having to jump through hoops to save the young women. "We need time, and we need them to ask for help. Right now none of them speak English, or if they do, they don't let on. They converse only in Russian, and all have visas and passports that indicate they're older than they are. Of course the visas and passports are fake, but again, we don't want to go rolling in there unless we're fairly certain we can take down the ROC group perpetrating this. Otherwise there will only be more ROC activity coming into Silver Valley, until the numbers are too great for us, or rather, local law enforcement, to keep up with."

"I'm sure Claudia or the other instructors told you this already, but Trail Hikers doesn't usually get involved in anything that local law enforcement or even the FBI can handle."

"Right. And I'm thinking we're back to the language ability—there aren't a lot of fluent Russian speakers in our area." Trina did think there would have to be a fair number of Russian speakers in TH, however, as it was a clandestine agency that helped go after ROC.

"Yes. TH has several agents who are polyglots and speak Russian, of course. But they're currently assigned to other ops, unable to break free."

"Trina is perfect for this." Rob added his opinion. "As a woman you may be more approachable for the girls. You and I do have a history of working well together."

"I read up on what you two did in the Navy. I knew about it peripherally as I was in the same Middle Eastern country then, too." Claudia addressed Trina. "Your squadron and the P-8 community in general provided a lot of support to our MEFs." Yes, Trina had flown many hours in support of US Marine expeditionary forces. Until she'd been assigned exclusively to support Rob's SEAL team.

"We did, as well as less frequent SEAL support ops. It was my privilege to fly those missions." Trina looked at Rob. "We worked together then because the missions had been deeply strategized many months ahead of time. What we did last week, what this might require, is much more fluid."

"If by 'fluid' you mean it could turn deadly on a dime, Trina, yes, you're correct. But so could any of your apprehensions as a US marshal, right?" Claudia was no-nonsense.

"Yes, that's correct." As Trina spoke, she felt Rob's

gaze on her and knew what he was thinking. He was asking that same damned question about why she chose law enforcement when she was a single mother. "And while some people might not understand why I'd take a job that involves some dangerous situations, law enforcement is my calling. I realized that during the war. Even though I was a pilot, I felt that I was doing something actively to bring justice to a part of the world that hasn't experienced it in a long while. And if we're going to talk about danger or life-threatening, simply driving to work on the interstate or turnpike can turn deadly in a heartbeat. I can't live in fear, and I'm not raising my son to live a fear-based life, either." Her voice shook with her conviction, and she forced herself to take several deep, slow breaths. Claudia was going to kick her off the TH team before she ever got started.

"I commend your resolve, Trina. And I'm grateful for your expertise. So, are you both on board for this mission? Together?"

Trina looked at Rob and found him staring at her, his brows lifted in expectation. He was leaving it up to her.

"Yes, of course. But how are we going to infiltrate this group of girls? The truck stop or strip club or both? Will I go undercover as one of them?" She imagined having to explain to Jake why Mommy had false eyelashes and heavy makeup on.

"We have a lead on that." Claudia rose off the desk and walked around to her executive chair, sitting to pull a three files from a small, neat stack. "Here you go." She handed them each one and opened her file. "The Silver Valley Community Church has an outreach program for human trafficking. Mostly, it deals with young women who came here under the guise of becoming nannies or housekeepers, but they end up working in the sex trade. They take hot meals and goodie bags with coupons, gift certificates and such into the strip club once a week, at lunchtime. The owner allows it and actually encourages the girls to attend. He didn't have any part in the women coming into the country per se. He does employ them now, though, and wants to give the appearance of cooperating with 'helping' these young women. The owner doesn't want to get caught breaking the law, and if any of the girls admits she's underage, or of age and wants out of the adult entertainment industry, he doesn't fight it. SVCC has volunteer families that take the girls in until they can be situated in regular jobs or college, working with a social worker." Claudia waited while they looked at their copies.

"Doesn't he lose all of his dancers this way?" Trina thought women would jump at the chance to get out of the adult entertainment industry.

"No. They're afraid of losing what they have—a decent paying job and a place to live. It's what they know, and safer than what they went through when they were transported here."

"What about the truck stop?" Trina couldn't get past the image of teenage girls having to turn tricks for aging truckers, risking their lives each time.

"That's a little more difficult, as the abused women know how to evade any kind of arrest. SVCC goes in every now and then and sets up a table outside with sandwiches and hot drinks, cold in the summer. Every now and then they convince one of the women to get help and escape their basic enslavement, but it's not easy. These are women who've been so abused they fear any change. It seems incomprehensible to us, as we know they'll have a better life going forward, away from how they were trafficked into the country. But they're in pure survival mode. We have had more success lately, however, as social media helps get the word out to the most disenfranchised that assistance is available."

"The women risk going up to the table?"

"Sure. They see the same volunteers there, week after week, and feel more comfortable around them. Don't forget the truck stops are also good places for the homeless to find a free meal. The church outreach groups also feed the homeless. Not all truckers are looking for sex on their rest time. Many work with the outreach program and pay for meals for the homeless. Many truckers dine with the homeless, when the homeless agree to it. Several other churches in the area reach out to the homeless at many different waypoints. The truck stops are a main location."

"Why are you telling us about the SVCC outreach, Claudia?" Rob's voice sounded rough. Something about this wasn't making him happy. Did he not want to work with her again? He'd seemed eager enough when he'd walked in here.

"Trina, you're familiar with SVCC, right?"

Trina held back a smile. There was nothing that TH didn't find out or know about its agents. "Yes, it's my parents' place of worship when they're in town. My brother and I go with them on the major holidays." And that was becoming more often as Jake grew and Trina wanted to give him some kind of spiritual basis on which to form an opinion. She was all for letting Jake choose his own religion as an adult but felt as his mother she needed to expose him to something regularly while he was young.

"Then it wouldn't be unreasonable for you and Rob to attend church there, behaving as, say, an engaged couple with a son?"

Trina sucked in her breath. "Are you sure this is a super classified law enforcement agency, Claudia? Because it sounds like a dating service on steroids."

Claudia laughed and so did Rob, although his sounded more like an expression of relief that Trina had said what perhaps he hadn't wanted to.

He was being extra careful, she thought. He was afraid she'd tell him he couldn't see Jake again, which was ridiculous. And maybe even a little worried she wanted more from him than he was willing to give. Rob would probably always have these kind of concerns, coming from the foster system. It made her care about him even more, because with each breath he was overcoming his past.

"What you two decide to do about your arrangement is none of my business." Claudia's high color indicated that maybe she was fibbing, just a bit. "But I think you'll be able to pull off being a couple, right?"

Trina looked at Rob, who was staring at the file on his lap. His tension was obvious in the way he gripped the chair arms. "Why a church, Claudia? Can't we pose as social workers?"

"I know you're not a fan of churches, Rob, but I think you'll see that SVCC is how a church is meant to be. Nothing like what you experienced in your foster home." She spoke firmly but with compassion.

Trina's heart pumped nothing but compassion for Rob. He'd mentioned he'd grown up in foster care, that his biological parents had died of drug overdoses when he was only five.

The same age as Jake.

Rob's foster parents had been churchgoers in the strictest sense, and he'd been forced to follow black-and-white rules to the point of abuse. He'd survived that time in his life and told her his happiest moment was when he'd enlisted in the Navy. He'd quickly been moved to officer candidate school and then to SEAL training. And never looked back, never cared to see his foster parents again.

It crystallized like old honey in her mind—Rob wanted to be a father to Jake because he hadn't had one. Rob didn't want to fail Jake the way he'd been failed.

And in Rob's eyes, he'd already failed Jake by walking away five years ago and never even considering Jake could have been his son.

"It'll be fine, Rob. We can be the couple that doesn't have a lot of time for church but wants to make a difference, so we sign up to be on the rotation for the strip club lunch meals. We'll offer to go to the truck stop together, too. Most couples with families probably don't want to spend prime time at the truck stop trying to draw in sex workers, I'm thinking."

Claudia shot her a grateful look.

Rob's expression was stony. "I'll do whatever the mission requires."

"Great." Claudia looked pleased as a groundhog in a vegetable garden. "So, not to rush you, but time is of the essence. We have to get these girls off their jobs quickly, before the ROC group thinks they're making a major profit. The third Wednesday of the month happens to be the morning the SVCC hosts its welcome reception for new volunteers on any of their committees. That unfortunately was yesterday. I suggest you two wait until next month to sign up for the trafficked worker outreach group, so that you don't look suspicious. In the meantime, attend SVCC services together. Become a staple couple in the community."

"We're supposed to blend in with all of these do-gooders?" Rob grumbled as if he were ten and being forced to endure a long, boring sermon. Trina stifled a giggle. After what they'd been through in less than a week, time with active, service-oriented people did sound a little sleepy.

Claudia smiled as she replied. "You'll be joining the Community Hand Up group. Report back as necessary. And Trina, I've spoken to Corey. You're free from going in to the Marshals office until we wrap this case. Keep training here, and you two coordinate daily on what intelligence reports come in regarding ROC and the smuggled sex workers. I trust you to know when to move in and break it all up."

"Thank you, Claudia. I hope we get it solved quickly." Trina didn't have any idea how long she and Rob would need to wait to be able to save more underage girls, but she'd do whatever it took.

"You will." Claudia sat with her hands on her desk, having obviously moved on mentally from their discussion. Trina couldn't begin to imagine how much Claudia was responsible for.

"Let's go." Rob stood first, and Trina followed him out of the office and into the parking lot. Only in front of her car did he turn to face her, his face resigned.

"What's bothering you so much, Rob?"

"A few things, but mostly it's the fact that I want to spend all my free time getting to know my son. I was hoping we'd tell him who I am sooner rather than later. But now with this case, that might be postponed indefinitely."

"It won't be." She decided to leap before thinking things through too much—her weakness had always been overanalyzing her actions. "Tell you what. We both need to eat dinner, right? How do you feel about hamburgers and hot dogs on the grill tonight? I have some fresh corn on the cob from the Amish market down the road, too."

Rob's eyes sparked with interest, the first positive sign she'd read from him since Claudia had mentioned the church involvement. "I'm not a charity case myself, Trina."

"I didn't say you were. My brother's out of town this week, and I hate using the gas grill my parents gave me for Mother's Day. Do you like to barbecue?"

"Are you kidding? I'm the best griller this side of the Susquehanna."

Chapter 11

"Mom, can we give Rob the red corn holders?" Jake placed two corn holders on the counter as he rummaged in the kitchen junk drawer. "You have clear and I'll have blue."

"Sure, sweetie. Sounds good." Trina was trying to stay present as she organized the kitchen for their impromptu barbecue. While she'd had the meal planned out well in advance, she hadn't known Rob would be their guest. She had plenty of food for three, but would have made more of an effort than hot dogs and hamburgers for Rob.

"Hello?" Rob tapped on the back screen door, just as she'd suggested.

"Come in, come in!" Jake ran around in circles, Renegade yapping his puppy head off as he raced after Jake. Jake stopped in front of the door. Trina didn't know whether to be glad that her son trusted Rob so much or worried that he'd let his guard down so quickly.

"Hey, buddy!" Rob knelt down to Jake's eye level and the two fist-bumped and high-fived. Seeing Jake's small hand against Rob's massive paw made Trina's heart lurch. Jake had Rob's hands—it was one of the first things she'd noticed when Jake was born. He had the same crooked thumbs, the wide fingernails, as Rob. The memory made her wonder when or if Jake would ever observe that he had many of the same physical attributes as Rob. Would Jake ask about Rob being his dad before she or Rob told him?

Rob stood and produced a huge bouquet of daisies from behind his back. "These are for you. Thanks for having me."

Unexpected joy leaped in her belly. "How nice. You didn't have to do this, but I'm happy you did. Jake, can you please find a jar under the sink for these?" As Jake slammed open a cupboard, Trina looked at Rob. "I have nicer vases, but they're in boxes. We've only been here a short time and I haven't been able to get everything unpacked."

"This is why I couldn't find you at first."

"Pardon?" The steely tone in her query wasn't on purpose. It was as if she automatically put up barbed wire fences whenever Rob was nice to her.

"I tried to find where you lived, to come see you. Your apartment in Harrisburg was still listed in the database I used."

"Oh. I mean, that's understandable, that it still has the old address. But I thought TH was up-to-date on everything?"

"I used a regular civilian database. I paid ten bucks to find you. How's that for a charming opening line?"

She couldn't stop her smile. "Needs some polish, Bristol."

"Is it hard for you to call me that?"

"Not at all. I keep telling myself it should be. But in reality you're still the man I knew, and then, you're not at all."

"What other man?" Jake reached on his tippy-toes to place an antique mason jar on the counter, next to the platters of food.

"That happens to have been my name once. Here, let's put the flowers on the table, away from the food. Unless you want them somewhere else?" Rob's smooth reply and the need to please his son was stamped so deeply on his expression that Trina felt a corner of her heart melt in one smooth plop.

"That's fine, or rather, how about on the plant shelves, over there by the window? The kitchen table's pretty small when we all sit at it."

"Got it." Rob filled the jar with water, his forearm brushing hers in the most erotic kitchen foreplay imaginable. Trina focused on getting the salad finished. She and Rob had to establish a solid friendship again, for Jake's sake. Her hormones needed to take a back seat. She let out a breath of relief when he moved across the room and placed the jar on the shelf, followed by the bouquet.

It's not just your hormones.

"What can I do?" Rob was back at her side, looking over the plate of uncooked hamburgers.

"Go ahead and fire up the grill if you'd like, and let me know when you want the hot dogs."

"I want my bun toasty!" Jake tugged at Rob's dark blue T-shirt, a touching gesture that pulled at Trina's composure.

"You've got it, buddy."

"His name is Jake."

"*Mom,* I like it when Rob calls me 'buddy.'"

"Don't worry, it's always easier being the new guy." Rob spoke quietly to her. He knew what she was thinking, that Jake had some serious hero worship going on. Rob apparently agreed. Their communication was mostly via eye contact and she remembered that this was why she'd taken so long to move on after she thought he'd died. Their unspoken connection by which they always seemed to understand one another. This had to be why she'd never fully accepted he was gone. Some tiny part of her had kept the flame of hope lit, believing he was still alive. As if she knew.

"You okay, Trina? You look like you saw a...ghost."

"Stop. We can't tiptoe around each other about this. Yes, it is like I saw a ghost. But you're not—you're here."

"That I am." Rob took the plate of hamburgers and the barbecue spatula she'd pulled out of the ceramic pot on the counter where she stored her kitchen utensils. "I'll have these done in no time. Want to help me, bud—Jake?"

"Yeah!"

"Take Renegade with you. Use his leash!"

"Come here, Renegade." Jake easily cajoled the puppy into the tiny harness. Trina shook her head as she washed the salad ingredients. That dang dog had made her run all over the house, chasing him, before she'd been able to leash him after work.

Jake chattered to Rob as they went out back, the screen door slamming against the weathered doorframe. There were plenty of upgrades Trina needed to have done in the old farmhouse, but a sliding glass door for the backyard and a walkout deck topped her list. The surrounding farm fields and rolling mountains were too beautiful to not make the most of the view.

"Here you go." She joined them outside, carrying the hot dogs and buns.

"Perfect timing. We do work well together, Marshal Lopez." She ignored Rob's banter and looked around for Jake, who was on an old tire swing that hung from the humongous oak next to the house. Renegade sat on the porch and watched him, his leash fastened to a patio chair.

"You always have to know where he is, don't you?" Rob flipped a burger.

"I'm his mother. It's called parenting."

"Whoa, it wasn't a criticism. I meant it from a place of appreciation—it's like you have a built-in radar."

She watched him work over the hot grill, and the heat waves rippling between them mirrored her doubt that she'd ever be able to trust Rob fully with Jake. Trust that he would take care of Jake and not harm him; sure, that was a given. But the sense that Rob would disappear again weighed heavy on her heart.

"Talk to me, Trina." His eyes slid to the side, and she knew he was watching Jake, too.

"I want to explain away your intense interest in Jake as part of the surprise of finding out you've had a child for the past five years."

"But?"

"I know it's deeper. You really do seem to care for

Jake in that natural bonding way. It's only been a few days and you have a rapport with him that's taken me his entire lifetime."

"First, I'm the shiny new dude around here. He's a kid, Trina—he likes to have all the attention on him. Second, this isn't something that's going to wear off. Jake is my son, I'm his father."

"It's all been so fast." She held the plate for Rob as he piled up the burgers. He opened the rolls and placed them on the grill's highest shelf.

"You know, for the last three months I'd planned to come here, one day during the week when you were home from work. I thought of calling first—TH can get anyone's number—but didn't want to scare you or have you worry about Jake's safety."

"Showing up here would have been a shock, that's for sure. And you're right—if you'd called first I would have thought it was some kind of twisted crank call. And I would have wondered from whom, as only my parents and brother know the entire story about the identity of Jake's father. About you, I mean."

"You never told anyone else?"

"I told people you'd been killed in the war, which on record you had. I wanted Jake to feel loved by both of his parents, even if one was deceased. I knew how painful you said it was for you as a foster kid, thinking that your mom and dad didn't love you, and I also wanted to honor your memory."

"Even though you couldn't legally claim that I was Jake's father."

"I named you as Jake's father on his birth certificate. I'm not all about what's legal or correct in this world, Rob. Sure, I'm in law enforcement, but it's more important to do what's right than what's legal at times. Don't you agree?"

"Maybe." He placed the toasted buns on a separate plate. "Looks like we're ready here."

"Jake, Ren, come on in." Jake loped up to the back door, the dog's tail wagging furiously as the boy untied the leash.

"Honey, put Ren in his crate and then wash your hands before you sit down."

As they climbed the three steps on the back stoop into the kitchen, it hit Trina that they would appear like any other regular family to an outsider. Coming in from the grill, ready to eat dinner, a dog at their heels.

It scared the tater tots right out of her.

Rob stayed quiet throughout dinner, joking with Jake on and off, watching how his son ate everything on his plate and asked for seconds. And the kid didn't expect dessert—Trina had instilled good nutritional habits, that was clear. But he was over-the-top jubilant about the biscuit raspberry shortcake Trina placed in front of him.

"Mom and I are going to go blueberry picking this weekend."

"Isn't berry season over?" He wasn't a farmer or gardener by any means but had seen the signs for local strawberry farms disappear from the main highway, one by one, over the past two weeks.

"Blueberries are the last to come in. We are a little late this year, too, because of the cold spring." Trina didn't meet his eyes, and her back was in that ramrod-straight position that told him she was cranky about something. He wondered if this was going to be the status quo until he proved he was trustworthy. That he wasn't going to disappear again.

"Blueberries stain your teeth real bad." Jake's exaggeration was so over-the-top that Rob reached over and tweaked his little nose.

"Is that so?"

Jake nodded. "Yes. First there are strawberries, then raspberries, then blueberries. But the blueberries grow on little trees. The strawberries and raspberries grow in the ground."

"Hmm." Rob didn't know what to say, he was having so much fun watching his son—his *son*—demonstrate his knowledge. Jake was only five years old but appeared and acted two years older, in Rob's opinion. Was this fatherly pride?

"Jake, I'm going to be working a lot these next few weeks, so Grandma or Uncle Nolan might have to pick you up from camp. Grandma will stay here if she drives down. I need you to take good care of Renegade if I'm late."

"Can't Rob pick me up from camp?"

"He's busy with work, too."

Jake nodded, his mouth full of whipped cream and berries. "Okay, Mom." His tone indicated this was a common conversation.

"You're growing up too quickly for your mom." Trina ruffled his hair, and Rob loved how Jake leaned into it, absorbing her affection. Had his parents ever done that to him, before their addictions killed them? His memories were fuzzy at best, and his younger brother never claimed to have any recollection of life before foster care. He'd been in touch with his brother since coming back from the dead, but he hadn't told him he was an uncle. Rob made a mental note to rectify that soon.

"I think I'll go after we're through. We have an early start tomorrow." He meant his words for Trina, but Jake missed nothing.

"You can't go, Rob! You have to read me my bedtime story." Pure happiness burst into thousands of feel-good thrills in his chest. His son wanted him to stay.

"Jake." Trina's voice elicited a side stare from Jake. Rob bit his cheek not to laugh.

"I'm happy to stay. I thought you'd want me out of your hair." Little had scared Rob, at least until a week ago. Now he measured each word he spoke by his desire to not overstep and lose whatever ground he'd gained with Trina on the Jake front.

You want to gain traction with Trina, too.

He did, but couldn't count on it. He didn't merit her love again. She deserved a man who didn't walk away.

"That's fine, Rob. I already told you, none of this—" she motioned at the table, including all three of them "—is an issue." She meant his time with Jake. Was he a lesser man because he wanted her to make it clear that what existed between her and him was just as important, if not more so?

"All done!" Jake pushed his plate away, a king in his castle.

"To the sink with that, mister." Trina was tough in the most loving way. Rob couldn't get enough of it. "Your choice tonight, Jake. Bath or shower?"

"Shower!" He answered so quickly Rob couldn't hold back his laugh this time. A reluctant grin lifted Trina's mouth, and he let his gaze linger there, the way he wanted his lips to.

"Go shower and come back in your pajamas, please."
Trina looked at Rob. "I have to get the shower going, get
the temperature right, for him." She stood up, taking the
remaining plates to the small laminate kitchen counter.

Rob followed her. "I've got this. You take care of
our son." He was behind her at the sink, her nape close
enough to kiss.

He heard her breath suck in and imagined two spots
of rosy awareness appearing on her cheeks. His hands
had a mind of their own as he stood more fully behind
her and massaged her shoulders. This was safer. If he
started to kiss her he wouldn't want to stop. There'd be
too many questions from Jake if he found them together
like that. It was too soon.

"That feels…wonderful." Her muscles relaxed into
his hands, and the satisfaction at comforting her was
almost as good as if she'd given him the green light to
make love to her again. Almost.

"Go on." He dropped his arms and kept his hand
from playfully swatting her bottom. It was a lovely ass,
and he knew instinctively that if he ever wanted to touch
it again, skin on skin, it had to be on Trina's time.

"We'll be in Jake's room in about twenty minutes."
She handed him the soapy sponge, and they stood like
that for a second.

"Take your time." He started to rinse plates and load
them into a dishwasher that looked like it was on its
last cycle.

"Okay, well. Thank you, Rob." She leaned up and
gave him a kiss on the cheek before she disappeared
up the stairs.

Rob whistled as he did the dishes, a sense of serenity he'd never experienced washing over him. A shoul-

der massage, a kiss on the cheek, all friendly gestures that could lead to more. Maybe. It was wait-and-see.

For the first time in forever, Rob was willing to wait as long as it took for something he wanted. For what was most worthwhile.

Rob loved reading to Jake and getting to be there again to watch Trina tuck him in. He stayed back near the door of Jake's bedroom, not wanting to come on too strong.

"'Night, Rob." Jake waved from his race car bed, and Rob winked at him.

"'Night, champ."

He went down the stairs and waited for Trina to meet him. He kept expecting a rush of anxiety at the weight of becoming a parent to hit him, but all he felt was joy. Pure exhilaration at knowing he had a son. And he'd been given a second chance to know him. It was easy to think he had a second chance with Trina, too.

But was it smart?

"Hey." Trina's bare feet hadn't made a sound until the last two steps.

"Hey, yourself." He drew her into his arms, grateful that she didn't stiffen or pull back. "I've been thinking."

"Hmm?" Her cheek felt so good against his chest.

"I would like to see more of Jake. Regularly."

She lifted her head, her expression wary. "Do you mean like custody?"

"Yes. No. No! Of course I want to take care of all of his financial needs, but I'd like a chance to spend time with him so that he gets used to me."

"I am totally capable of providing for his financial

needs. Isn't time like tonight what you're talking about? Coming over, getting to know him?"

"I want to do more than be your dinner guest, Trina." Her eyes flared with heat at his words, and the energy went straight to his dick, already invested in the conversation as it was. He was going to need a long, cold shower tonight.

"That's—that's mutual." She chewed her lower lip, and frustration made him place his hands on her shoulders, his forehead to hers. It had been their signature move in the desert all those years ago, and while this was a new beginning for them, he wanted her to know he meant what he said.

"Babe, I want you so bad I could take you up against this wall. But we're going to go slow, so that we both know it's for the right reasons."

"What, no more frantic coupling in the middle of a family campsite?" She tried to be jovial, but he heard the pain that threaded through her question.

"That wasn't frantic, it was pure instinct. Existential. We'll talk about it for years to come." He rubbed the insides of her wrists with his thumb. "Whether we're able to make a go of it this time or not, it's important that Jake know we're here for him. I won't have him be part of a family with two parents who don't get along or worse, fight in front of him."

"Rob, you're not a bad parent. You've only been one as far as you knew for what, a week? Give this time."

"Exactly. Will you let me help you? Can I be the other parent Jake never had until now?"

"I don't think you're giving me any other choice, are you?"

"You have every right to say no."

"That's not how I roll, Rob." Her voice was husky with emotion, and he thrilled at the jolts of awareness that hopped across his chest and down to his very hard, very focused dick. He sighed before he could stop it.

"What?"

He gently stepped back and let go of her. "I've got to say goodbye now or risk permanent blue balls."

The next morning she stared at the daisies Rob had given her as she drank her first cup of coffee. Jake would come barreling down the stairs at any minute, and she appreciated the quiet before the day started.

A rap at her back door startled her. Her mother was two hours north in Williamsport, and Nolan hadn't texted he'd be by. Heart hammering, she stood up and walked to the door. Relief was followed by curiosity as she opened the door.

"Good morning!" Rob held out a potted flower.

"Come on in." She accepted the plant, its ceramic container a beautiful work of blues, greens and golds that swirled tighter into a heart on the side. "Thank you. At this rate, I'm going to be able to open my own florist's shop."

"I noticed you're in need of plants and flowers for the house. Where's Jake?"

"He's upstairs brushing his teeth. I don't want to be rude, but I thought we'd agreed to meet at TH?"

"We did, and I changed my mind. Being a part of my son's life isn't the same as borrowing a library book. I'm sorry if I gave you the impression I was only interested in seeing him in short spurts. I want it all, Trina."

"That's fair."

"And I want my brother to know him. Jeremy is Jake's only uncle on my side, and it's important to me."

She was touched by how much Rob had thought this out. "I don't have a problem with that. Where does your brother live?"

"Believe it or not, less than two hours from here. He works at a resort as their head chef." Pride laced his words. Trina loved how Rob might only have one relative but he made the most of it, never complained about losing his family of origin so young.

"He sounds a lot different than you."

"Because he's not LEA? He was in the Navy as a cook, for a short time. He used his GI bill to go to culinary school. It sounds different, cooking versus bringing down bad guys, but they both require a level of focus and attention to detail."

She thought about how Rob's attention to detail, crucial in a successful mission, translated to the bedroom. What was she going to do with her feelings for this man? They were discussing Jake's custody and parenting, something that could become so contentious. And yet, even knowing they might not make it as a couple, she wanted him. Needed him.

"Rob, I've been thinking, too. I can't, I won't let Jake think we're all going to be together when the chance is so slim."

His gaze met hers and she saw his understanding. But there was more. A simmering heat that she knew was reflected in her eyes, too.

"Is it, Trina? A slim chance?"

Desire exploded between them, and Trina's body reacted as it always did to Rob. From the exquisite friction as her nipples rubbed up against her sundress to the heat that pooled between her legs and made said limbs wobbly, she was a goner.

He moved in, his lips meeting hers with no other touch involved. The kiss was hot, expert on both their parts. But it wasn't the sexual arousal that made Trina's insides melt, that tugged at the walls around her soul. It was their connection. Her physical compatibility with Rob was due to this enigmatic link they'd shared since he'd climbed aboard her P-8 in Iraq.

"Mom! Are you okay?"

Trina and Rob jerked apart, and to her extreme dismay, Jake stood right next to them, toothpaste on his mouth.

"I'm fine, honey bunny." She let out breath and knelt to his level. "Rob and I are very good friends."

He shrugged. "I know, Mom. Hey, Rob!" He hugged Rob's leg tightly, and another brick in her wall crumbled. What was she doing? It was one thing if she had to face the reality of not making a lifetime with Rob because of her own trust issues. But to ever have to see Jake grieve over the loss of a father—unthinkable.

"Mom, we have to get to camp. We're collecting bugs with exoskeletons today." Jake had lost interest in the kiss once he knew his mom was okay. And he soaked up Rob's friendly attention like a dry sponge.

"Okay, let's go. Rob, you can come with us since we're going to work together today. Jake, Rob and I work together at our job."

"You told me that, Mom. So Rob, you're a marshal like Mommy?"

"Ah, yes. In a way."

They got out of the house, and as she buckled Jake into his booster seat she felt Rob's gaze and met his eyes. They'd shifted from lovers to parents as if it was a natural progression. As if she could somehow over-come her fear that he'd disappear again.

They dropped Jake at his day camp with little fan-fare, as he was still pooped from last night's excite-ment. Other than family, Trina explained to Rob that she didn't have a lot of folks over for dinner during the week, and he was the first person they'd had to dinner in the new house, period.

"Bye, Mom." Rob watched Jake hug Trina on the sidewalk with his big-boy persona. A surge of delight hit him when Jake looked over Trina's shoulder and waved at him. He waved back, smiling in spite of his churning gut. Dread filled every corner of Rob's being as he watched the quintessentially familial scene. He couldn't tamp down the pure love he felt for his son, the incredible sense of ownership he had as Jake jogged away from the car at the drop-off point and joined the group of children sitting in a circle.

"Bye, honey." Trina waved, her dress swaying about her sexy body.

"He really likes you." Trina slid her sunglasses back onto her nose and drove away from the school building.

"Does it ever get easier?" He spoke around the huge lump in his throat.

"What?" She shot him a quick once-over. "Dang, I forgot that all of this is brand-new for you. You're upset at having to watch him go off to a group of strangers, right?"

Yes, that was part of what was bothering him.

"Yeah."

"It gets easier. I remind myself that it's healthy for

him to have a break from me, and vice versa. Plus kids need other trusted adults to be authority figures. And of course the bottom line has always been that I have to work, so it's part of our life."

"You'd never be a stay-at-home mom, not full time. I don't see you doing that."

"It's easy to think that, I get it, but when he was very tiny I wanted out of the Navy so badly, wanted to be able to spend every moment with him. Reality set in at about six months. I'm a much better mom when I've taken care of myself first, and yes, for me that means my career."

"Have you thought of a safer one?"

"As I've said before, I'm called to this profession, in one form or another. You of all people understand that. And consider—would you ask a man the same thing?"

"I wouldn't question any other man's choice. Or woman's. But you're my son's mother." A mental scene flashed in front of him. What if Jake had a full-time dad? What if Trina didn't have to worry about child-care, after-school care, who'd drive Jake to his sporting events?

"Don't go there, Rob."

"Where?"

"You're thinking you could be his full-time parent, right? Trust me, I've put myself through all the scenarios. It's tough no matter what job you leave for in the morning. You'll figure it out. Give yourself time."

As Trina continued to train with Trail Hikers over the next month, she and Rob fell into a routine with Jake. Rob asked to split up the schedule as far as drop-off and pickup, and they went to his summer soccer league games together.

"It's more like pee wee or bumblebee soccer." They stood at edge of a small soccer field. Rob spoke from the side of his mouth, his gaze riveted on Jake in the early-evening light. Trina stifled a giggle.

"It's not the World Cup, but the kids seem to really enjoy it." Jake got the ball and started to dribble it stiltedly up the field for a few steps before he was swarmed by a half dozen other players, all no more than three feet tall. It was pure American little-kid soccer, and she loved it.

"He's a natural. Look at how he's able to maneuver it out of that group." Rob sounded as though Jake was performing brain surgery instead of making his earliest attempts at playing the game.

"I have to admit that if this turns out to be his favorite sport it's from your genes. I never wanted anything to do with running. I was a tree climber."

Rob turned to her, his attention rapt. She still hadn't gotten used to his intensity in a civilian, downright family setting.

"You're still pretty good at climbing."

"Hey, keep it G-rated, mister." She slapped lightly at his upper arm, aware of the other parents checking them out. She was usually the lone single mother out here, with Nolan or one of her parents with her. Rob's good looks and graceful physicality drew attention wherever he went, and in Silver Valley word traveled quickly. She wasn't ready to explain exactly who Rob was in her life and what he meant to Jake. Not until Jake knew Rob was his father. Although their behavior lent itself well to the op, as an engaged couple.

"Relax. You care more than anyone else." To prove his point he nuzzled her shoulder, bared by her tank top. The summer heat did nothing to her compared to Rob's lips against her skin. He stood behind her and wrapped his arms loosely around her waist, waiting for her to let go and trust the moment.

They hadn't made love again, but their kisses were becoming more frantic as the weeks wore on. Part of her wished Jake already knew Rob was his father, and that maybe, just maybe, she and Rob could agree to give their relationship a fighting chance.

She leaned back so that he'd hear her as the parents around them cheered on their little tykes. "I'll let you get away with it this time. I trust you not to do anything too blatant."

Trust. The illusive criterion for her to even begin to consider a serious relationship with Rob, beyond sharing parenthood. In his arms under the softly falling twilight, with fireflies sparking and cicadas singing, it seemed possible.

Chapter 12

The day finally arrived for Trina and Rob to show up at Silver Valley Community Church for the Community Hands Up committee meeting, scheduled for ten in the morning. Even her mother didn't know she was doing this, and unless Carmen heard about it through the grapevine, Trina didn't see a need to tell her or her father. There would be too many questions, and her mother would get those three lines across her forehead that were mom-speak for "Trina's getting overextended again."

It was different for her to dress as a suburban fiancée. Conservative enough to appear responsible but with enough flair to not be boring. Because of the summer heat she decided on a floral sundress with a short-sleeved white cardigan and her favorite multicolored beaded sandals. She'd sent Jake up to her parents in

Williamsport, safely out of reach of what could become a dangerous mission in Silver Valley.

She and Rob had agreed to meet at TH headquarters first to read over any new intel reports before they headed out together to begin their first civilian mission. It was actually their second, but she didn't count the ROC chaos in the Poconos as it hadn't been planned.

Once at the headquarters building she made it inside, through several security devices that were biometric- as well as human-guarded, without trouble.

Rob stood in the middle of the entry foyer, looking as if he'd chosen his clothing with the same thoughts as her.

"Nice polo shirt."

Rob feigned hurt. "Hey, this is my favorite color." The rich butter yellow brought out his eyes, and she felt the familiar zip of sexual attraction. Familiar in that she associated this pounding heat with Rob. No other man had ever turned her on this easily, this effortlessly.

"It looks good on you. I'm only teasing."

"That's all right. You, by the way, look like a slice of heaven."

She looked around to see who could overhear his compliment, but the receptionist appeared engrossed in something on her computer screen and no one else was in hearing distance.

"Relax. We're supposed to be a couple, remember? I'm just getting prepped for it."

"Should we go to one of our offices to go over what we'll say?"

"Yes. Let's get some coffee first, if you don't mind. After you." He followed her and they went to the lavish kitchen area that looked like it belonged in an issue of *Architectural Digest*. While the office building itself was all straight lines and contemporary design, the break area looked like a French country kitchen. Claudia was heating up something in the microwave and smiled warmly as she recognized them.

"Hey you two. Good luck today."

"Thank you."

"Thanks, Claudia."

They spoke in unison, and Trina helped herself to the fresh brew, adding a good dollop of half-and-half to the black mug that had the Trail Hikers logo, a single pine tree with two hiking poles crossed over it, emblazoned in gold. Very subtle. No one would suspect they were anything but some kind of tourist agency related to the Appalachian Trail, which ran through Silver Valley.

"I look forward to your report." The microwave dinged and she took out a bowl of oatmeal, her hands protected by a kitchen towel.

"I'm surprised her assistant doesn't do that for her." Trina wouldn't have expected to see a former two-star general so at ease in the company break room.

"I'm not. She's very down-to-earth and practical. She wouldn't hesitate to ask her assistant to bring it to her if she were in the middle of an op or important meeting. But when she isn't, she fends for herself. With Claudia, the mission always comes first. Well, that and her employees."

"I picked up on that." Trina had the clear impression that Claudia would never ask her to participate in a mission she wasn't entirely comfortable with.

As they carried their coffees and two pastries back to Rob's desk, Trina realized that she'd missed this. The easy way they fell into working side by side. Being with a man who understood her and didn't think she was odd for having a lifelong desire to serve either in the military or law enforcement. The very few men she'd tried to date since Jake was born had been civilians and thought she'd want to "settle down" into a more "stable" job. What she'd wanted was a partner who'd accept her for who she was.

Rob always had, and even though he'd prefer she transition to a less dangerous position, he supported her in this op.

They started by reading the intelligence reports that had come in overnight via emails, courier delivery and texts. Trina almost dropped her cup of coffee when she read the worst news possible.

"Vasin escaped!" Quickly, she scanned the intelligence, absorbing that he'd gotten free while being transferred from one federal facility to another. Rob read the same information from his computer.

"ROC has endless money and contacts. That's the only way this happened." His mouth was grim, the lines around his eyes pronounced.

"Rob, he's not coming after us, is he?"

"He may be. Thank God you sent Jake to his grandparents."

The reality of their mission would have been frightening if Jake were still in Silver Valley. ROC's information network was far reaching, but they'd be hard-pressed to find out exactly where Jake was.

Rob was already on his phone. "I need complete attention to this." He gave her parents' address and described Jake. "I'll have his photo to you ASAP." He disconnected and looked at her. "Trail Hikers security group. They'll disperse agents immediately. We can't trust local or even federal LEA. There's a mole, probably more."

"Jake. I have to go be with him." She couldn't think of anything else but protecting her son.

"You can't, Trina. If Vasin's after us, and you go to your parents', you'll lead them right to Jake. The best thing you can do is work with me. Let's catch this bastard and save as many of the girls as we can."

She wiped a tear off her cheek. "You're right. I know Jake is safe, but this is different, isn't it?"

"We're in it together, babe. We'll be back with Jake and Renegade in no time. And you won't have to worry about Vasin." He reached for her hand, and she gave it to him, along with her trust. This would work out.

"At least we don't have worry about that silly dog." She forced a laugh, but really, she was grateful she'd thought to send the dog with Jake instead of putting him in a kennel, because Jake needed someone, something familiar to comfort him. If anything happened to her or Rob—

No. Don't go there.

"I, um, stopped by the department store on the way here." She shoved her hand in front of him, a fake diamond solitaire on her left ring finger. "This is to make our cover more solid." An unexpected well of sorrow overflowed from her regrets at what could have been, if Rob hadn't been hurt in the war, and she blinked rapidly, cursing her emotions in the midst of work.

Rob's free hand engulfed hers and infused her with warmth. "It's okay. I get it." His voice was huskier than normal and she peeked at him. His eyes held the same sadness as her heart. He regretted their past, too. But she also saw a twinkle.

Hope. A chance to heal.

"You do get it. Thank you." She sniffed and wiped her nose with a tissue from her purse.

Rob tapped the side of his mug.

"Okay, let's go over our plan one more time. We've got an hour until we have to be at the church, and it's only five minutes away." Rob placed his coffee on his desk and pulled out a chair for Trina to sit next to him. His computer was on a side table so they had a work-table between them, the surface spread with timelines and maps.

"I would have thought you'd be more into technology." She fingered one of the larger maps of Silver Valley.

"Old habits die hard. My SEAL training always emphasized that with an EMP detonation, we'd lose all of our comms. Hard copy is always a good backup."

"I agree." She still hadn't gotten into the habit of keeping notes on her phone as many of the newer, younger marshals did. A small notebook and pen were always in her purse or back pocket.

"We've picked the perfect time for this, as today is not only the welcome meeting but one of the days the outreach program goes both to the strip club for lunch, and the truck stop for dinner. We'll say we took the day off work to help find our church home, and since we've been looking at SVCC we wanted to participate in one of its charity groups."

"That's fair. My mom and dad like SVCC when they're in town. I don't go every Sunday, but I've been trying to attend more now that Jake's older." She steeled her resolve as she met his gaze.

"I'm okay with that, Trina. I like the idea of my son,

our son, having a familiar place to learn about something bigger than himself."

"You surprise me. When I met you, you were agnostic."

"And I may still be, but that doesn't mean I want my kid to be any less educated or experienced in a traditional way. What religion it is or isn't doesn't matter to me as much as he's learning right from wrong. Getting love from more than just his family. Kids only listen to parents so much, for so long."

"Did you attend church while you were in foster care?" She spoke quietly, as if her words risked cracking open his bad memories.

"Yeah, it was the one good thing that the bastard who was my foster father did. He let his wife take us to church. It was an escape from his brutality and a place to relax and play like a kid. I did the children's Sunday school and Vacation Bible School in the summers. As I got older I taught classes in both."

"You've never mentioned if your foster family wanted to adopt you."

"Are you kidding? Hell no. They wanted that regular check coming in from the government, and adopting me would end that."

"So you knew you were just a paycheck to them?" Her heart hurt at the thought of anyone treating Jake like that. Rob had made it against all odds.

"Yeah. And I wasn't stupid. I knew I was biding my time, too. Once I got too old for the old man to beat on me, because I'd grown taller than him, he continued with the verbal abuse. I knew they wanted the money my presence in their home brought each month, so I mouthed back to him. What was he going to do, kick me out? I spent very little time under their roof after I was fourteen or fifteen. It was a place to lay my head at night and claim as an address so that I could go to the public school in their district."

"I'm so sorry you went through that."

"Don't be. It's history." Rob ended further discussion, and she let it go.

As they went through their notes, Trina studied him. She didn't believe his childhood in foster care was all "history" for Rob. Not if he was so intent on saving underage girls. It was one of the reasons she loved him. His compassion and sense of justice.

Wait—had she just admitted she loved Rob?

Rob treasured that he didn't have to tell Trina what this mission meant to him. What a thrill the possibility of being able to rescue underage girls from their sordid life was. Not an adrenaline rush, though that was there. It was more a sense of complete justice, of knowing he was using what he'd learned from his own rough and tumble experiences to reach out and lift someone else up. Being able to share this work with Trina elevated it to more than work or an op; this was his life's calling.

He didn't want to scare her off with his deep thoughts—they were shaking him up enough.

"We didn't say if we're going to say we live together or are engaged." Rob casually wrapped his arm around her waist as they walked up to the church's community room entrance. He loved that she didn't move away or stiffen but relaxed into him. As if she, too, wanted this engagement to be more than an undercover op.

"Either one works. Maybe with Jake in the picture,

and since so many of these parishioners know my family, we should say engaged. To keep it looking serious."

"What will we tell them later, after the op?" He wanted her to want what he did.

Her spine stiffened, and now she moved away from him, stopping the middle of the walkway. Trina's eyes sparked with defensiveness. "Relationships end. It shouldn't be such a shock to anyone."

"They'll eventually find out I'm Jake's father. Everyone will."

"What do you want from me, Rob? Yes, everyone will know that you're Jake's father, but not until you and I tell him. We haven't even sat down with my family yet."

"I don't see why your family needs to be involved in this." He spoke too quickly and wished he could suck the words back in. "Trina, I don't mean they aren't important. You know me, it's my hang-up. I'm not used to having a family that cares so much about me."

"You're not used to family, period. If you'd been raised differently I doubt you'd have walked away from me and Jake five years ago without a word. You'd have used your brain to see that there was a good chance it was your kid."

Red-hot anger flared deep in his chest, and he wanted to lash out. Not at Trina—never at Trina—but at the world and life. He breathed in and out, counting backward from twenty before he replied.

"I deserve that. However, I can't do a damn thing to change my distant or recent past. I can only change today and going forward. You know what my plan is, Trina—I've made it clear that I'm not going anywhere. I'm here for Jake for the rest of my life."

Her stony expression eased a bit and he knew he'd cornered her, put her on the defensive by mentioning how his relationship with Jake was sacred to him. Again. No matter how frustrating it was for him to have to keep repeating his intentions, he had to remember that Trina had suffered the most of anyone in this hot mess. Jake hadn't missed what he didn't have, and Rob had known Trina was alive and well.

Trina had grieved his death, birthed their son and started her life over.

"You've got no reason to trust me ever again, Trina. And yet you're here, ready to put your life at risk to save the lives of innocent girls. I don't expect it to happen overnight, but if you could extend a little bit of the working trust we share to our personal relationship, it would be easier on both of us."

"That's fair." Her annoyance was clear in the lines around her mouth, but at least she didn't walk away or change her mind about working with him.

"Thank you."

"I know your childhood was messed up, but that doesn't mean I don't think you're a good father. You've already invested more in your son over the past month than a lot of dads do during an entire lifetime. And I'm not ignorant, either. I know that Jake could be a shiny new toy for you, one that you'll grow weary of putting all of your effort into. But that's not you. I do trust you, Rob. I'm just not very good at showing it."

Relief made him want to shout out loud "Yes!" Instead he held his hand out to her and smiled. "So we're engaged, huh?"

"Yes. And we'll celebrate later." Her eyes promised so much more than just making love. He pulled her to him and kissed her, needed her up against him, on top of him.

"Rob."

"Hmm?"

"We're in front of the church's main entrance."

Trina had never seen so many silver-haired ladies go gaga over a man before. Dimly she remembered her mother saying that the nursing home where her grandmother resided was full of fit, active women all vying for the affections of a very few senior men of equal ability. It had seemed foreign, nothing she needed to think about, until she saw Betty Laurel shove her sagging, albeit smooth for an octogenarian, cleavage under Rob's nose.

"Here you go, sugar. Sign this list for the committees you want to serve on. This one meets on Wednesdays, as you know. We have outreach to the homeless on Fridays, and the meals-on-wheels committee meets daily as necessary." Betty's heavily made-up eyes ate up the sight of Rob. Trina watched Rob handle the attention with aplomb, treating Betty and the other senior women as if they were his age and eligible.

He had them eating out of his palm.

Trina loved Rob's hands and his palms. Especially when they were on her breasts.

"Trina, honey, what made you decide to come in on this committee? I thought working for the Marshals would make you sick of helping out people, at least on your downtime." Mildred Maple sat next to her in the church cafeteria where on Sundays after services the congregation was treated to oversize doughnuts and hot soup.

"There's always more work to be done, right? And since Rob is interested in doing more for the community, I thought this was a good place to start."

"I'll bet your parents are thrilled that you're getting married."

"Oh, um, we've only just gotten engaged, and we're in no hurry."

"Why wait? Your little boy is so darling, and he's the perfect age to be a ring bearer."

Trina gave her a wobbly smile, but it was her best at the moment. Thankfully a woman on Mildred's other side started talking and distracted her from grilling Trina further.

A warm hand squeezed her thigh. "You handled that perfectly." Rob's mouth was next to her ear as he assured her they were blending in. The heat of his breath made her squeeze her legs together against the rush of awareness.

"How soon can we get to the bar?" she whispered back to him, breathing in the scent of his soap and shampoo. He grabbed her hand and held it between them, giving her another reassuring squeeze. She could get used to being supported like this. Mentally she counted the hours until they'd be done with the outreach tonight. It was the perfect night to show Rob exactly how much her trust in him had grown.

The man who'd greeted them at the door, Carl, stood up in front of the almost dozen people gathered and clapped his hands smartly, twice. "Okay, folks! I see our two newest members—welcome. As a brief reminder, not all of our efforts have been successful, so when we're allowed in one it's on us to be polite and professional to all we meet. The owner of the local club doesn't have a problem with us being there, for now, because he wants to give the appearance of being above the law and not tied into any illegal actions. Another reminder—we are not law enforcement or vigilantes. If you see anything troubling, wait until we're out of there and then tell me. I'll report it to SVPD or go with you as you report it. Unless it's an emergency situation, of course." Carl made it a point to make eye contact with each volunteer. "Let's get going. Mary is going to run down who's assigned to which station today, and then we'll drive to the bar. Anyone in need of a ride, please join us in the church van. I'm driving." The ladies all chuckled, sharing some inside joke.

"Will there be room in your car?" Mildred leaned so far in front of Trina to see around to Rob that Trina imagined poking her with her index finger, just to see if she'd topple.

"I'm sorry, but Trina and I have to get Jake from camp right afterward, so we'll drive on our own."

"Well, phooey. I'll take the van, I guess."

Trina walked over to Rob, who stood at the assignment table. "We've got the dessert spread."

"Sounds good." She slipped her hand into his, cozying up next to him like a good fiancée.

"Anyone ever tell you that you could make it on the stage?" His murmur was low and urgent.

"I'm not a good actor, FYI."

Trina had been inside the strip bar twice since working the Harrisburg office, and it hadn't changed. There was new carpet in the front lounge and it was very quiet, since it was a weekday before opening time.

"Does this place usually draw a big crowd?" Rob

took the tray of cookies and placed them at the edge of the table, next to a pile of smaller paper plates and napkins.

"When I've made my apprehensions here it's been booming. The music's so loud, it's like a rock concert. There are always at least half a dozen girls on the stage." And probably more in the back, doing private dances. But she hadn't been interested in that when she'd come in, as she'd had specific people to arrest.

"I'd like nothing more than to bring the bastards down who would even think about putting an underage girl in here." Rob's growl was louder than the crunch of her bite into a particularly good snickerdoodle cookie.

"I agree. I love what I do for the Marshals, but I've often thought I wouldn't mind doing something a little different."

"Trust me, if you stay in TH long enough, you'll do a lot of different things."

"Better be quiet." She smiled as Carl approached their table. "Hi, Carl. We're all ready!"

"Okey-dokey. The women will start coming in over the next twenty minutes. Some days we get no more than two or three who are willing to grab a bite—other days we've had as many as twenty. And not all are trafficked, or here illegally. Some are legit, and enjoy the meals and goodie bags just as much."

"That's a lot of employees for one bar." Rob shook his head, playing the suburban fiancé to a T.

"What did you say you do, Rob?" Carl knew Trina's parents and they'd met on occasion, so he knew what she did. Everyone at SVCC did, it seemed, so she'd had to play up her desire to do community service more than she'd expected. For some reason they all thought her job was enough. She had a hard time making the correlation. She was a US marshal, not a minister or physician. Those were professions that she admired.

"I'm actually between jobs at the moment. I was in the Navy, and have worked law enforcement. I'm looking into a few options locally." Rob's sincerity wasn't an act. And for some reason Trina didn't think he was talking about Trail Hikers.

"What's your passion?" Carl got to the point, that was for sure. Trina had noted that seniors tended to do this. As if small talk was a luxury of youth.

"At-risk youth."

"No kidding! My son's a counselor at Silver Valley High School." As the two compared notes, she was shocked to hear Rob state that not only did he know Carl's son but he'd worked with him when he'd volunteered at the school.

The men finished up their conversation, and Carl turned back to Trina. "Keep the smiles coming for these girls. I really think that this is the best meal of the week for a lot of them." He rapped his knuckles on the front of the table.

"Will do." She waited for him to be out of earshot. "What the hell, Rob? You never mentioned this before. Did you make that up? Because if you did, Carl is going to find out. He's probably texting his son right now."

"And he'll verify that we've worked together." Rob's enigmatic smile unnerved her.

"I don't get it." She'd pictured him as solely an undercover agent.

"I've gotten my Master of Social Work degree over the last five years, mostly at night and online. I had to finagle it here and there between the course load and my ops, but it's worked out. You were briefed by Claudia about how all Trail Hikers need a real, solid job outside of these ops, right?"

"Well, yes, she said my position as a marshal was ideal, as it was the perfect job and cover to dovetail with my work as a TH." Realization dawned. "So you're really settling down here?"

"I was going to do everything on a temporary basis until I saw you again. Now that I know about Jake, it makes sense that I make Silver Valley my home base. I still have a condo in Arlington that I'm renting out for now. I could opt to sell it or use it as a pied-à-terre, depending upon how the workload goes here."

"How do you justify your absences to the kids you help? To Carl's son and the other counselors?" The Silver Valley school district was large, encompassing several elementary schools, two middle schools, and one of the largest public high schools in the state.

"They think I'm still on reserve duty in the Navy. I've told the school that I could be called to active duty at any time due to my skill set. And that's not entirely untrue, as TH calls me in when I'm needed."

Rob watched Trina absorb the information that he'd earned his degree and was already putting down semi-permanent roots in Silver Valley. And the funny thing was that as he explained his status to Carl, he hadn't been just answering the elder's question. He'd been serious. With all of the attention on first the ROC op and then getting know Jake this past month, he'd never told Trina what else he did. She'd assumed all he did was work Trail Hikers ops, and he allowed her to. He still hadn't taken her to the apartment he rented, as they spent their time mostly at her place. Where Jake was.

"I meant to tell you sooner, Trina, but I didn't want to put any extra pressure on us, or on our start of parenting together. It wasn't important."

"Not important? You figuring out what you want to do with your life is incredibly important." She fidgeted with the edge of the tablecloth. The sunshine-yellow plastic looked out of place in the dark strip club. Rob had the urge to grab Trina and haul her out of here.

His protective instincts had been on overdrive since meeting Jake.

Baloney. It's about Trina and Jake. Your family.

"Yeah, well, it came in bits and pieces. I don't even have an income from it yet. What I'm thinking about is opening up my own office and getting a contract with local government and mostly the schools. I want to provide a sanctuary for the kids who don't have the safety net they need."

"I think that's wonderful, Rob." Her words didn't match her disconcerted expression.

"But?"

She shook her head. "No 'but.' This explains why you've been so great with Jake. Why you've given me time and space to let you in as his father. You're a professional."

That stung.

"Whoa—I'm not a professional dad. My relationship with Jake is from the heart."

"I know." Quiet, a small smile. Had he destroyed her trust again by not telling her sooner about his social work? She placed her hand on his. "It's okay. I know why you didn't tell me. You said so yourself. It would have spooked me."

"Babe, I'm here. And as much as I enjoy getting a rise out of you, I'd never do anything to betray you, Jake or this." He motioned at her, then him.

"About that, Rob." Oh God, she was going to tell him to forget it all. That his relationship was going to be with Jake only.

"Go ahead."

"I've been thinking...you know Jake is in Williamsport with my folks, and we won't be at the truck stop all night." Hope flickered again as he watched her lick her full, rosy red lips. "I think it's time we had an adult sleepover."

Rob's expression went from wary to hungry in an instant. It wasn't hunger for a meal, but for her.

"Trina, are you sure? Because I'm willing to wait as long as I need to."

"I know you are. But I'm not."

She stared at him a heartbeat longer before a movement in her peripheral vision drew her attention. "First girl, dressed to look about seventeen years old, your six o'clock." She used the analog clock face as a reference to indicate that one of the dancers was behind Rob.

"Roger." He replied quietly and slid into the chair next to Trina so that he could have the same view. "She looks a lot younger, more like fourteen."

"And she probably is." Compassion tugged, but Trina shut that part of her heart down. If she was to save any of these girls, she had to be a professional first.

The girl approached the dessert table, reinforcing

their assessment of her age. Younger teens often had a bigger sweet tooth.

"Hi, I'm Trina. Please help yourself to whatever you want."

Her eyes were pale blue against a porcelain complexion. She was slight and petite, her movements jerky as she took three cookies off the plate.

"Thanks." She didn't make eye contact, and Trina recognized a heavy Russian accent.

"Do you speak Russian?" Trina gave her a chipper smile, and began to explain, in that language, that she was studying it and always needed more practice. She introduced Rob as her fiancé and said that he was trying to learn but wasn't so good at it.

Rob glared at her and the young woman laughed.

"What's your name?" Rob asked in English. Trina stifled her giggle. Rob was fluent in Russian.

"Stacia." Trina would bet her full name was Anastasia but didn't press her luck. The girl was talking; that was enough for now.

"It's so nice to meet you, Stacia." Both she and Rob held out their hands and Stacia shyly shook them. "Do you live around here?"

She shook her head, then drifted over to the sandwich table with no further conversation.

"Smooth," Rob teased her, and she bit her cheek.

"I messed that up."

"Relax. There's still the truck stop."

As several more women came by to eat and pick up the goodie bags filled with toiletries, healthy snacks, local restaurant and grocery gift certificates, Trina refrained from asking any deep questions. She could kick herself for such a rookie mistake with Stacia but then it was only their first day, their first time with this group of ladies. And as her experience with the Marshals and training from TH taught her, nothing happened as quickly as she wanted it to. Patience was the key character attribute of any law enforcement officer.

But there were lives at stake here. She was certain the girls had been told that they'd be hurt or killed if they talked about how they got here.

After lunchtime ended, Rob placed his hand on her shoulder. "Have you stopped beating yourself up yet?"

"Never."

He said nothing as he regarded her. God, she loved how he looked at her. "We have a few hours before we're due at the truck stop."

She consolidated the remaining cookies onto one dish and stacked the empty plates as she waited for him to catch her vibe.

"As in we have your house to ourselves for the afternoon?"

"As in it's time for an adult sleepover."

Rob leaned in and gave her a quick kiss on her lips. Chaste for the church crowd, but the contact heated her as much as any kiss from Rob did.

"I'll bring the popcorn."

The drive back to Trina's passed in a blur. When Rob pulled up to her front porch, she turned to him. "This doesn't have to mean everything to you, Rob, but I want you to know that it can. Mean everything. If you want it to."

"Get out of the car, Trina." He couldn't answer her, because he couldn't look at her. It was the same as it was in the Poconos at Camp Serenity, the way his need for her shook him to his core. But it wasn't the same at all. That had been closure on their old days.

This was their beginning.

Trina said nothing more, but he knew she was as juiced as he was by the pink color on her cheeks and how her chest rose and fell in ragged, quick motions. As she unlocked the door, he was so close to her he felt the heat of her body along his front. The door spilled open and he'd never been so grateful he'd seen the inside of her house already. He used his foot to slam her door shut and immediately pulled her back up against him, his arms reaching around her front.

"Rob, God." She reached above and behind her to grab his head, and he kissed her from behind as his hands held her breasts. Her nipples pressed against his palms through her sundress, and it felt like his head would explode if not for the grip of her hands in his hair. Their tongues fought, lapped, twisted together as their bodies wanted to. As their souls always had.

"Trina, your room. Now."

"No." She took the two steps to the back of her sofa. "Here. Now." As she playfully repeated his request, she looked over her shoulder at him. She'd hitched up her skirt, revealing black lace thong panties. Her ass, her beautiful ass, drove him mad. But nothing did more to him than the look of pure desire in her eyes. The impish grin.

"Those panties aren't made for church, Trina." He reveled in her gasps as he pushed the scrap of fabric away and quickly tore open the condom packet he'd had enough foresight to shove into his front pocket. As soon as he'd unzipped and donned the protection, he touched the small of her back. "Are you sure?"

"Always. *Now*, Bristol."

Rob didn't need to be told twice. Trina was wet and open for him, and he plunged into her, his hands on her hips, pure sensation rocking him with each pump. He saw her hands as they gripped the back of the sofa, saw her head swing around to encourage him.

"Faster, Rob. Faster."

He wished it could last forever, but knew he'd always remember the flush on her face, the smoothness of her ass, the pure connection between them. Trina's moans grew deeper, and she let out an ecstatic scream just as he went rigid and his own release quaked through him. She kept pulsing around him until every last nuance of his orgasm faded.

He bent over her back, mirroring her position on the sofa but not wanting to crush her with his weight.

"You're beautiful."

"Mmm. I could get used to this." Trina moved to stand up, and he backed away, not ready for their "adult sleepover" to end. She turned and faced him. "Don't look so sad, Rob." She looked at her watch. "We've still got two more hours."

Trina stood under the shower and allowed the water to massage her shoulders. She and Rob had made love two more times since they'd gone at it like animals on the sofa. Soaping herself up, she laughed.

"What's so funny?" Rob stepped into the shower and took the bar of soap from her, lathering her back.

"We were like two rabbits when we came in."

His deep chuckle filled the space. "More like dogs, if you ask me."

"Do you think it'll always be like this with us?" His hands stilled. She'd surprised him.

"I hope so, Trina. I'm counting on it."

Chapter 13

It was hot and muggy at the truck stop the next week, when Trina got the call from Carl, the ministry leader, that she and Rob were needed again. The stop's owner allowed them to set up outside the main entrance, off to the side. The tables were away from the larger throngs of motor travelers coming in and out of the combination fast-food/convenience store/coffee shop establishment. Trina did a quick walk-through of the building, re-familiarizing herself with all entrances. There were full showers and lockers in the back for the truckers, all rentals. When she was done, she sat down at one of the outreach tables.

"I'm thinking I should pose as a trucker and go hang out in the shower. Don't you think there'd be conversations to overhear?" Rob spoke as yet another eighteen-wheeler drove into the huge lot, pulling parallel with another humongous trailer truck. It had freshly painted fruits and vegetables on the side of its trailer, with a popular grocery chain's name painted over the images. At least three dozen trucks with connected trailers were parked in parallel, making the parking lot look more like a village.

"I think that the women who come here to turn tricks do it inside the truck cabs, or even outside in the woods over there. Less chance of being caught, and if the cops show up the trucker can always say he knows the woman. You might overhear something else, though, that could help us track the girls." Evidence that would put Vasin and Ivanov behind bars for good, once they caught them. If Trina had anything to do with it, she'd see Vasin in cuffs right now. It still chafed that he'd sprung free.

"There are female truckers, too, you know." Rob poked fun at her, and she smiled.

"I do know. And yes, I know that some of them indulge in the sexual market as well. We'll just have to keep our eyes and ears open. And if we're very lucky, we'll get a break sooner rather than later." She forced her gaze on the lot, away from Rob's handsome face. They'd have their sexy time later. The anticipation simmered between them.

"Where did Carl go?" Rob strained his neck to see past the trucks and highway traffic that routed into the station.

"He said something about needing coffee." She shooed away a yellow jacket, intent on the sugary treats that were now individually wrapped in plastic instead of being on open display.

"It's been twenty minutes." Rob looked agitated.

"Go check on him if you want. I'll be fine."

"Text me with anything odd." His voice was stern as he stood up. "Do you want coffee or tea, a soda?"

"No, I'm good. Thanks, though." She kept scouring the area in between the trailers.

"I'll be back out in a minute." He walked off, and Trina allowed herself the pleasure of taking in his form, his shape, his butt. This was so easy, falling into working with Rob again.

And she'd fallen in love with him as he was today.

As much as her heart sang at the thought of being with him as a lover and maybe more, her brain existed for a good reason. To keep her heart from breaking into an infinite number of shards again. Because no matter how much she wanted to believe Rob was here for the duration, for the hard times as well as good with his newfound son, she couldn't shake the deeper worry that something awful would take him away again.

Rob stood in the bathroom at the sink and washed his hands. He'd had to force himself to stay here, wait for a chance to listen in on the truckers' conversations. He was in a hurry to get back outside to the table, to the outreach post, to a chance to break the trade that had insinuated its way into what had to be the nicest slice of small-town America he'd ever had the chance to experience. He saw someone walk in and pretended to be examining his face.

Who are you kidding, man?

Aw, hell. It was *all* about Trina. Trina made everything more exciting, the colors of the Appalachian Mountains a deeper green, the contrast of postthunderstorm steam a smokier blue. He heard the sound of footsteps from the shower area and ducked his head. With a ball cap on he looked like any other trucker or fast-food customer.

"See anything yet?" The guttural Russian came from a corner of the wide room, past the stalls, near the showers. Rob froze. *Vasin.*

"Two of our girls are out there. I verified."

How the hell had they verified?

"Stupid bitches don't know enough to cover their ink."

"They're the two we delivered to the club? And we allow to live with the others in the apartment? And they're trying to two-time it?" Rob heard the indignation at what ROC would consider a blasphemous act. They usually kept their working girls separate—a group for the club, and a group for the truck stop. And he'd bet a dozen women were living in one squalid apartment, the cheapest available. He wondered if the women had somehow gotten together, because it sounded like the criminals were being outsmarted.

"They forget about the tattoos that show they're ours."

"They are crazy to think we wouldn't figure out what they're doing."

Ah. Tattoos. And Rob thought the Russian mobsters were the stupid ones, assuming no one would be able to understand them. They sounded angry, though, and that meant danger for the two girls who were no doubt trying to make extra money on their terms so that they could escape their life at the club. They weren't the first to attempt it, from the reports he'd read.

"Do we grab them now, or at the club later?"

"Later. Monitor the situation and make sure we have names."

"I don't know their names. Not all of them." Rob thought he knew that voice, too—

Minsky. There were two of them, then. Manageable. He wasted no time on wondering how Vasin's number two henchman was here when he was supposed to be in jail. The intel reports had said Vasin was free but didn't mention Minsky, so he'd probably never been caught the other day. Both men would recognize him, so Rob quickly entered a stall and shut the door. It cut against his instinct to linger in the restroom. He wanted to be out in the parking lot with Trina. Of course Trina could handle herself and any jerks who came along, but it didn't stop his protectiveness from clanging alarm bells.

"They used to be good girls. Did their jobs. Got regular jobs later. Now everyone wants to save all the victims." Minsky's sneer when he said "victims" pretty much summed up the attitude of ROC toward any suffering on the part of their captives. For ROC, it was all about the bottom line. Cash trumped women trafficked for sex, as well as the fates of the inner cities where their smuggled weapons and drugs were sold. Anger simmered in Rob. Vasin's operations had reached its venomous tentacles into Silver Valley. The town where the mother of his child had chosen to raise their son.

He couldn't act yet, though. It was best to wait out these two ROC bad guys and catch them in the act of trying to kidnap the girls again, or as they assaulted them at the club, arrest them on the spot. As soon as he heard them depart through the shower room, he left the restroom and made a beeline for the exit. Trina was still out at their spot, and he wasn't about to trust the other couple from church with her safety.

Rob had to know Trina was safe.

"How many women actually trust us enough to take some of the food?" Trina spoke to Binnie and Chuck, the seniors who were pulling the outreach shift with her and Rob. Carl had stopped by earlier to check on things but left the evening shift to his fellow church goers.

"They never come up to me if Binnie has to run into the restroom, or get a snack." Chuck looked bewildered, as if he took it personally.

"That's because they're scared, sweetie." Binnie patted her husband's knee and lowered her voice for Trina. "He forgets his hearing aids and then shouts and it scares the truckers, let alone the ladies. It's no wonder they won't come up to him."

Trina loved this couple, and she only knew them peripherally from Silver Valley Community Church. She liked to think it was how she'd be with her partner one day. Two peas in a pod.

"Where's your young fellow?" Chuck leaned around his wife, speaking in a modulated tone as if to deny what Binnie had just said.

"He went in to get something to drink." Trina noticed a movement out of the corner of her eye and turned to see two young women approach the table. They walked with their heads down, eyes averted from Trina but definitely focused on the sandwiches in wax paper and the plastic-wrapped baked goods.

"Help yourselves. Our volunteers baked the goodies and the truck stop provides the sandwiches." Trina spoke up.

They said nothing but each took a sandwich and a couple of cookies.

"Thanks." The mumbled word was accented and Trina instinctively knew it was Russian.

"Are you thirsty? There's cold soda and water here." She opened the cover of the cooler that the truck stop filled with donated ice and beverages.

As the women bent over the cooler and reached in for their drink, Trina saw that one of them whose hair was pulled back in a high ponytail had a tattoo of what looked like a crescent moon. The symbol was just behind her left ear. The girl straightened quickly and met Trina's eyes. *Caught.*

"Nice tat." Trina kept it easy, not wanting to spook them. Drawing out a potential witness wasn't easy and required the patience of someone far saintlier than her, but she had to give it a try.

"She likes my sickle." The girl spoke in rapid-fire Russian to the other girl. A *sickle*. Of course. Not the moon. Was it a symbol of their native land for them? That didn't make sense, not when Ukraine had split from the former Soviet Union. The girls had all been shipped in from Ukraine, if the Trail Hikers intelligence reports were accurate. ROC had branded them with these tattoos.

Trina played ignorant, tilted her head in interest. "It's a crescent moon, right? I love anything to do with the sun, stars or moon."

"I have one, too." The second girl spoke better English and lifted the fall of her black hair to show Trina her tattoo. This time Trina made out the thin hammer that sliced through the sickle's center. It had to be linked to ROC. There were so many tattoos with each factor of the criminal organization that she didn't have a chance to know all of them.

"Are you sisters or best friends? Is that why you have the same tattoo?" Trina silently prayed they'd open up. She noticed that Binnie and Chuck were being quiet, watching her interaction.

Both girls laughed. Not the silly adolescent giggles they deserved to enjoy but harsh barks that only the jaded were capable of.

"Tell her we're sisters. It's okay." Again, the quick Russian meant to be under the radar.

"Oxana and I are sisters, all right." The young woman rolled her eyes. "I have to keep her out of trouble."

"What's your name? I'm Trina, by the way."

"Ekaterina."

"That's so similar to my name, you know." Trina saw they were losing interest as their eyes shifted past her and back over their shoulders toward the long row of trucks parked for either a short rest or the night. Trina imagined it didn't matter how long any of the truckers were here as the women made their money and moved on to the next client. It was almost hard to believe something so dark and lurid went on in the truck cabins as the blaze of the summer sunset in Silver Valley lit up the sky with fuchsia and lavender streaks.

Keep them talking.

She opened her mouth to ask where they were from, in a very open, curious American way. She saw Oxana's mouth drop open at the same time she dropped her food onto the gravel lot and screamed.

Trina twisted to see two burly men bearing down on the young women, their faces intent.

"Come now. No fight or you will regret it." The taller

of the two men spoke in Russian. Their faces were obscured by the brims of their hats, but Trina knew the voice of the man she'd failed to apprehend in the Poconos. *Vasin.*

The men were only strides from the girls. Trina was certain they were underage, and since they each had the tattoos that might indicate the gang who'd sold them, she wasn't about to watch them be taken in by ROC.

"Call the police." She spoke directly to Binnie and Chuck before she leaped over the table and ran after the group of four. The girls bolted for the safety of the parked trucks, which would give them a place to hide and stall their attackers. The men were fast for being so beefy, and they ran right behind the girls, their dark shoes spitting up gravel. Trina closed in on them, fists pumping. As the girls slid between two long trailers, the men heard Trina and stopped in their tracks. She saw them each reach for a weapon—one a pistol, the other a knife—as they turned around to face her.

Adrenaline pumped through her, and she sucked in deep breaths to stay steady, focused. As long as these brutes were looking at her, the girls had a fighting chance to get away.

Rob walked out to the outreach table, and when he saw Trina's empty seat, Chuck and Binnie excitedly moving their arms, and Binnie with a cell phone to her ear, his stomach lurched.

"She went that way! Two men are chasing the girls!" Chuck's septuagenarian voice was surprisingly strong.

"Have you called the police?"

"Yes. Go get her!" Chuck's concern was palpable.

And more justified than he could imagine. Rob ran

out into the lot that served as the truck rest stop and saw Trina's slim figure standing approximately two hundred yards away, her legs in a wide stance and her arms up in front of her. She aimed her pistol at Vasin and Minsky, as Rob would expect. Trina was a warrior.

What made his mental warning alarm clamor like an air raid siren was the sight of each man holding a lethal weapon. Vasin held a Beretta in one hand, shouting something Rob couldn't hear over the continuous purr of the parked trucks as they ran air-conditioning in the summer heat. Minsky held a blade, its surface reflecting the streetlamps that had begun to flicker in the waning light.

Rob had seconds to figure out how to save Trina's life. Because while she'd had the Trail Hikers indoc, Trina was at heart a US marshal. She wasn't going to go home until she had these criminals in cuffs. She'd never cut her losses and run away.

The rumble of a Mack truck engine broke through his concentration, and he ran in front of an eighteen-wheeler preparing to leave the rest area. He waved his arms and flashed a badge—also that of a US marshal, like Trina's, as it made a great front for both of them as they worked as undercover Trail Hikers. The truck's brakes engaged with a hydraulic groan and the cab lurched to a stop. Wasting no time, Rob reached up and opened the driver's door. "US marshal. I need your vehicle. Please get out."

"What about my dog?" The female driver pointed to a large pit bull in the passenger seat.

"He friendly?"

"If I tell him to be." She grinned.

"Best take him with you." Rob didn't want to put any civilians at risk, human or canine.

"You're going for those jerks messing with that woman over there? Keep Rosie with you. In case you need backup." The woman slid out of the seat and Rob jumped in.

"Clear the area, ma'am." The woman backed away from the rig, her eyes wary as she probably just realized she'd given a supposed US marshal her superb piece of machinery, her entire livelihood. As well as her dog.

Rob slammed the door shut and immediately shifted into gear, turning the wheel to be able to bear down on the trio of armed adversaries. "Hang on, Rosie." The dog let out an enthusiastic bark from the passenger seat.

His hands gripped the wheel and he drove straight ahead, picking up speed but retaining control. But no matter how controlled, how well executed, the next several seconds were, he couldn't escape the reality of what was at stake. One wrong move and Trina would be dead.

Trina heard the motor approach and didn't flinch. She needed only a split second, maybe one full heartbeat, of distraction on the part of these losers. The full beam of headlights hit the eyes of the guy holding the knife, and when he squinted she quickly kicked the knife out of his hand. He swore in Russian, bent over and cradling the hand she'd made contact with. She turned and aimed her weapon at Vasin.

"Drop your weapon or you're both dead." She'd take out Vasin first, since he still held his pistol, but she was prepared to shoot his accomplice, too, if need be.

Vasin grinned malevolently before he turned and took off between the rows of distribution trucks. Trina couldn't risk a shot with so many civilians around and the possibility of a bullet ricocheting into a trailer or worse, an occupied cab. The majority of the cabs were sleepers, and the drivers slept on bunks in the back. Vasin knew this, of course. She'd have to secure the knife dude and then go after Vasin.

"Stand up. Turn around." The thug grunted at her but didn't move from his hunched position. Familiar steps on the gravel behind her were followed by a sense of security she'd never experienced once she saw their source.

Rob.

"You heard her. Turn around and put your hands up. I will shoot."

The thug lifted his arms and turned. Trina went cuffed him. He swore in Russian that she was hurting him.

"Stop being so melodramatic." She pushed him toward the front of the lot, away from the trucks.

"That's right, Minsky. Get ready to dish it all to the cops. As you can see, Vasin didn't hang around to save you, did he?" Rob said in Russian.

The high pitch of sirens filled the night as several SVPD vehicles arrived on scene, followed by an ambulance.

She looked at Rob. "I had Binnie and Chuck call them in." She wished they'd be able to get all the girls out of the club, off the streets, safe from the horrors of a trafficked life. But that was a job, on a more regular basis, for other law enforcement agency like FBI and ICE. Trina was grateful to help even two of the girls. She secretly hoped she'd be asked to help rescue more of the women, though. Maybe TH would call her to.

"Good work. You want to read him his rights?"

"No." She nodded at a Silver Valley PD officer who approached. "Hey, Nika. I've got this guy cuffed, and he needs his rights read."

"Sure thing, Trina." Trina had worked with Officer Nika Pasczenko on a few cases, and they'd hit it off. Nika had promised to take her and Jake kayaking now that Trina lived in Silver Valley.

She walked over to Rob, who was briefing Chief Todd. The chief assessed her with sharp eyes. "You okay, Marshal Lopez?"

"Yes, thanks. I appreciate your officers coming in and cleaning up. There's still one on the loose, and I have no idea where the girls went. I'm going to search the trailer lot now."

Colt nodded. He was fully briefed on all TH ops in the area that could involve his department, so he didn't ask any questions. He knew the deal—all TH ops were need-to-know only. And a lot of his officers had no idea about the Trail Hikers' existence, so it wasn't something they could discuss in such a public place.

"You'll get it done, you two." As the chief walked away, Trina looked at Rob. And it hit her that she would do whatever it took to keep him here with her. Behind her. Having her back.

Even risk her heart. Again.

"We're going to need to split up." At his shocked expression, she quickly added, "No, not us. I mean break the surveillance of the lot up amongst all of the LEA here, including us."

"Right." Relief registered on his face before he said more. "As much as I hate it, you're correct. I'll stay out here, in the truck I just drove. I'm sure the owner won't mind if I tell her it's for everyone's safety. You head toward the rear of the lot. We'll have a better chance if we can see two levels of activity." Rob's response reassured her. Everything about him, about them as a couple, as Jake's parents, made sense to her.

"What?" Rob must have seen what was in her heart.

"I love you, Rob."

"I know. I love you, too." He pulled her against him at the same moment she lunged for him. The kiss was hard and fast, the promise of their future in the warmth of his lips on hers. He lifted his head a half inch. "Now let's go get the bad guy."

When he let her go he swatted her butt, and Trina smiled.

They'd survive this and they'd go back home. Together.

Trina waited in the field beyond the paved lot, no more than a hundred feet from where the nearest trailer rested. It seemed peaceful, the hum of the engines to support the electrical systems in the truck cabs, the vast majority of which were privately owned and came complete with bunks behind the seats, where the truckers took their overnights. In the ninety-degree night, air-conditioning was a must. It was a safety precaution, too, as the truckers had to keep their windows up and doors locked while they slept. Many had dogs, like the woman Rob had borrowed the truck from. That had been brilliant on his part. Trina wondered if she would have thought that quickly. She was a well-trained and experienced marshal, but still a newbie as far as the Trail Hikers went.

She'd grabbed a pair of night-vision goggles from

Nika and used them to check underneath the trailers, between the large truck tires. A slight movement caught her attention, near a large fuel trailer. The cylindrical carrier had pulled in within the last few minutes and parked on the far edge of the lot, nearest to her. As she watched, the driver seemed to drop from view. One second he'd been sitting behind the wheel of his cab; the next the spot looked vacant. As she watched, her heart hammered in her chest; her instincts told her to run to the truck and see what was going on. Her training made her wait. It paid off when she identified the silhouette of one woman, and then another, as they climbed into the truck cab. They each disappeared, and one more figure appeared in the driver's seat.

Vasin.

Trina spoke to Rob on her headset, standard gear that she carried in a small fanny pack, as she ran in, weapon drawn. "It's him. He's got the two girls who stopped for food in the oil tanker on the far side of the parking lot. I think he may have shot the driver."

"Do not go in alone. I'm driving around." She saw the headlights of the truck Rob drove in the distance, saw the truck move toward her.

"I'll wait for you." She ran to the back of the oil carrier, careful to stay low and out of the reflection of the rearview mirrors. To her dismay the truck began to move.

No, no, no! She ran faster, and calculated how many tires she'd have to blow out to stop it. *Impossible.*

The truck increased speed too quickly. Vasin was getting the hell out. No way was Trina going to let him get away with this. The girls had to be scared out of their minds. They couldn't defend themselves, not against Vasin's physicality or his weapon.

Vasin put the vehicle into the wide turn it needed to leave the truck stop and head out onto the main highway. Trina didn't think but instead relied on pure instinct. She shoved her weapon into its holster as she ran. She closed the distance between herself and the back of the tanker, willing her legs to move faster, faster. As she came within an arm's reach, she tried to grab for the ladder that went to the top of the round end, but the truck was picking up speed, widening the distance between rescuing the girls and their certain death.

A mental image of what Vasin would do to the girls flashed in front of her, and she dug deep, reached for the last of her reserves.

Instead of putting her arm out to catch the truck, she jumped. Her palms slammed against the steel rung and instinctively gripped, holding her to the back of the rapidly accelerating truck. Trina couldn't risk looking over her shoulder to see if Rob knew what was happening. Her entire mission was to get to the truck's cab and take out Vasin before he hurt the girls.

Rob thought if hearts could rupture, his would at the sight of Trina hanging on to the back of the fuel tank, her body no more that a third the height of the trailer. He worked his truck's gears, grateful that Rosie had gone with her owner this time. His gut told him this was going to get ugly.

"Trina, hang on. Do not climb that tanker."

"Too. Late." He heard her breathing deepen as he trailed behind Vasin and saw her ascend the narrow ladder. There were overpasses and bridges and umpteen other ways she could be killed while traversing the fuel tanker. And he was powerless to stop her.

"Talk to me, babe." He had to hear what she was thinking.

"I'll get him to stop. If you take him out, I can drive the truck." She'd been trained to operate heavy machinery and trucks just as he had. He'd learned a lot of it in the SEALs and knew that Trail Hikers covered it, too.

"It's too dangerous to fire a weapon. The fuel."

"Gas. I just read the label on the side." Her voice was strong, but the wind interfered with their comms. He had to strain to pick out her words.

"Get in the cab and stop him if you can, Trina." Rob wanted to scream. No, not scream. He wanted to get Trina and take them far away. Where they could live safely with Jake. Nothing else mattered.

"Damn it!" He knew it was his primal resistance flaring, knew that he'd complete this mission to the best of his ability. But he didn't know if he'd survive, or worse, if Trina would. He'd never stared into such desolation.

Trina made it up to the cabin. This was a fancy rig, complete with a sunroof over the sleeping compartment. She looked into the back of the cabin through the glass and saw Oxana and Ekaterina, huddled together. It wasn't easy hanging on to the top of the cab. She preferred the ladder. At least the rungs were sturdy. The slippery top of the cab was nothing but treacherous. But this was also the only way she'd save them.

She pounded on the window twice and the girls looked up, their faces full of fear. A shot rang out and she realized that Vasin had heard her, too. He was shooting at her from the driver's-side window. No concern about the probability of nine thousand gallons of liquid natural gas behind him. Trina had to get the girls out. She clung to the top of the cab, flattening herself against it as they neared another overpass. The three they'd already cleared had been so close, so tight a fit that she'd thought she was dead. This was no different. She looked up after her ears popped from the harrowing passage and saw where Vasin was headed. Silver Valley View Road.

Vasin turned the gas rig onto the four-lane country route, and Rob knew it was now or never. He had to draw alongside the tanker or he'd never catch up in time to make a difference. The road had wide enough shoulders for other vehicles to use as needed. Thankfully it looked clear for the next mile or so.

It was all he'd need. He engaged his engine full throttle and eased into the left lane. Vasin immediately tried to edge him off the road, but Rob's truck was more maneuverable that the huge can of gas. Within thirty seconds he was parallel with Vasin's cab, and was rewarded by a bullet shattering his passenger-side window.

Rob had ducked, anticipating the shot. When he risked another look, Vasin appeared to be distracted, and the criminal fired a shot into the air. Trying to get to Trina. Rob kept one eye on the road and one on Vasin. He had to keep his truck in the right position. He had to trust Trina that she'd paid attention during the moving vehicle portion of her Trail Hikers training, when she learned how to keep her balance while atop a truck going sixty miles an hour. Except at Trail Hikers they never practiced with trucks going faster than thirty miles an hour.

* * *

Trina saw Rob's cab, and her training kicked in. All she had to do was get the girls over to his truck. They'd hang on until he stopped the trailer. She motioned at them through the window to break the glass and follow her, glad that at least she didn't have to worry about overpasses on the country road. But the frequent hills made keeping her balance difficult.

Oxana held up a fire extinguisher. *Good girl.* Trina crawled back six inches and held her breath. It took three hits but the sunroof shattered, the tempered glass disintegrating into clear shards that smarted as they whipped against her face. She waited for Vasin to shoot, but heard nothing. Reaching down, her hand was immediately grasped by one of the girls and she pulled, then up came Oxana.

"Stay flat, right here," Trina shouted as she moved forward again and reached down. Ekaterina followed Oxana's example and was flat on the cab in seconds.

"You have to jump onto the other truck." Both girls looked at her like she spoke the gospel truth. It was the shock and fear. Pure survival mode.

Trina lifted her head and then crawled backward until she could reach the ladder in the back of the cab. Standing between the cab and fuel tank, she grasped Oxana's ankle and squeezed. Rob was next to them, far enough back that Vasin couldn't get off a good shot with his weapon, but close enough to the tanker that they could drop onto his cab.

Trina was loath to leave the girls alone and exposed on the moving truck, but there was no other way. She'd have to catch them once on Rob's truck. Trina saw the top of the cab, knew that Rob was in it. All she had to do was trust.

She jumped.

Rob heard the first thud on the cab's roof and hit the ceiling with his fist. Yes! Trina had made it. He listened for the next two thuds, which came surprisingly quickly, one after another. He immediately slowed the truck down, praying all three women would hang on.

"We're all here." Trina's shout rang through his headset.

"It's just another couple of minutes, ladies." The truck shuddered and shimmied on the weathered road as it slowed down. He watched Vasin continue to drive off and figured the crook was going to take the truck as far as he could as a means of escape. Rob would call it in to TH as soon as he stopped his truck. His speedometer read thirty miles per hour, falling.

"Rob! Trouble!" Trina's scream broke through his training protocol. He looked out at the road and saw that the tanker had made a U-turn at the only place wide enough in three counties to do so, a median pull-off area. Vasin was headed back straight toward them. Rob reached for his weapon, but he'd never get a good shot off, not from inside the cab.

They were all dead. Vasin was going to run right over them, obviously not caring if he died along with them. It was a matter of honor to ROC. The truck finally came to a halt, and Rob put it in Reverse. The two Ukrainian girls climbed down from the top of the cab and got in via his passenger door.

"Ladies, you need to make a run for it. Now!" The

girls didn't argue but slid out of the truck. There were plenty of trees to hide behind until backup arrived.

"Trina, come down. I'm backing up. There's no time!"

"Rob, stop the truck. I've got the perfect shot from here."

"Damn it, Trina, get down." He put the engine on idle and opened his door. If she wouldn't listen, he'd go get her himself. Before he got a foot on the running board, he heard the sound of Trina's gun firing. Two seconds later the night lit up with a light brighter than Fourth of July fireworks as the propane truck Vasin drove exploded.

"You okay, Trina?" It had been an hour since Vasin's fiery death and there hadn't been time to check in with each other until now.

"What?" She looked at him like she'd seen her life pass in front of her as she watched EMTs tend to the girls. They'd already checked Trina out and save for a few bruises from climbing onto a moving fuel truck, she was fine.

Rob wrapped his arm around her shoulders, willing his body heat into her. "Come here, babe." Maybe she needed to sit down. Shock could affect a law enforcement agent at any time, no matter their level of experience. He lifted her chin with his finger and peered into her eyes. Under the glare of emergency spotlights, her pupils were dilated, but no more than would be expected.

She shook him off. "I'm fine. Thanks, by the way, for the truck bit—you got me out of an awfully tough spot."

"You did it on your own." As she always did.

"No. Rob, this time I was in a pickle, really. Did you see how he was driving it?" She nodded to where Vasin had breathed his last breath. The charred frame of the rig was still on fire, the Silver Valley Fire Department smothering it with foam.

"If one of his shots had ricocheted and hit his tanker before I got the girls away, we wouldn't be having this conversation."

" It's okay, Trina. You're safe, and you saved the girls. Vasin got what he deserved."

"I never like seeing someone die, no matter how awful or downright evil they are. And for the record, Rob? *We* saved the girls. Did you know they belonged to him, to ROC?"

"Yes." He told her what he knew about the tats, and what he'd overheard in the bathroom.

Her eyes widened. "Rob, both of the girls have tattoos behind her left ear. It looks like a crescent moon to the untrained eye, but I heard them say in Russian that it was a sickle. When you look really closely the line of the hammer is there—it has to be what you overheard. It must be the symbol of Ivanov's girls."

He brought her in for a hug. "You can put it in your after-action report. All I care about is that you're alive, and my son's safe from a very bad man. We also have two young women we know will have a chance at true freedom, if they want it." Trina knew the women would be offered witness protection if they wanted.

Trina's phone vibrated with a text from SVPD.

"It's SVPD. They've verified that the truck driver is dead. Vasin isn't ever going to hurt another girl or woman." She looked up at him. "But Ivanov is still out there, Rob. He could come after us, or punish the other girls as an example."

"Not likely. ROC will lie low, at least for a while. Ivanov doesn't even get briefed on all of the awful things his subordinates do. It's unlikely Vasin ever told him about us, period. It would only make Vasin look bad."

"I'd say Vasin had a lot more power than we thought, then."

"That's not our problem any longer, Marshal Lopez. We solved our part of the case."

She looked bemused. "My first Trail Hikers op. Our first one together since the Navy. But Ivanov will be back, we know this. We'll have to fight him again, Rob."

"Let's celebrate completing our first TH op together. We can't control what happens next with ROC. No one can."

"We can control what we do together, Rob."

He couldn't wait any longer—he kissed her. It was in the middle of a truck stop, in front of first responders and the church volunteers, but Rob only cared about Trina's reaction. Which was getting as heated as his.

Trina pulled back enough to meet his gaze. "It's our beginning."

"Yes." He'd never let her go again.

Three days later, Rob knocked on Trina's front door. His heart pounded in his chest as if this were his first undercover op. He laughed nervously at his unintentional joke. This was indeed an *uncover* op—it was time to tell Jake who he was.

He heard the sound of Renegade's barks followed by scampering feet, the sound he'd memorized that first night he'd met his son. The door flew open and revealed the boy who'd cemented a permanent place in Rob's soul since the minute Trina had revealed he was a father.

"Rob!" Rob knelt down and the little boy launched himself at Rob, wrapping his arms around Rob's neck in what was now a familiar gesture.

"Hey, Jake!" He hugged his son back, savoring how good it felt to be able to receive love as much as give it.

"Hi, handsome." Trina was behind Jake and Rob stood, lifting Jake with him. He leaned over and gave her a warm, lingering kiss.

"Hi, yourself."

"Ick." Jake's observation made all three laugh.

"Trina, do you mind if Jake and I have a man-to-man conversation? You can be there, but it's just going to be us guys talking." He watched his son as he spoke. He and Trina had already agreed that this was the time and place to tell Jake the truth.

"Sure thing. How about the backyard?"

"Yeah!" Jake wiggled out of his arms and raced through the house, heading for the back door. Renegade followed him, tail wagging.

Trina hugged him tight. "You've got this, Rob."

"Thanks." He wanted to stay in her arms forever, and he would, but first things first.

Trina stayed on the back porch, where she sat on the steps holding Renegade as Rob walked toward the huge oak tree where Jake swung on his tire.

"Do you want to try it, Rob?"

Rob shook his head. "Not now. I need to talk to you about something, first." He knelt next to the swing.

"Okay." Jake stopped swinging and stared intently at Rob.

Rob swallowed. "Jake, do you know how your mom

told you your dad was in the Navy and did a lot of military missions?"

Jake nodded, never taking his wide eyes off of Rob. Rob didn't think he'd ever get used to his son staring at him like this, as if everything he said was the Gospel.

"Mom said my dad wished he could be here."

"Well, that's just it, Jake. I am here. I'm your dad."

Rob started to go on, to tell Jake all that he'd memorized to include how different circumstances had kept them apart. But his son had a different take on things.

"You mean you want to be my dad? I know that you love my mom."

Rob laughed. "You do?"

Jake nodded.

"Yes, I want to be your dad, Jake, but in fact, I am your dad. I'm the Navy guy your mom told you about."

"You're the hero?" Jake's eyes grew even wider.

"I'm not a hero, Jake."

But Jake didn't hear him as he slid through the tire to stand next to Rob. "You're my hero, Rob."

"You can call me Dad, if you'd like."

"Is Daddy okay for now? And Dad, too?"

Rob couldn't speak past the lump in his throat so he nodded and opened his arms to his son.

"Daddy or Dad, whichever you want, son." As he hugged him he felt hands on his shoulders. Trina knelt next to him, joining their embrace. She kissed Jake on the cheek.

"Mommy, why are you crying?"

"I'm happy. These are tears of joy, Jake."

When she sought his gaze he saw the tears streaming down her cheeks. Rob still couldn't find words, never having faced so much love in his lifetime. Trina smiled. "I love you so much."

"I love you, too."

Jake patted both of their cheeks with his hands. "Guess what, guys? I mean, Mommy and Daddy." He giggled. "This is our first family hug!"

"Yes, it is." Trina's voice was soft, her eyes luminous. Rob knew he must look the same. Besotted.

"So are you going to get married or what?"

Trina looked at him and Rob found his words. "If your mom will have me. But that's an adult conversation that your mom and I will have later, Jake."

"Fine. But Mom, please say yes."

Renegade jumped up and started licking Rob's face, as if showing his agreement to the plan. Rob fell backward, dragging his family and dog with him. Amidst the barks and laughter, Rob knew he'd finally found his forever family.

Epilogue

Three months later

"To the bride and groom!" Nolan Lopez held his glass of champagne high, and the wedding guests followed suit, echoing his toast.

Glasses clinked and people laughed. Rob could not care less. All he wanted, all he ever desired, sat with him at the head table of his wedding reception. Trina and Jake. To his utter delight, she'd accepted his proposal of marriage and they'd put together a ceremony that they'd all appreciate, Jake included.

His bride smiled over his son's head. "How you holding up, Mr. Lopez?"

"Wonderfully, Mrs. Bristol." They kissed over Jake's head, laughing as they did so. Unable to decide whose name to take with the reality of Jake bearing Rob's original name, they'd decided to legally keep their current names, Trina Lopez and Robert Bristol. It was a necessity, as Rob was going to continue his civilian job as a social worker, and Trina would continue with the Marshals in a desk job. They'd both take Trail Hiker assignments as offered, sometimes together as long as her mother was available to watch Jake. And many women kept their maiden names, so it wasn't anything major. Still, it made for good teasing between them. And if it got him an extra kiss from Trina, Rob was all for it.

Rob was particularly pleased that they'd all agreed to change Jake's name to Justin Lopez-Bristol. It was time for a new beginning for all of them. He watched his son charm Trina's mother, who couldn't resist adjusting the bow tie on Jake's tux. He and Jake wore matching tuxedoes, and he felt it cemented their relationship so far. Today was a celebration of their father-son bond, which had grown leaps even as Rob stumbled over basic things like adhering to Jake's set bedtime and not allowing him to have all the sweets he wanted, whenever he wanted. Trina helped him see that boundaries with his son were a good thing, and helped respect and love grow on both sides.

He saw his brother-in-law, Nolan, raise a glass of champagne, saluting him again for marrying his sister. Rob nodded and hoisted his glass, grateful for the family he'd gained in Nolan and Trina's parents. He and Trina had told them both his true identity, and Jake would know when he was old enough to know what "classified" meant. Of course, by then, it would most likely be unclassified. Time had a way of making all secrets impotent.

"Dad, is it time yet?" Rob's eyes filled with tears.

Jake had started calling him "Dad" the minute he had told him he was his real father, by the tire swing. He called him "Daddy" when he was tired or especially needy. Rob was learning that a five-, almost six-year-old had a lot of needy times. Which made him more determined to make sure Jake felt a part of his and Trina's wedding. Trina had agreed.

Today was Jake's day, too.

"*Daaaaad.* Is. It. Time?" His son looked at him with exasperation. Not easy in his kid-size tuxedo, perfectly matching Rob's.

"Time for what?" Trina sipped her champagne, and Rob couldn't wait to share a bottle of bubbly in private with her. Later.

"Go ahead, son." Rob nodded at Jake, who pulled out a box from his coat pocket. It looked big in such small hands.

"Here, Mommy. This is from me and Daddy. It's a surprise wedding gift."

"Rob, we said we weren't doing this." Her eyes glistened, turning their gray depths silver.

"Jake insisted."

She opened the box, which Jake had carefully wrapped in racing car paper last night. When Trina lifted the lid, she gasped. "Rob. Jake. Oh my."

Rob reached over and lifted the gold charm bracelet from her hands. "Here, let me." He fastened it on her wrist and kissed her hand. "The charms are special."

"Yeah! The dog is from Renegade." That one had taken a while to find, as had the small race car with Jake's birthdate engraved on it. Trina smiled and thanked them for each one.

"And I know what this one is." She fingered the gold

camel, from the necklace that had broken at Camp Serenity.

"Not quite. Look on its belly." Trina turned the charm over, and tears spilled down her cheeks. "It's today. Our wedding day."

"Our new beginning."

They met again over Jake's head and kissed.

* * * * *

Don't miss the other thrilling romances in
GERI KROTOW'S SILVER VALLEY P.D.
miniseries:

SECRET AGENT UNDER FIRE
HER SECRET CHRISTMAS AGENT
WEDDING TAKEDOWN
HER CHRISTMAS PROTECTOR

All available now from
Harlequin Romantic Suspense.

Get 4 FREE REWARDS!

We'll send you 2 FREE Books plus 2 FREE Mystery Gifts.

Harlequin® Romantic Suspense books feature heart-racing sensuality and the promise of a sweeping romance set against the backdrop of suspense.

FREE Value Over $20

SPECIAL EXCERPT FROM

HARLEQUIN®

ROMANTIC suspense

*Armstrong Black doesn't do partners, and Danielle Winstead
is not a team player. To find the criminal they're after, they
have to trust each other. But their powerful attraction throws
an unexpected curveball in their investigation!*

Read on for a sneak preview of
SEDUCED BY THE BADGE,
the first book in **Deborah Fletcher Mello**'s
new miniseries,
TO SEDUCE AND SERVE.

"Why did you leave your service revolver on my bathroom
counter?" Armstrong asked as they stood at the bus stop, waiting
for her return ride.

"I can't risk keeping it strapped on me and I was afraid one of
the girls might go through my bag and find it. I knew it was safe
with you."

"I don't like you not having your gun."

"I'll be fine. I have a black belt in karate and jujitsu. I know how
to take care of myself!"

Armstrong nodded. "So you keep telling me. It doesn't mean
I'm not going to worry about you, though."

Danni rocked back and forth on her heels. Deep down she was
grateful that a man did care. For longer than she wanted to admit,
there hadn't been a man who did.

Armstrong interrupted her thoughts. "There's a protective detail
already in front of the coffee shop and another that will follow you
and your bus. There will be someone on you at all times. If you get
into any trouble, you know what to do."

Danni nodded. "I'll contact you as soon as it's feasible. And
please, if there is any change in Alissa's condition, find a way to

let me know."

"I will. I promise."

Danni's attention shifted to the bus that had turned the corner and was making its way toward them. A wave of sadness suddenly rippled through her stomach.

"You good?" Armstrong asked, sensing the change in her mood.

She nodded, biting back the rise of emotion. "I'll be fine," she answered.

As the bus pulled up to the stop, he drew her hand into his and pulled it to his mouth, kissing the backs of her fingers.

Danni gave him one last smile as she fell into line with the others boarding the bus. She tossed a look over her shoulder as he stood staring after her. The woman in front of her was pushing an infant in a stroller. A boy about eight years old and a little girl about five clung to each side of the carriage. The little girl looked back at Danni and smiled before hiding her face in her mother's skirt. The line stopped, an elderly woman closer to the front struggling with a multitude of bags to get inside.

She suddenly spun around, the man behind her eyeing her warily. "Excuse me," she said as she pushed past him and stepped aside. She called after Armstrong as she hurried back to where he stood.

"What's wrong?" he said as she came to a stop in front of him

"Nothing," Danni said as she pressed both palms against his broad chest. "Nothing at all." She lifted herself up on her toes as her gaze locked with his. Her hands slid up his chest to the sides of his face. She gently cupped her palms against his cheeks and then she pressed her lips to his.

Don't miss
SEDUCED BY THE BADGE by Deborah Fletcher Mello,
available June 2018 wherever
Harlequin® Romantic Suspense books and ebooks are sold.

www.Harlequin.com

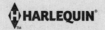

Need an adrenaline rush from nail-biting tales
(and irresistible males)?

Check out **Harlequin® Intrigue®**
and **Harlequin® Romantic Suspense** books!

New books available every month!

CONNECT WITH US AT:

Harlequin.com/Community

 Facebook.com/HarlequinBooks

 Twitter.com/HarlequinBooks

 Instagram.com/HarlequinBooks

 Pinterest.com/HarlequinBooks

ReaderService.com

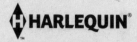

**ROMANCE WHEN
YOU NEED IT**

SGENRE2017

LOVE
Harlequin
romance?

Join our Harlequin community to share your thoughts and connect with other romance readers!

Be the first to find out about promotions, news, and exclusive content!

Sign up for the Harlequin e-newsletter and download a free book from any series at

www.TryHarlequin.com